YEAH, BUT I DIDN'T

YEAH, BUT I DIDN'T

ANN SWANN

WordCrafts Press

One

THE SECOND RUNG

That day—the second to last rung on the ladder of events that changed everything—when the doorbell *bing-bonged*, I didn't think twice about answering. At the age of 14, I was plenty old enough to stay home alone in our small town of Lawson, Texas.

I opened the storm door.

Paul from geometry stood on the side porch. His choppy bangs grazed his eyebrows and framed his dark eyes. A few weeks ago he came to school with burnt orange streaks in his hair. I remember how my gaze kept drifting over those surprising bits of color, picturing them in my own brown hair.

Later I wondered if my fascination with his highlights was what made him come over that day. As if something in my gaze had invited him, or perhaps *invoked* was a better word.

The empty house yawned behind me.

Paul stood on the bottom porch step. "Hey, Benji-girl." His eyes were opaque. Unreadable.

The skin on the back of my neck grew cold. I stood there chewing my cuticle like an idiot. The branches of the pecan tree behind his head swayed in the sudden breeze. A spring storm cloud crouched on the horizon. There was just enough sun left to rake the shadows of the leaves across the porch. And across him.

He grinned.

I tried to think of a polite way to ask what he wanted. Instead, I blurted, "What's up?"

He stared at me through those jagged bangs. "Wanna hang out?"

I shifted my feet. "I can't have anyone over when Mom is gone."

"We could stream a movie." His snake charmer's voice rolled toward me across the narrow space.

Something coiled in my gut. Did he not hear me say no one could come in?

I watched—dumbfounded—as his hand darted forward and grasped the edge of the door. Before I could react, he pulled it open and stepped past me into the hall. His shadow grew horns and scales on the paneled wall. "Kinda hot out there," he said. "Got anything to drink?"

Neon PANIC flashed in my head. Thunder boomed in the distance. If Mom came home now, I wouldn't just be grounded from my phone, I would lose it forever.

I finally came to life and rushed around him. "Wait here." I pressed my hands against the air in front of his chest. "I'll get you some water."

In the kitchen, I yanked open the fridge, grabbed a bottle of Dasani, and pushed the door shut with my hip.

When I turned around, there he was. Directly behind me. Without a word he grabbed my shoulders.

The bottle of water slid from my fingers and hit the tile with a thump. "Stop! What are you—"

He pushed his wordless mouth against mine and forced

my lips apart. I whipped my head from side to side. Our teeth crashed together. Blood salted my tongue. I couldn't push him off. His hard hands crushed me against the wall. He shoved his knee between my legs and I crumpled and slid downward, my long hair creating a kind of slide on the oak paneling.

Falling on me with all his weight, he smashed me to the floor. My forehead smacked the doorjamb as he shoved his fingers inside the waistband of my shorts.

The denim held. His short, dragon-hard nails clawed my skin as he became enraged. He continued to grapple with the single tough sheaf of fabric.

Bing-Bong

Bing-Bong

The doorbell. UPS. The driver always placed the packages on the side porch for safety. Thunder boomed again. Rain splatted the door glass. I could almost hear the loud, brown truck, its engine always running.

I tried to yell but his palm covered my mouth.

On instinct I bit down.

Bing-Bong

A third ring of the bell.

Paul's weight left me. His palm disappeared. A rush of air found its way into my lungs. I heaved, gasped, tried to scream.

Running footsteps preceded a blast of moist air as my attacker burst out the back door into a small Texas storm.

I pulled myself to my hands and knees. My elbows sang with scraped pain. Long brown hairs waved at me, stuck in the tiny imperfections of the oak paneling. I ran my fingers across my forehead, surprised at the lump forming there. The bitter tang of bile burned my throat.

Dazed, I used the wall to pull myself all the way up. I staggered to the door in shock. No sign of the Big Brown Truck, but three boxes rested on the mat. Thank God Mom was a one-click addict.

With shaking fingers I latched the storm door and pushed the wooden one closed. I shoved home the deadbolt. I'd worried about losing my phone privileges, but I'd never worried about this. Not *this*.

My vision blurred. I tried to quell the panic. What just happened? Why did he come over, why did he try to—because I stared at his *hair*?

A stray thought hit me like a hammer. Could Kera have talked him into doing this to get me in trouble? Could Will? Oh my God. *Could* they? I steadied myself against the wall. A single drop of blood glistened on the floor, probably from my tongue.

The back door gaped. I hurried across the kitchen, snatched the handle, yanked it shut, locked the screen and slammed the big door closed, just as I'd done in the hall. I glanced through the open layout toward the front door—the one we never used—it was closed and locked like always.

As I turned back toward the hall, my toes bumped the bottle of Dasani and kicked it across the tile. I couldn't believe I'd thought I could get rid of him with a bottle of water. I picked it up and held it against my throbbing forehead. It was still cold. The clock chimed four. The whole thing had lasted less than five minutes. Janie's shift at her part-time job was just ending.

I perched on a barstool. The *chunkle* of ice falling through the automatic maker in the fridge door trickled through my shock. Holding onto the kitchen island, I climbed off my stool, took a baggie from the cupboard, filled it with crushed ice. I held it to the throbbing spot on my forehead then jerked it away, wrapped the baggie in a thin kitchen towel, and tried again. Better. I opened the Dasani and gulped.

Where had he gone?

No sign of him out the kitchen window. Should I call the cops? Would he come back? Worrying about it hurt my head. I just wanted to lie down and close my eyes. But first, I had to check all the windows. Should have done it already. Not thinking clearly.

Through my fog I forced myself to check every lock. Then I carefully made my way to the bathroom to assess the damage. The wide mirror reflected wild eyes and a small blue knot in the middle of my forehead. Was that me? It didn't feel like me. The entire day had taken on the hue of a barely under-stood nightmare. One of those dreams already fading when you open your eyes.

I wet the cup towel and put the ice directly inside. The cold seeped into my skin quicker, less painfully. Tears surprised me, as warm and salty as the blood on my tongue. I sank to the fluffy pink bathmat, sobbing.

Should I call Mom from the landline? She had my cell in her purse. Kera had talked a long time last night, too late. Trying to get me to say I didn't hate her for taking my boyfriend.

But should I disturb Mom with her clients? What would I say, Paul came in, he tried to— No. I couldn't tell her that on the phone. I didn't think I could tell her that, ever. She might call the cops. They might make me have an exam; *a rape kit*. I'd heard about those, but I didn't need that. It hadn't gone *that* far. I was lucky—one-click-addict lucky. Would

Mom freak out and make me do it anyway? Would she make me say his name?

I felt a softness swish against my ankle. A scream clawed into my throat, but it was just Maggie May, my little cat. I reached down and scooped her up, held her to my chest. "Did you see that?" I murmured. "Did you see that—that monster?" I hoped she hadn't. Already I was so embarrassed at the thought that I'd let him in, that I'd somehow encouraged him—

From the back of the house I heard the screak of the side door.

My heart froze. I crawled into the shower and pulled the frosted door closed. The scream was back in my throat, needing to be let out. Too late, I realized I'd cornered myself in the shower. There was nowhere to go. No escape. I clutched Maggie tighter.

Footsteps sounded in the hall.

"Ben?"

Relief flooded my body. I pulled myself up and stepped out of the shower. Maggie slid from my grasp and dashed out of the room.

I turned on the faucet and jammed my hand under the flow, then rinsed my mouth with cold water. "In here, Janie."

My sister appeared in the doorway. "Why was the side door locked?" Noticing the bruise on my forehead, she leaned forward as if to touch it. "What the hell?"

I flinched away.

"Fell." The lie tumbled clumsily off my sore tongue. "Running to get the packages, slipped on the rug."

She nodded, one hand on her hip. "So that's why the rug's all twisted." She looked me up and down. "The ice helping?"

I nodded, still holding the dripping cup towel in my hand. "Bit my tongue, too."

Janie stood quietly assessing me. "Your shorts—"

I glanced in the mirror. My blue jean cutoffs were twisted sideways, rumpled like the rug.

"You sure you're all right?"

I nodded again. "Just fell. Never even got the packages."

Two

Monday at School

Thankfully the next day was Sunday. I lay in my bed relieved that Mom hadn't noticed my bruise; relieved I didn't have to go to school; relieved I didn't have to see *him*, or Kera, or Will.

But what would I do on Monday? I couldn't avoid them all. Would he say anything? I spent the whole morning in bed, my head sore, my life in tatters. *Why me?* still echoed through my mind.

We used to go to church sometimes, when Janie and I were little, and I'd gone sometimes with Kera after that, but lately we couldn't seem to get there as a family. Nowadays, Mom seemed even more exhausted than me. I finally got up around 11:00 and wandered to the kitchen in my fleece sleep pants and old tee shirt. I examined my forehead and the bruise was barely noticeable.

I slathered concealer on it just in case.

Janie sat in the window seat with her laptop. She didn't speak. We seldom did unless it was unavoidable. She appeared to be doing research. Her goal was to get an academic scholarship to Baylor. She didn't want to be a doctor, she wanted to do radiology or become a P.A. When I asked what a P.A. was she gave me one of those piteous looks that made me feel like an imbecile. "A physician's assistant, of course."

After that, I didn't ask her anything else. I couldn't understand why anyone would want to be an assistant to a doctor instead of just becoming a doctor, but Janie made me feel so stupid I wasn't about to inquire further.

I took two Tylenol and spent the rest of the day catching up on homework and trying to watch *The Walking Dead*. I had them all recorded. But after a few minutes, I gave up. Doing my homework caused my head to feel worse in spite of the Tylenol.

Mom lounged around in her robe drinking coffee and talking on the phone. Around five o'clock we ordered pizza. Without fanfare, she gave me back my phone. "I'm surprised at Kera calling so late." Her eyes searched mine for an explanation. When I said nothing, she went on, "She knows the rules—I mean she practically lives here."

"Yeah."

I couldn't say more. All that best-friend stuff was in the past. Yeah, Kera *used* to almost-live-here. She'd always said her favorite place on earth was the little day bed on my screened-in back porch. We'd even called it "her room," and us her "second family." She and I, we'd had our first clumsy sexual encounter on that little day bed back in elementary school. It had been awkward beneath the screened-porch stars. But it hadn't changed anything between us. We were just experimenting. Exploring. Even more than Will, I'd thought we were forever. Kera and me.

Then she'd betrayed me. With Will.

After her lengthy apology in which she'd told me she thought Will might be *The One*, I'd hung up on her. She knew damn well he'd always been *My* one. Mine. Not hers.

Something in the pit of my stomach clenched when I took

my phone and saw my little message icon with the number four beside it. I didn't get many texts anymore. I had completely insulated myself with Kera and with Will. I talked to a few people in Art and Choir, but we didn't text much. Not like Kera and I had done. Not like I had with Will, for hours on end. I didn't want texts from anyone right now. Not from Kera. Not from Will. Definitely not from *him*.

What if he had messaged me? What would I say? What would I do?

The PANIC sign blinked on again.

My headache throbbed up a notch.

I touched the message icon and relief coursed through me. The texts were innocuous. A couple were from games I played on the internet telling me it was my turn, and the other two were from Mom yesterday asking me if I wanted anything from Dairy Queen. She must've forgot she had my phone in her purse, turned off.

The irony of that one made me smile. I wondered how long it had taken her to realize why I never answered her texts.

I went to bed early that night.

But I didn't go to sleep. Not for a long, long time.

Monday morning came way too soon. I'd fallen asleep with my TV on. The low voices of an old movie had helped to cover up the voices in my head. Voices and now images. Voices because Mom saw me taking more Tylenol and said I needed to get a grip, I was just an over-achiever suffering low-grade anxiety. Images because *hard hands, a slimy tongue...*

Will and Kera at school. Now *him*. Shadows on the wall. In my head. Covering my heart, squeezing my soul.

"Get a grip, Benji," I whispered to my reflection. *Get a freakin' grip.*

Janie drove us to school like always. Kera looked up when we passed her in the parking lot, but she didn't wave. Sergio from World Lit did, though. When I got out of the car, he fell into step beside me. "Hey, Ben."

I raised my hand. "Hey."

"Did you finish *Wuthering Heights*?"

"Yeah. It took *forever*."

He laughed. "Is that why they call it a classic? I couldn't believe it when I finally understood what 'wuthering' meant."

"Me either. I thought it would be something, I don't know, *profound*." We strolled through the double doors together and I felt something tighten across the back of my shoulders as if I'd slipped on an even heavier backpack. An extra one.

I almost turned around and ran back to Janie. My body longed for the cocoon of my soft bed, my fuzzy, leopard-print bedspread. The warmth of my little Maggie curled into the bend of my knees.

Right now I would even settle for the inside of Janie's little Ford Focus. But of course by now she was already driving around to the senior high side of our small-town school. She might even be out of the car and gone, meeting up with her boyfriend, Shawn, at the senior high doors. She had no idea what had really happened at our house on Saturday.

Sergio stopped me just inside the doors. "Hey! Is that a bruise? What happened?" He stared at my forehead.

I quickly smoothed my bangs down. I'd layered on concealer again, but since Mom hadn't noticed last night, I hadn't worried too much. Maybe I hadn't been as careful as I should have.

His fingers went toward my forehead. "You okay?"

Stupid tears popped into my eyes, jack-in-the-box moisture threatening to give me away. "I'm fine. Just clumsy." I smiled a watery smile to let him know I appreciated the sympathy.

Sergio looked away, dropped his hand.

He probably thinks my mom or dad slapped me, or my boyfriend. He probably doesn't know I don't even see my dad anymore, and my mom wouldn't slap a flea. A boyfriend? He should know I don't have one of those anymore. Wait, is that why he's suddenly so friendly?

OMG, Is that why Paul had come to my house, because he'd heard Will was out of the picture? Had he mentioned that? It was hard to remember now, but it didn't matter. Even if he did know, it didn't give him the right to do what he did.

I hurried to the bathroom to check the mirror, piled on even more concealer, sprayed my bangs into place so they wouldn't blow away again, tucked my makeup bag back inside my purse.

Shelly Shumaker floated in on a cloud of perfume. She ignored me and pulled mascara from her bag and went to work on her lashes. Shelly was a cheerleader, the *head* cheerleader of the JV squad. She didn't know my name. I preferred it that way. I scurried past her out the door, one hand holding my bangs in place, just in case. I hoped Sergio hadn't mentioned me to anyone.

He looked up and smiled a tiny smile when I entered homeroom. We both sat near the back, not side by side but in the same row. I ducked my head and took my seat. Had he told anyone about the bruise? I couldn't concentrate on anything the rest of the period. The announcements went over my head and I had to be prompted to respond when

Ms. Allenby called the roll. My desk might as well have been sitting on a stage. Everyone seemed to be looking at me. I found it impossible to keep my hands off my bangs.

When the bell rang, I made certain Sergio and all the other students left the room ahead of me before I made my way to first period, World History, just down the hall. No big deal. Memorize some terms, read about some dead guys. Watch a video. The teacher was also a coach. He didn't assign much that wasn't multiple choice and those we traded and graded. He was into football; he didn't have time for essays or projects. Lucky us.

Second period was World Lit, *Wuthering Heights*. Everyone in the book was related to everyone else—sort of. Everyone was dying or wishing someone else was dead. What a story. We were doing a review today, before the final exam. I couldn't keep up. My thoughts kept straying to the rumpled rug in the hallway, those long hairs waving from the rough paneling, the sore spot on my forehead.

"Benji?" Karma Jones snapped her fingers in my direction.

I turned my head, my hand falling away from my bangs. As usual, I sat near the back of the class, but this time I had a window. "Sorry. What?" All I could think of was next period. Geometry. *Him.*

Karma jerked her head toward the seat beside her. Sergio gazed at me with a question in his eyes.

I raised my hands in a *What?* gesture.

"Your review notes," he mouthed. "Can I borrow them later?"

I nodded and looked down at my notebook. I'd written a few one-word reminders. Fortunately, Ms. Kestrel had passed out a complete study guide. I think she knew everyone was in danger of flunking this one.

"I'll text you," Sergio mouthed, making texting motions on the palm of his hand. We didn't dare pull out our phones in this class. History, we could get away with it, but not here. Ms. Kestrel's vision was as sharp as that of her namesake. And she didn't mind writing referrals and calling parents.

I nodded okay at Sergio. But I was getting suspicious. Before today, the most we'd ever said to each other was hi, and that was usually in response to literally bumping each other in the hall or going through classroom doorways at the same instant.

I shoved the question to the back of my mind and tried to concentrate on Ms. Kestrel's wrap-up. She was a good teacher. Strict and fair, but she didn't cut corners when it came to grading, and she sure didn't mind assigning essay questions.

"You've got to know how to write essays and explore topics for your college entrance exams," she'd said the first day of class, gazing over her half-rim glasses at us, one wiry strand of graying hair curling about an earpiece. "You are all *going* to college, right?"

No one dared say otherwise, although in reality we all knew that some of us would be lucky to even graduate high school. Still, Ms. Kestrel's class was the one place I felt absolutely safe. In light of what had happened at my own home over the weekend, I felt doubly safe here. If I read the material, I could do the work. And if I did the work, then I could succeed. No hidden agendas, no secrets. No one would leave, no one would start a new relationship, no one would betray me.

God. It always comes back around to that now. First Dad with his new wife. Then Will with Kera. Now *him*. Three deserters and one wanna-be-rapist—

The bell rang and I gathered my backpack and my books and waited for the room to clear. Maybe I *should* have called Mom, let her call the cops—

Sergio fell in beside me outside the classroom door. "So, how did you like the party?"

My skin tightened up around my flesh. "Party?"

"Yeah, at Todd's the other night?"

"You were there?" That was the one Kera and I had gone to after my breakup argument with Will. Todd invited her because they'd lived on the same street for years. She pulled me along out of pity, or so I thought. Looking back, I'd say that was the first rung on the ladder to despair.

"Yeah," Sergio continued. "I saw you there with Kera."

My stomach flip-flopped. What was he getting at? Had he witnessed the whole embarrassing episode where Will came in and sat down behind us and started talking to Kera and me? Did he hear Will come right out and ask if I wanted to take a walk with him, which we all knew was a euphemism for go somewhere and make out? Did he see me shake my head, giving my loyalty to my best friend, Kera, the one who had invited me to the stupid party in the first place?

I shrugged, trying not to let Sergio see how the question rattled me. "It was okay, I guess."

He bumped my elbow with his. "I didn't even know you and Will had broke up until I saw Kera leave with him."

My face burned. Had he seen how I'd had to call my sister and feign an illness so she would come and pick me up?

The fluorescents buzzed overhead. The new paint on this renovated wing suddenly seemed suffocating. Before today, the odor had smelled clean.

I veered off toward the restroom. "See you later." I dropped my head. The memory of Kera hopping up to catch Will after I'd declined—"I'll keep you company," she'd purred—made me literally sick to my stomach.

Crashing into a stall, I stabbed my backpack and purse on the door hook and bent over the toilet just in time to vomit bits of breakfast into the bowl. Chunks of horribly fragrant cinnamon roll floated in the water. The sight and smell made me heave all over again.

From the stall next door I heard, "Oh my gawd," as someone slammed out without stopping by the sink.

I could only hope it wasn't anyone who recognized my shoes. More humiliation and embarrassment I did not need. The internet would go wild. There would probably be pictures of the stall door. Audio of me retching. The caption would say MORNING SICKNESS or KNOCKED UP, something like that.

I thought about my Instagram page. Mom kept such a tight rein on it I seldom posted anything other than happy little memes and cat videos. And since Kera and Will hooked up, I hadn't even been doing that. I'd been tempted to get offline completely. I did not need to see pics of the two of them kissing or laughing, strolling around arm in arm like they'd done outside the party.

When I was certain the other girl had left, I came out of the stall, washed my face and rinsed out my mouth. I hadn't worn much makeup that day other than the concealer on my bruise. Now, I took out my eyeliner and darkened my eyes and brows. The contrast with my too-pale face seemed to capture my inner turmoil. My heart felt broken, my soul felt dead.

I dug through my purse for gum, but found only a tiny

box of orange Tic Tacs. I popped two of them instead. The taste was vile, but at least they would cover the scent of regurgitated cinnamon roll.

Exiting the bathroom, I inhaled through my nose and started down the hall. For one wild moment, I considered turning away from the math wing and walking toward the exit. I'd only skipped school once before, with Kera, and it hadn't been successful. We got caught sneaking into the closed water park on a whim. It had been such a kid thing to do, but my mom had blamed it all on her inability to be both Mom and Dad. She seemed to think I was headed to Hell in a hand basket and it was all her fault. Actually, those are some of the exact words she said, or rather, sobbed.

I'd felt so bad, making her cry like that. But it hadn't been anything evil, or twisted, or rebellious. It hadn't been about her breakup with my father or her lack of discipline. If any-thing it had been about a bright, sunny day in May and a severe case of boredom. It had been about spring fever more than anything else.

I turned away from the exit and walked toward M-3. Geometry. My heart seemed to be stuck up under my ribs. I didn't want to face this class. Everyone was in it. Sergio. Kera. Will. Even Paul. They were *all* in here.

Of course it would be *this* class. My favorite.

At the start of the year, I'd dreaded Geometry. I'd always heard it was tough, killer. All those planes and angles, the weird terms. A new language.

Turned out, I didn't mind it at all. Kind of liked it, actu-ally. Geometry made so much more sense to me than I had thought it would. Of course Will had made fun of me—in a joking way. "Nothing's ever hard for you," he'd said. "Even pre-Algebra was a breeze, am I right?" He was right. I'd been the tutor in that class.

One more reason I missed him even though he'd killed me. He'd always kind of reveled in my intelligence. At least he'd seemed to, until the fight, until he'd accused me of not loving him. "If you really loved me, you'd want me the same way I want you," he said.

I'd thought he would get over it in a day or two—surely he could tell I did want him the same way—just not yet. Kissing, cuddling, making out, all that was fine, I loved it. It made me feel special. Just because I was afraid to go further, he belittled me. Said I didn't love him.

But I wasn't stupid. Weren't you supposed to *both* want to do it before you had sex with someone? I didn't say that to him. I just stayed quiet, thinking he'd get over it. Then came the party.

The soul-slaughtering party.

I hadn't told Mom what happened, even though she'd commented on Will's and Kara's absence more than once. I couldn't tell her. It made me feel like a failure.

And I wondered if that's how she felt when Dad had left us for his old girlfriend. I couldn't ask her. I didn't even know how.

I inhaled, squared my shoulders, smoothed my bangs, and stepped into Geometry.

Kera and Will sat in the corner, near the windows. They weren't holding hands, but their heads were leaned toward each other, almost touching, looking at something on Kera's phone. Even from across the room I recognized her Penny-wise phone cover. I'd given it to her for her birthday.

My stomach churned. Thank God it was empty.

Sergio sat in the back row near the desk where I usually sat. I took my seat and tried to ignore his glances.

So far, there was no sign of *him*. I hoped he had dropped out of school, fallen in a river, stepped in front of a truck, or flew off the face of the earth completely.

He slunk in just before the bell and took his usual desk in the center of the room. Kera and Will were on my left near the windows, Sergio sat almost right behind them on the same row as me, and now *he* was in front of me and to my right. It took all the courage I could muster to keep from bolting from the room like a gazelle from a pack of hyenas.

Sergio kept looking around, smiling at me and shooting glances at Kera and Will who studiously ignored everyone. Their chemistry was so sexual it felt like a sauna. I couldn't hope to concentrate on geometry, no matter how much I liked it.

Three

Third Rung on the Ladder

To my relief, *he* acted like I didn't exist. If anything, he so carefully avoided looking at me that I got the idea *he* was afraid of *me*. Afraid I might say something, or do something, maybe. He looked horrible. Grease flattened his coppery hair and his chalky face made every blemish pop out like ugly art on dirty canvas. Even the back of his neck, the strip of skin above his shirt collar, showed a crop of angry scratched-at pimples.

I can't say I immediately breathed easier, but it was one minor hurdle cleared. He wasn't going to say anything or come after me or push me up against a wall again. *He* was afraid of me. I closed my eyes and tried to get rid of the memory of his nasty tongue squirming its way into my mouth. I didn't know it then, but that would be the last time I'd ever sit in a classroom with Paul Ackerson again.

"Benji!"

My eyes flew open. "Yes, ma'am?"

Mrs. Peterson stood at the front of the room, pointer raised. She'd obviously asked me a question about what she'd written on the white board.

I scanned the problem, trying to figure out the missing piece, but it appeared complete. What had she asked? The silence in the room thickened. My throat closed tight.

Sunlight filtered through the far window, dust motes danced as each person in the room turned to look at me, to see why I didn't answer.

Mrs. Peterson opened her mouth to say something else, something scathing no doubt—she had absolutely zero tolerance for *slaggards* (her word)—but something in my expression must've stopped her.

I shook my head and looked down at my desktop. "Sorry..."

"Are you all right?" Her voice was not unkind. "Would you like to go to the nurse?"

Once again, I shook my head. No way I could get up and walk to the front of the room with all those eyes fastened to my back like little round leeches. "I'll be okay," I mumbled. "Thank you."

She shifted her focus to someone else and asked that person the question she'd probably asked me, but she took a pink nurse's pass and scribbled on it anyway. Walking it to me, without making a scene, she said in a low voice, "If you feel you need to leave, just get up and go." And then she smiled and patted my shoulder.

I almost fainted. Mrs. Peterson was one of the toughest teachers in school. I must really look sick. My hand strayed to my forehead. Could she see the bruise?

After a few moments she made certain everyone turned their attention back to the problem on the board. I couldn't have solved it now if my life depended on it. Apparently the other student hadn't known the answer either.

In a burst of courage, I gathered my things together and headed for the door. I tried not to make any sound as I threaded the aisles, but of course my backpack clipped Sonny Riser's desk and knocked his book to the floor.

"Sorry." Tears blurred my vision. I could feel questions coating my retreat as surely as the warm shafts of sunlight stretching across my path.

I'll never forget that day, the way the shafts of light gave way as I rushed through them in my desperate quest to escape that room full of traitors. I imagined myself playing those bars of sunlight the way a harpist's fingers play across the strings, lightly, but with unforgettable impact.

Unforgettable.

My last normal day.

I rushed headlong down the hall toward the exit. No intention of going to the nurse and telling her the reason I couldn't stop retching inside. Memories of being smashed against the wall, to the floor, memories of Kera hopping up to follow my boyfriend, their tongues—no doubt—entangling as they clutched each other in lusty help-me-I'm-drowning embraces. Memories of Will putting his hands up my shirt as he kissed me on our screened back porch and me, pushing him away, older memories of a girl named Susanna whose big brother, Keenan, jokingly running his hands up and down my body as I lay cowering, covers pulled to my neck, in the bottom bunk at her house the one and only time she'd ever asked me to spend the night with her in fifth grade.

At least *she* wasn't in Geometry. Somehow, she wasn't in any of my classes. Nor Keenan. But that's because he was in Janie's grade.

And over all those memories, like strangling cellophane wrapping, an image of my Dad and Sharla-the-slut—the one he tossed us away for—lying on the reclined front seat of her car in the driveway of *our* house the night I had come home early and Mom was at a convention in Dallas.

The image of her bare leg wrapped around his back, his pants halfway down his hips—

I whammed the silver push bar with my forearm half-expecting an alarm to go off as I fell out the rear exit door into the sunshine. I'd never left school during class before. Kera and I had skipped out at lunch that one time. Surely someone would see me now, stop me, know what I was doing, but nothing happened. My pounding heart nearly broke my resolve, but my feet continued their forward trajectory, and the doors swung shut behind me.

I knew if I turned and tried the handles they would be securely locked. There was no going back now.

Rushing down the long shaded side of the building, I felt like a prisoner who'd just escaped from jail. I kept expecting a siren to go off like in the movies.

Turning the corner, feeling exposed, I made my way around the school to the senior parking lot. When I spied Janie's car, I almost cried with relief. The sun beat down on my arms and face as my fingers flew across the keypad and then I was inside.

The interior wasn't stifling yet, but it definitely wasn't cool. The black seats and dash held onto the spring warmth and amplified it, trapping it, turning the interior into a warming oven. With no way to roll down the windows, I simply left the door open and hoped for the best. When the next bell rang, I would get out and go to lunch like always.

I thought about going home, but it was a few miles walk. Mom would be furious if I did that without calling her. And I did not want to call her and tell her I was sick. The first thing she would do... put her hand on my forehead. Then the jig would *definitely* be up. I hadn't told her my fake story about falling, and for some reason, neither had Janie. Fortunately, my blonde, blue-eyed sister was quite involved in her own classes, her job, and Shawn. I wouldn't call her self-centered but I'm pretty sure her radar screen didn't include a blip called Benji.

When my heart stopped pounding and my stomach settled a bit, I pulled a bottle of water from my backpack and opened it. For a moment I wondered if the blue-labeled bottle could be the same one I'd dropped on the kitchen floor when *he* first grabbed me. Then I recalled sipping it later, during the lull I now thought of as The Aftermath.

Closing my eyes, I touched my forehead. It wasn't nearly as sore as it had been. An image of his ugly, scratched-up neck popped into my mind. Had I caused any of those scratches? I hoped I *had*. I wished I had somehow marked his face so everyone would know what a monster he was. If only I could have scratched a big R across his face for Rapist—like a scarlet letter—or at least a W for wannabe.

Had he done this to other girls? Surely I wasn't the only one. If so, then there really was something wrong with me.

I tucked that thought away, pulled out my notebook, and concentrated on the geometry assignment I'd written at the beginning of class. But the thought that I had somehow caused him to come to my house that day would not leave me alone.

It reminded me of the incident with Keenan and Susanna.

I'd been thrilled when Susanna invited me to sleep over that weekend. Shy was my middle name, and Susanna was so confident and self-assured. I knew she had two big brothers, the older one a standout star on the football and basketball teams. I didn't see him that night; he was away on some sports trip, but the other brother, Keenan, hung around the whole time.

My sister's age, he had straw-like blond hair and pale green eyes. I liked the straight line of his jaw, but when he appeared in Susanna's room that night after her parents went to bed, his attractiveness wore off, fast. Not having any brothers nor even any older male cousins, boys fascinated me, but I didn't flirt. I didn't know how. My middle name was Shy with a capital S.

Susanna and I were only in fifth grade. Keenan was in seventh.

He began that night by standing in the bedroom doorway cracking jokes. When I laughed, he said, "Oh you like that?" And before I realized his intention, he was kneeling beside the bed, tickling me, making me squeal.

Then suddenly he was no longer tickling; he was running his hands all over me. Leaning in close, trying to stick his tongue in my ear.

When his fingers found my breasts, I pushed his hands down and wriggled away from him toward the wall.

He crawled up on the bed saying, "Why've you got your hands on your ears?" It had been next to impossible to cover my ears *and* keep my grip on the quilt.

When Susanna threatened to call her mom, Keenan finally left, but not before giving my left breast a hard pinch through the quilt. Susanna didn't say another word. Eventually I shivered myself to sleep. At breakfast, things took an even nastier turn. Keenan didn't bother me. He slept in. It was Susanna who twisted the knife.

"Why *did* you have your hands under there?" Susanna asked out of the blue.

I stopped, strawberry Pop-Tart halfway to my mouth. "Huh?"

She looked at me coldly, no sign of the warm girl who had invited me over the day before. "Why did my brother keep telling you to get your hands out from under there?"

For a few seconds, I had no idea what she meant, and then it hit me. She thought I'd been encouraging her brother. She thought I had my hands in some inappropriate place. I shook my head. I couldn't even say *AreYouKiddingMe?* My brain had stopped working. Finally, I choked out, "He kept asking why I had my hands *on my ears*." I took a breath and decided to tell her the truth, though how she could not have known, being right there in the room with us was beyond me. "He kept trying to stick his tongue in my ear—"

"That's not what I heard," she interrupted. And that was the end of that. She never spoke to me again. Ever. Her mother dropped me off at my house with an invitation to join them at church on Sunday, and that concluded my brief friendship with Susanna Denae King.

After that, I kept to myself until Kera and I got partnered together in Science lab. We clicked immediately. It was the best thing that had ever happened to me. Kera always said my house was her house. She said she'd rather be there than anywhere, even her own home. We loved playing UNO and Life, watching stupid YouTube videos, streaming movies. Sleeping out on the screened porch. And doing each other's makeup.

For Halloween last year she made me into Alice Cooper and I made her into Gene Simmons from KISS.

And when I started hanging out with Will, I always invited her to spend weekends like we'd always done. Sometimes she did, but after I got my own phone and Will and I started texting all the time, Kera claimed she was texting, too. A boy named Anthony. A tenth grader.

I was thrilled for her. Secretly, I might have also been relieved. It freed me to spend even more time with Will. When we weren't on the phone with each other, he was at my house.

He loved the screened porch, too. We sat for hours on end sharing music on our phones, watching videos, and talking. Will is the one who told me Kera wasn't really dating anyone. He said the boy named Anthony didn't exist. That's when I knew she was simply saving face. Maybe she didn't want to be like a third wheel.

I felt guilty.

I went back to trying to include her in our plans. The only time we left my house—since everything we did depended on parents, older siblings, or our own two feet—was to go to the movies, someone's house party, the neighborhood pool, or the game room at the Pizza Palace.

Kera didn't go with us very often. She told me she was dating Anthony and I didn't tell her what Will had said. I never wanted to embarrass her.

But all that was in the past.

Now, sitting here in my sister's car, I couldn't help thinking how fickle everyone had turned out to be. And I couldn't stop wondering why boys seemed to think I wanted them to paw me, to kiss me, to feel me up. Was I one of those victim types that attracted these bullies? What if I had gone farther with Will and then he'd left me like Dad left Mom? Or what if he'd acted like Keenan, what if he hadn't stopped even when I told him to?

It didn't matter now. I'd seen him and Kera together. They obviously didn't stop.

They both got what they wanted.

Four

Rumors

Five minutes before the lunch bell I stuffed my things back in my pack and tossed my empty water bottle in the back seat with the rest of the junk. Later I would discover why leaving class that way turned out to be the third rung on the ladder—it led to so many rumors.

A couple of kids came out the back door, heads bent over their phones, and went straight to their cars. I watched for Keenan. If he came out, I didn't know what I would do. Janie came out instead. For once, I was glad to see her.

She didn't look happy to see me. "What the hell?"

I hung my head. "I got sick and Ms. Peterson sent me to the nurse, but when I went there, some kid was in her office throwing up and I just couldn't go in. I came out here instead." I crossed my fingers at the white lie just like we'd always done when we were little. When we used to sort of like each other.

She looked me up and down. "You're not pregnant are you?"

Shades of my earlier fear, in the bathroom, came back to me. "Of course not!"

"Well, you've been acting weird. If you are, you better tell me now while we can do something about it."

I felt my face flame. "God. I'm not. I couldn't be."

"Virgin, huh?" Her voice was a sneer.

Tears flooded my eyes. So much for being glad to see her. She killed that feeling in a heartbeat.

I grabbed my stuff and headed back toward the building, trying to be invisible. Seventh, eighth, and ninth graders were supposed to stay together in the front of the campus. There were concrete picnic tables outside under the live oaks. That's where we used to always meet for lunch. Kera, Will, and me.

Now, I avoided that area and chose a new place at the edge of the yard. Jenny or Steph, two of the girls from Art, might join me. I'd seen them sitting there before. But today I was late. And I didn't have the nerve to go to their table.

I was beginning to think I was too nice. Too shy to stand up for myself. Up until now I would've said that was impossible, not even necessary, but things were beginning to come clear. As if a cloudy wrapper was being pulled off the truth, a little at a time. The way of the world. The path of a grown-up.

I didn't think I liked this path. If this is how the world really operated, I wasn't sure I wanted to be a part of it.

Arriving at my new place at the edge of the yard, I wasn't surprised to see the table covered with bird poop. Mourning doves populated the live oaks all over campus. Today, their mournful song was a perfect counterpoint to my day.

I swiped the table clean with my old Literature spiral and then sat down and pulled out my bag of Doritos and my cheese sandwich. I'd already finished my Dasani in the car. If I went inside for another bottle from the machine, I'd lose my table.

Karma Jones plopped down opposite me. "Girl, you look like shit. Are you okay? What'd the nurse say?"

I almost choked on the first bite of my sandwich. I hadn't

even seen her coming. Shaking my head, I covered my mouth with my hand. "I felt horrible for a few minutes, but after I barfed, I was okay."

She drew back. "Ewww, are you like, really sick?" Her eyes grew wide. "Or something else?"

Damn. I'd just added to my own rumor. "No, it's not that. I'm not—I just got a stomach bug or something. Probably should have gone home, but—"

Karma didn't wait to hear the rest. She hopped up and blew me a kiss as she hurried away. "I'd give you a hug, but I don't want to catch anything. Feel better soon!" And then she flitted away.

She landed at a nearby table where Shelley and her team sat, ignoring everyone else. When they began to glance my way, one after the other, I knew Karma had told them I might be pregnant.

Smoothing my bangs over my forehead, I wondered how this day could get any worse. Then Kera and Will strolled by, hand in hand, and my misery was complete. I let my hair fall forward across my face, as if that would hide me.

I immediately flashed back to how it had felt when Will and I first started holding hands. When I'd walked into the choir room that first day, the day I spied him standing there beside the risers, all of a sudden, I'd felt self-conscious in a brand new way. Everything in the room went away and the space between the two of us had taken on a new definition. Like looking through Alice-in-Wonderland-binoculars.

He wasn't shy. I felt him noticing me all through class. He didn't stare, but every time I glanced up he glanced up, too, and smiled. He had the best smile.

I was thrilled to walk down the hall with him after choir

that day. It immediately became a ritual. He would walk me over to Spanish even though he had to turn and sprint to his next class on the opposite side of the campus.

Will was such a charmer he never got in trouble for being late, or for anything. He just smiled that wide, white smile, flashed those perfect dimples, and sailed on through. Being with Will had been easy until it wasn't. Until he wanted more, and more, and finally, everything.

I pushed my hair behind my ears, smoothed my bangs down for good measure, and stood, picking up my lunch remains as I did. Kera and Will pretended they hadn't seen me, or maybe they were so wrapped up in their own little world, they really didn't see me, or anyone.

My stomach roiled.

My heart hurt.

The girls at Shelley's table began to gather their things.

I squinted up at the rays of sunlight falling through the leaves and found myself smoothing my loose shirt down over my flat stomach and hips. It was a self-conscious gesture, one my injured psyche made without my foreknowledge. A couple of the girls looked my way, but they didn't comment.

I hurried back into the building just before the bell rang. Thank God Art was my next class. Kera once jokingly admitted she felt a little jealous of the way I could capture faces and shapes with just a few charcoal lines. "It's like your brain is hardwired to your fingers."

I remember feeling my face grow warm when she said it. Now it just felt like more betrayal. Rushing into the bright, open Art room, I shouldered off my backpack along with thoughts of Kera. I clipped a new heavyweight sheet of water-color paper onto my standup easel.

Mr. Stanford allowed us to work at our own pace after he taught us new techniques, like arabesque or chiaroscuro—working with deep, contrasting shadow—and he also allowed us to choose our final projects each quarter, in addition to our general sketchbooks, of course. That's where we kept all the lessons and examples he taught us each period.

Surveying the new page, I grabbed my red Conté stick and slashed figures across the blank white space. With a few harsh strokes I depicted a couple strolling hand in hand—making certain no faces were visible—then I did something I'd never done before. I took crimson watercolor and splashed blood dripping from between their clasped fists. Inside their grip, I imagined my beating heart. Now, if I could show it pulsing there, still alive, but dying. That was my aim for this piece. After all was said and done, years down the road, I'll think that I should have titled the painting *The Fourth Rung on the Ladder*.

I didn't look up when the other kids entered the class. I didn't notice if Mr. Stanford spoke or took roll—he had only to see who wasn't at their easel to know who was missing—and I didn't even look at the clock once. In fact, it wasn't until I felt the breath of a dozen people heating up my space that I noticed the oppressive silence.

Glancing up, I blew my bangs off my forehead. I'd been working feverishly since the moment I walked in.

Mr. Stanford stood with his arms crossed lightly across his chest, studying my mixed media art. "Well done, Benji."

My hand went to my forehead and smoothed my bangs down. I'd been somewhere else. Not in the room at all. Not even in myself.

"Thank you."

The other kids actually sighed. Someone clapped. That's

when I realized they were standing around me in a semi-circle, watching me work.

Completely embarrassed, I backed away from the easel to see what I had done. Red. The overall theme of the piece was the color red. The clasped-hand figures were barely visible, as if through a cloud of red watercolor fog. The pulsing heart had taken center stage, albeit off to the left of the paper just a bit, where the true heart resides in the living chest, and yes, I could see that I had somehow captured it. Captured the beating of the ripped-out-life being cruelly, nonchalantly, squeezed to death by the two figures.

The bottom of the work appeared to be a lake of blood. The figures were walking on it. Not in it, but on it. I remembered doing that because I wanted them walking on water like the Savior. Like they were the light, and the way. As if I'd put my faith in them and was now paying the price.

I couldn't find anything wrong with the painting. I'd never used watercolor so carelessly. The red foamed and spattered and dripped across the graphite figures, across the entire page. And somehow, behind it all, I had created a dark, looming shadow, horns and scales and too many arms for one figure. Like that day on the entryway wall. But where had that image originated? It was almost an overlay, so faint it was almost invisible—holding sway over everything.

I didn't have time to think it through. People were crowding me. Murmuring.

It was done.

The painting was complete.

I'd never finished an entire painting in one class period. My usual style was to start and stop and try to perfect every single line and angle.

Mr. Stanford stood off to my right. "It's really something, Benji. I knew you had it in you, of course. I'm just glad I could witness it coming out. You were possessed." He patted my back and if there was a slight hesitation at the end of his sentence, on the word *possessed*, I didn't let myself dwell on it. It seemed fitting.

Later that day, Kate Gonzales found me in Choir. She tracked me down to ask if she could photograph my painting for the school bulletin.

I should have said no, but I was flattered. What a mistake. Before I knew it, I would be the talk of the entire school. Everyone thought they knew whom the Conte-couple represented. Everyone assumed they knew what the shadow meant. And everyone believed Karma Jones when she began to spew her must-be-knocked-up tale. Even Sergio got into the act. He had a field day with his party story.

I should have seen it coming.

But I was so thrilled at the praise for my painting I couldn't get past my own hubris. Will stood off at a distance as Kate interviewed me and took my picture to go in the article alongside my painting.

If he knew what she had come to see me about, he gave no indication. We didn't talk. Not once since the horrid party. It was like he'd never built a fire in our barbecue. Like we'd never roasted hotdogs on real sticks from the back yard, like we'd never kissed and necked and whispered our dreams to each other in the twilight. It's like *we* had never existed. I didn't know how easy it was to be thrown away. But I'd seen it with my own father. I shouldn't have been surprised. I wanted to ask my Mom, but I didn't. We didn't really talk either. Not about real stuff anyway.

Five

JANIE

By the time I got back to the car after PE that day—Ms.
Jung had us doing yoga and interpretive dance, not co-ed
thankfully, very progressive my mom said—Janie had already
heard the rumor.

"So you *are* pregnant." It was a statement, not a question.

I slung my backpack into the floorboard. "I told you I
couldn't be." This crap was getting old. Why was she so certain
I didn't simply have a stomach virus?

She slid into the driver's seat and started the engine.
"Everyone is saying you were the one barfing in the bathroom. And that you ran out of class to do it." She glanced
at me from the corner of her eye as she queued up to leave
the parking lot.

"Besides, Shawn's cousin is in your Art class and he showed
us this." She held up her phone. Someone had posted a
picture of my painting on Instagram. The caption read #Will-
Kera #preggers #oopsie #Benji. "Kyle said you were painting
like a fiend. Like someone on meth."

I looked out the window. Who had posted my painting?
I didn't recognize the username but they sure knew mine. I
dug my phone out of my backpack and there it was. Guess
they scooped the school bulletin. Can't believe I thought it

would be okay to put it out there, but then, I hadn't really thought about it at all. Just did it.

Could Katie be the one who posted? She'd been the one taking pictures of both the painting and me.

"Well?"

I shrugged. "It's only art. It can't hurt you. Besides, I was possessed." I chuckled deep in my chest. I had a tee shirt with the logo, ART CAN'T HURT YOU, but now I wondered. This was not funny. Especially not the #preggers hashtag. Nothing about this day was funny, nothing about the whole thing, but I couldn't help laughing because it really was just art. A way for me to let go of the horrid feelings seeing Will and Kera together had brought out in me.

Maybe it's true about artists needing to suffer. Look at Van Gogh. Damn. I hope I'm not going insane. My insides felt crushed, a Coke can under the heel of the student body.

Janie remained silent, but her phone buzzed almost constantly with texts.

I got a couple, too. One from Sergio wanting to know if I'd really painted that (and no, I hadn't texted him those notes. I didn't know how he got my number), and the other was from Steph. She'd been there in Art when I was painting. "You okay?" It was the kindest thing anyone had said all afternoon.

I told her I'd be okay, and then I repeated what I'd told my sister; about it just being Art and that I simply had an upset stomach. Then I turned my phone off.

Mom always said I had a high IQ. The elementary school tested it when I was five so I could qualify for Speech Therapy. It was 138 or something like that. It hadn't helped me much. It only made Mom expect more from me. And it made Jane resent me, I think.

I often wondered if they'd gotten my scores mixed up with another kid's. Those scores were the reason I skipped most of second grade. Mom wanted me to skip another grade, too. But I came down with a headachey fever that lasted nearly all summer and she made the correct assumption that I was stressing out about it so she finally put away the nonsense about me skipping another grade.

Even the school counselor agreed. "You don't want to make her a pariah."

I'd had to look that word up.

A pariah. It hadn't happened then. But at that age it didn't seem to matter that I was a little younger than most of the class. As I got older, it became more and more apparent. Especially in fifth and sixth grade when all the other girls began to develop and get their periods and I was left behind.

Pariah.

I hoped I wasn't headed that way now.

I took my phone out and turned it back on. Glanced at the messages icon. 16. That wasn't good. I hadn't had 16 messages from different people at one time—ever.

The atmosphere changed completely after that. It felt like the period of time immediately after Sharla-the-slut had moved back to town.

Her husband had been killed in Afghanistan and she'd moved back home. In no time at all, my dad was spending all his time away from home. Things between my parents went south.

Then came the realtor's convention and Dad and Sharla in the driveway. After that, Dad moved in with her and Mom filed for divorce. He never even looked back. It felt as if our family—Mom, Janie, me—had simply been disposable. I'd felt the same way watching Kera and Will getting all hot and heavy in the corner of Todd's basement game room that night. I'd been disposable.

Thrown away. Worthless. Trash.

As for my dad, I still couldn't let myself remember how I used to sit on his lap for a bedtime story—*Winnie the Pooh* had been a favorite because Dad could do such funny voices—it was impossible to understand how none of that made any difference to him now.

Oh, he pretended to still want us, Janie and me. Even made us come and visit sometimes, because the judge gave him that right, but the *new* soon wore off when we weren't that easy to get along with. I hated him after the incident in the driveway. And now he finally had his son, a little boy named Alvin who had been named after his real dad, the war hero.

I had to wonder if Dad did the chipmunk Alvin voice when he read to him at night. I knew in my heart that he did.

"You don't need Ben anymore, do you?" I'd said on one of the first visits. I hadn't meant it to be *that* ugly; it had just shot out of my mouth like a bullet. He had always joked that I was the son he'd never had. According to Janie, that was the reason he'd named me Benji. Mom had tacked on Marie because it had been my gran's middle name.

We hadn't had much contact after that weekend. For a while, I'd been glad. It was easier on all of us. But the house seemed so quiet when mom had to work late, and Janie was at work or out with Shawn. At those times, I often wondered what my dad was doing with his new kid. His new wife. His new life. I couldn't help it. I missed him. The old him. The one that belonged to me and not to Alvin, the Chipmunk.

When we got home, Janie went inside with me. She'd forgotten her uniform shirt. It usually lived in the backseat with all her other junk so she could just drop me off and go straight to work, but wonder-of-wonders, she'd taken it home to wash it.

My heart slowed back to normal when she walked inside with me. I hadn't even realized how much I'd been dreading coming home to an empty house. Just having her there, while I surreptitiously checked out every room, made everything all right.

I'm smart, okay? I knew *he* wasn't there, hiding, waiting to finish what he'd started, but still. All those unread messages on my phone, all those stares and whispers at school, everything had just unnerved me.

Janie didn't say anything when she left, just put on her shirt, brushed her hair, touched up her lipstick, and took off.

"Bye," I whispered, locking the side door behind her.

I watched her get in her car and leave before I started reading messages. Texts, Instagram posts, Facebook. Twitter, Snapchat. I had accounts on all of them; I just didn't use them much since Mom watched everything so closely. Now, my painting and my picture were plastered everywhere. I'd never wanted to be famous. Just wanted to express myself.

I sat at the breakfast bar to read. The first one said:

COOL PIC but WHEN'S THE KID DUE?

Nice color, blood red

And my favorite:

AWW, BWESS YOUR WIDDLE BWOKEN HEART
A couple said things like:
#coolnotcool or
#ewwww
And then there was one I was certain came from an account just started by Kera or one of her friends. I didn't recognize the username truthfortruth. The post read:
#thatsRude #bloodymess and #notalentsourgrapes
But the worst one of all, sort of threatening, came from a different account. It showed my painting with a huge black X across it. The caption #bloodforetellsblood made my skin crawl. It scared me. Reminded me of Paul. I longed for someone to help me sort things out, someone like my old besties; Will, or Kera. But of course they were the problem. They were the reason I'd painted the thing in the first place.

By the time Mom got home, the number of messages on my phone had tripled. I didn't want to read them, but I couldn't seem to stop. I cycled from one social media platform to the next. I didn't reply to any, I just lurked, watching, hurting, deleting.

I barely noticed when Mom swept in on a breeze. "The wind's really picking up out there." She carried a bag of groceries. "How about baked spaghetti for supper?"

I sat on my barstool, every muscle in my body tense, telling me to show her the messages. But my lips seemed glued together. I nodded and slid my phone into my pocket.

Mom filled the spaghetti pot with water and set it on the stove. "Everything all right, kiddo?" She didn't turn completely around, but I knew she was not just making idle conversation. Something about the straightness of her spine told me she was wise.

"Um. Yeah. Everything's okay." My fingers snuck to my forehead, to the almost forgotten bruise, to make sure it was still covered.

She turned around. Something in my voice, perhaps.

"What's the matter?"

Uh oh, I could see the hand coming toward me, searching for fever, a mom's first response. I hopped off the stool and headed for the bathroom. "I'm okay. I'll be back to help in a second." I tried on a smile, hoped it fit. I didn't want her to see the embarrassing messages or my painting. What had seemed like nothing, like a school project (or a necessity, truth-be-told, as if I could have kept that feeling inside), now seemed like the world's worst mistake. How would I ever show my face in school tomorrow?

An idea struck me.

In the bathroom, I made certain my concealer still covered the bruise, then I dusted a pale, white powder lightly across my entire face, careful not to get it in my brows or lashes.

By this time the sun had dipped low in the sky. The kitchen, once our favorite place in the house, was draped in shadow. A couple of bulbs had gone out of the overhead light fixture—it was an old fashioned wagon-wheel, retro, Mom said—and it still had a couple more, but for once, I was glad none of us had bothered to replace them.

I took the loaf of French bread she'd brought out of its brown paper sack and slathered it in butter before wrapping it in foil and placing it on a cookie sheet. "It's ready to warm," I said.

Mom nodded. "We can have regular spaghetti if you're hungry. Baking will just take extra time."

"That works for me. I'm looking forward to the sauce and bread mostly."

"And salad, of course."

I got the hint and took out lettuce and tomatoes.

"Just a small one," she reminded me.

As if I didn't know it would only be the two of us for supper.

"Maybe we can eat out on the back porch?"

I shrugged, putting together the salad. Once mine and Kera's favorite place. Tainted now. "If it isn't too windy," I said. My phone buzzed in my pocket. I had turned off the ringer but left it on vibrate. I pulled it out and looked at the screen. It was Janie. She never called me.

"Hello?"

"This is ridiculous." Her voice was cold. "How could you do this to me? Everyone who comes in feels the need to show me a picture of that stupid painting."

I clicked the END icon without thinking. How could I do this to *her*? What had I done to her, or anyone? I felt sick to my stomach all over again.

With a moan, I pressed a hand to my middle. Mom came around the kitchen island. Her hand went right to my forehead.

"I knew something was wrong. Is it the stomach flu? What did you eat for lunch?" Her face looked the way it had when I was six and fell off the swing, cracking my elbow.

Thank God for shadows, I thought. She didn't seem to notice the bruise.

"You're awfully pale, but I don't think you have a fever." She stepped back and examined me from a distance. "Why don't you go get comfortable in the recliner, turn on the TV. I'll bring you a plate when it's ready. Do you still feel like eating?"

I nodded. Lunch seemed like a distant memory. Maybe the thick bread would help my stomach stop rolling.

Mom didn't question me anymore. I turned my phone off completely. I didn't open my computer at all. Instead, I put the TV on Nick at Night and pretended I was ten years old and everything would be all right in the morning.

The smell of the rich spaghetti sauce brought me out of a doze.

Mom placed a lap tray across my legs as I sat up. She smiled, went back to the kitchen, and brought her own supper on a tray, too. Not eating in the living room had always been her one cardinal rule. But now she was willing to break it. I must've done a bang up job on my makeup.

Suddenly, I was ravenous. Mom had also brought iced tea in our good cut crystal glasses. It seemed as if she needed someone to take care of. "Thanks, Mom." I dipped a hunk of bread into the thick sauce and devoured it. The taste was sharper, sweeter, than I remembered. As if all my senses were heightened because of my anxiety. The spaghetti was tender, the tea cold and sweet, and for the moment at least, life was good.

Mom twirled spaghetti onto her fork. "Maybe this will make you feel all better." She popped a bite in her mouth, chewed, swallowed, sipped tea, and then asked, "Everything all right at school?"

The bite of bread I had just swallowed turned to a solid lump in my throat. I took a huge gulp of tea to wash it down, began to sputter instead. Droplets of tea sprayed from my lips as I tried to stand. My tray began to slide. I was choking. Literally choking. The bread wouldn't budge.

"Honey!" Mom grabbed my plate before it hit the floor.

She couldn't get the tray. My knife and fork bounced on the hardwood. The tray hit with a hard thump.

Holding my drippy plate with one hand, Mom began to pound me on the back with her other hand. "Should I do the Heimlich?" Panic edged her voice.

I shook my head, uncertain. I could breathe through my nose so I tried to focus on that. Leaping to my feet must have jarred the lump. Somehow it went down. I inhaled raggedly, began to cough.

"Benji. Damn. Are you okay?"

I could see Mom from the corner of my eye. She had one hand pressed to the center of her chest.

"I'm okay. Too big a bite. Bread. Greedy-gus." I wished I hadn't said that last part. It was one of Dad's old jokey sayings, Greedy-gus, greedy-gus, soon you'll look just like a bus. But Mom didn't seem to notice.

She set my plate on the coffee table and patted me gently. "I thought you were really choking."

"Yeah," I said. "Me, too." I felt stupid. My stomach revolted and I ran to the bathroom and threw up the few bites I had managed to get down.

Afterward, I put on my fleece pajamas—the ones covered with smiling cats—and crawled into my bed. The *Love Bear* Will had given me for Valentine's taunted me from the corner. I'd thrown it away once, right after the party, and then I'd gone and got it back out, thankful there hadn't been anything nasty in the laundry room garbage.

Mom came in and I closed my eyes, certain she couldn't see me in the dim room.

"Ben?" Her soft voice almost made me answer.

I played possum.

"Let me know if I can get you anything," she said. "I'll check on you before I go to bed." She pulled the door shut, carefully, quietly.

A tear slipped from the outside corner of my right eye and made its way toward my ear. If I had tried to answer, I might have told her everything. And I couldn't do that. Too humiliating.

I watched the fat white moon rise behind my thin blue curtains. How had everything gone so wrong?

Six

Don't let the Bastards get ya Down

I must have been asleep when Mom came in later. It wasn't until the next morning that I realized I'd slept.

"Ready for breakfast?" Her voice held a hopeful lilt.

I groaned. All the events of yesterday came rushing back at me. I slid my hand beneath my quilt in search of my phone. I'd tucked it there thinking I would look at it after Mom left my room last night. Somehow, I never had.

Now, I felt it, I felt it's power. I felt its possibilities. Could I face those possibilities? Was it possible that things had changed overnight, that the trolls had gotten it out of their systems, that I would click that little icon and see nothing but good?

I believed in my painting. It felt like the realest thing I'd ever created. The realest thing I'd ever done. Is that why people were reacting to it this way? Or were they just evil minions looking for a victim?

Mom stepped closer to the bed. "Waffles?"

I stretched and used that as an excuse to turn my face away, bruise already on my mind. "Toast? Coffee?"

Mom laughed. "Coffee, huh? Maybe that would be best. Come on in as soon as you're ready."

In the bathroom, I showered and pulled on fresh jeans

and a plain blue tee shirt. When I looked in the mirror, the effect was blue. That wasn't exactly my intention. Not blue. I just wanted one solid color. Monotone. Today, I didn't want anyone to notice me.

At the breakfast bar, Mom placed a mug of coffee the color of caramel in front of me. It was in my old SpongeBob mug. That made me smile. It also made me homesick for when I was a little kid. As she buttered toast—she often went out of her way to spoil us when she didn't have a house to show, sort of like her way of making up for the times she had to leave us to our own devices I think—I took out my phone and touched the screen. I'd put it off as long as I could. The desire to know was greater than the fear of not knowing.

The number 43 popped up with my message icon.

My heart sank to the pit of my stomach. My pale coffee sloshed and threatened. This wasn't good. It couldn't be good.

I clicked on the first one.

Hey, did you see this? Someone else must have had the same thought I did. An altered picture of me popped up. Van Gogh's bandaged ear had been pasted over one of mine. The caption read, *Crazy much?*

Strange how it was almost the exact same thought I'd had.

Am I crazy? Was that one painting the work of a crazy person?

I quickly scrolled through the rest of the messages. They were almost all versions of the Van Gogh meme. Some had my painting as a meme, too. They all had similar remarks. Some much worse than others. The *#Crazymuch?* hashtag had been repeated over and over.

Just before I clicked off the messages completely, one text jumped out at me. It was in all caps from a number I didn't recognize. It read: DON'T LET THE BASTARDS GET YA DOWN!

Who could that be? The quote was from a Rhianna song but I'd also read it in *A Handmaid's Tale* by Margaret Atwood. Was someone actually on my side? If they were, they obviously didn't want me to know their name. But that quote was one Will had jokingly said many times when things didn't go my way. He'd chuck me under the chin and say, "C'mon, Ben. Don't let the bastids get ya down." He'd say it in a funny, New England accent and I never asked him why. It just seemed to make it that much funnier. Could the text be from Will?

I must have made some sort of noise because Mom turned around, butter knife still in hand.

"Honey?"

I flung myself off the stool and ran for the bathroom. There was no way I could go and face all those hashtaggers. No friggin' way. Not even with someone (Will?) on my side. Not even in my monotone, blend-in blue.

Mom came and stood outside the bathroom door. "Benji, sweetie? What's the matter, are you sick?"

I made garbled, gagging, noises. Strings of coffee-tinged bile followed by dry heaves. I'd never had this sort of chronic stomach upset in my life. Even my long hair was sticky with bile. I hadn't pulled it back quickly enough.

After a moment I grabbed a washcloth and ran it under the cold tap, blotted my lips, my cheeks, my green-going-yellow forehead. "I'm all right," I called through the door. "Just a minute."

The coldness felt so good (how could simple text messages and memes make my skin burn with shame?) that I gave up and stuck my face down toward the faucet and splashed myself with handfuls of cold water. When I raised my head, someone else's haunted eyes peered at me from the mirror.

After another minute, I heard Mom move away from the door. I dried my face and reapplied the concealer to my forehead. I knew the way my mother's mind worked. Big bruise followed by bouts of nausea and vomiting would = concussion. I'd be in the ER before I could puke again. It never occurred to me the two really could be related. Not until much, much later that is.

I checked my reflection one last time before I opened the door. There was no way I was going to school. Not today, maybe not ever. I would beg to be homeschooled. Here's where the IQ would come in handy. Yes, I'd play the IQ card. I'll study on my own, I'd tell her. Self-paced. Abe Lincoln-library-card-Internet-self-taught-early-graduation, you name it, whatever it takes. Just let me stay home.

I made my way back to my bedroom determined to pull the covers over my head and hide from the world. But I had to pass the kitchen doorway first.

There stood Mom, holding my phone, scrolling, scrolling, scrolling, a look of horror on her face. Even from where I stood I could see the blood-red memes flying by. The phone must have slipped out of the kangaroo pocket on my pajama top. I know I didn't leave it there on the breakfast bar when I bolted for the bathroom—did I? Could I be that stupid? IQ? Hah. I rubbed my forehead gently. A headache had settled there like an old friend. One like Kera.

Mom looked up. "What is all this?"

Tears sprang to my eyes. I didn't let them fall, but they blurred my vision. I shook my head. "It was just a painting I did in Art. I don't know how it went so viral."

She held the phone in her palm. "Such ugly messages, why?"

I shrugged and sank to the floor. "Kera and Will." I let the names hang there. "They're dating now. I saw them walking together, holding hands, right before Art." I sniffled back a sneaky tear. The coolness of the tile floor seeped through my pajama bottoms freezing me to the floor like a wet finger stuck to an ice cube. My back sliding down the wall reminded me of the awful monster-moment from days earlier.

Mom must have seen me shiver. She came and pulled me to my feet. Even then, I tried to keep my face turned so that she wouldn't see the bruise. No need to drag that crappy day into this one. The two things had nothing to do with each other.

Walking me to my room and tucking me into my bed like a toddler, Mom seemed to make it a point not to seek eye contact. "So you painted the picture in Art?"

I nodded. "I felt possessed. My heart hurt so bad to see my two ex-best friends like that. The paint flowed onto the page like magic."

Moisture plopped onto the back of my hand and I looked up to see my mother wiping her eyes, too. I shifted my hips so she could sit beside me.

"I know how you feel, honey. There's nothing that compares with the pain and anger of betrayal. It's horrible." She hesitated and I knew she *did* understand. She didn't berate me or tell me I shouldn't have put my feelings on paper. "It's a beautiful picture," she said. "Heartbreaking." Then she laughed. "No pun intended."

I smiled at that, recalling how I'd tried to make the heart appear to pulse as the two entwined hands crushed it between them. A tiny sliver of hope began to worm its way into my brain.

But Mom's face didn't mirror hope. "I don't quite under-stand all these ugly messages, though. Why are they saying—"

My eyes closed on the idea of hope. I interrupted her before she could ask the rest of her question. "Seeing Will and Kera that way made me sick at my stomach." I opened my eyes and looked at her. "Just like today." My glance took in the phone still clutched in her hand. "Someone heard me retching in the bathroom, from that and my painting they added two and two together and came up with pregnant." I actually had the two incidents reversed, but I didn't try to explain that part. It didn't matter which happened first. Just that they had.

Mom blanched. I'd never used that old-fashioned word in real life, but it immediately came to my mind when all the color ran out of her face as if poured from a glass. Her eyes, now as haunted as my own, stared into mine. "Are you?"

This time my tears would not be stopped. "Of course not!"

"No possibility? You and Will were so close."

I shook my head so hard the tears flew from my eyes like rain. "We didn't. I never..." My stomach began to churn again. The nausea was always there, just waiting.

Mom reached out to touch me but I blocked her hand, pushed it away. "Don't!"

"Benji—" Her voice belied her hurt.

Guilt flooded my gut. I'd never been rude to my mother on purpose. Since Dad left, she was my everything. "Sorry," I mumbled. "I just want to go back to sleep. I don't understand why everyone got so bent out of shape. It's just *art*." The real reason I suddenly wanted her to be gone was because she assumed I'd slept with Will when in reality that was the reason we'd broken up—because I wouldn't. Is that irony? I'd say yes.

Mom stood. My bed creaked ever so slightly. "Okay." I heard her exhale as she walked away. "I'll be back to check on you in a little while."

I thought she'd gone, but then she said, "Does Janie know about this?"

"Yes," I muttered. "She's mad at me, too." I didn't see what that had to do with anything. In my opinion, Janie was part of the problem.

I didn't go to school that day.

Mom followed up on her promise and came to check on me throughout the day, bringing me iced tea, patting my shoulder beneath my quilt (I did not shrug or push her away this time), telling me she loved me. She had taken my phone with her. I didn't care. She'd already seen everything anyway. I'd deleted all of Will's texts from when we were together. There had been a few in which he'd declared we were soul mates. *Soul mates.* Is it any wonder my heart felt crushed?

I slept all day. Mom left me a sandwich at lunch, but she didn't force me to eat it. I just turned over and buried my head again. Pretty sure I heard her talking to Janie at one point, whether on the phone or in person, I don't know. I braced myself for an onslaught of questions, or bits and pieces from school.

But Janie didn't come in and sit on the edge of the bed the way Mom did. I didn't look at the clock, just rolled over and went back to sleep.

When I awoke, the room had dimmed and I knew the sun was on the other side of the house, headed toward the western horizon. My light blue curtains hung down as if they'd never been new, never been washed or freshened by a breeze from an open window. It stunned me to realize I'd slept straight through the day. I hadn't done that since I was a kid with fever.

I got up and staggered to the bathroom that joined my room to Janie's.

Mom must've heard me stirring. She knocked on my door and stuck her head inside just as I crawled back into bed.

It surprised me to see that she was dressed in work clothes. She also had her hair done and her face made up. Had she gone to work after all?

"What time is it?"

She crossed to the window and opened the curtains a bit. "It's just after four. A little storm blew in around noon. I'm surprised it didn't wake you."

I cocked one eyebrow at the window. "That's why it's so dim."

Mom nodded and pulled the sash up a few inches.

We both inhaled the fresh scent of rain and I was glad to see the hem of the curtain flutter to life.

Her back still to me, Mom said, "I've been to your school."

My whole body froze. The fresh rainy scent turned to ice that broke into crystals inside my blood. "Why?" The word clinked in the air between us.

Of course I knew why. All those texts and posts. The very reason I hadn't shown them to her to begin with, because I knew she'd have to do something about them. I wondered if she'd mentioned them to my father. They didn't speak much, unless it had to do with Janie, or me, and then only in emergencies, like when Janie had appendicitis and had to be rushed to the hospital. I didn't think this was on that level though.

"What did you do?" I didn't mean it to sound accusatory, but it did and I couldn't take it back.

Mom turned. "There won't be any more ugly messages. The counselor took it very seriously. She was appalled. We went to the assistant principal who took us directly to Mrs. Gloss. They made an announcement over the PA that all the pictures and texts would be deleted immediately—with random spot checks—or parents would be contacted and suspensions would abound."

I knew they could do it. Our school had a new system that would let them send a text message to every parent with a cell phone all at once. It was a phone tree they'd created after Joe Rickover was caught with a gun in his pickup. He claimed he'd only been hunting rabbits the day before—Sunday—and forgot to take it out at home. We all believed him. Everyone knew Joe liked hunting and fishing and anything outdoorsy. Nevertheless, the incident had brought my hometown into the here-and-now in terms of what could have happened.

I felt my eyes growing wider and wider as Mom spoke. My fist jammed itself into my mouth to stifle the scream clawing its way up my throat.

"Honey, what's wrong? This is a good thing. You won't be bothered any—"

"Mom!" I shook my head, my tangled hair slapping my cheeks. "They'll hate me. Everyone will hate me. And it won't even matter. It will still be on Facebook, Instagram, Twitter—it doesn't matter what they do at school. This. This is so much worse. Now, everyone will think I asked you to go up there. They'll think they got to me." I clenched my fists and dug my nails into my palms as hard as I could, until the pain there took my mind off the pain inside me, at least for the moment.

Seven

Mom came across the room. "But now there won't be any more ugly messages."

She seemed stuck on that, like a mantra. We both heard the door open and close as Janie came in. I expected her to go straight to her room to change for work; instead, she stomped into my room, brandishing her phone. "What the hell, Benji?" She shook it at me.

I couldn't believe she'd just cussed in front of Mom.

"Janie Lynn! What—"

Janie pointed at me, her forefinger trembling. "She. Has. Ruined. My. Life!"

Tears popped into my eyes. Again. How could there be any more? Shouldn't I be dry by now? No. They'd been there all along, hiding, waiting. Now they ran down my cheeks in rivulets. I felt flayed, my feelings hanging in tatters; even then I couldn't seem to defend myself; I just kept shaking my head, like with Mom.

"You went to the principal? Told them you were being *cyber*-bullied? All because of that freaking painting?" Every sentence ended on a high-note question, as if she couldn't believe it herself. Her face wore a mask of pure hatred, her blue eyes almost black, her entire body hard as stone. "I'll never forgive you for this. Everyone started laughing, looking at me when the principal made the announcement—" As she spoke, she stalked closer and closer to my bed.

Mom stood. "That is enough!"

Janie turned her eyes on Mom. She hadn't even noticed her until that moment. "I hate her! She ruins everyth—"

Whap!

Mom slapped her, hard, shocking us all.

Janie's head rocked sideways, her free hand flying to her face to examine the damage.

"I told the principal," Mom said. "Not your sister." Her voice sounded as hard as Janie's posture.

My sister looked from Mom to me as if trying to understand this new information. When she took her hand away from her face, a bright red palm print decorated her cheek.

"Then it's your fault as much as *hers*." Janie whirled on her heel and rushed from my room.

Mom sank to my bed. Her shoulders slumped. In all our years, she had never slapped either of us. I could only recall one or two spankings when we were really small. Once when I pulled away from her and ran into the street in front of a car, and another time when Janie took a candy bar from the convenience store and then lied about it.

"I can't believe this." Mom looked down at her hands lying in her lap as if they belonged to someone else. "I didn't mean to slap her, but those words, that tone of voice..."

I didn't care that she'd slapped Janie. I wanted to slap her myself. She said she hated me. As if I'd done this painting just to make people talk, or look at her. Didn't she care that *my* life was over? That I couldn't possibly go back to school? She could just send a few texts, *oh look what my ignorant little sister did*, but what could I do? My heart had bled out onto the canvas for the whole world to see—and they had laughed. And pointed. And said awful things.

Stunned and exhausted at this turn of events, I curled back into my quilt and covered my head. A black pall closed around me, darker than the rain clouds, shutting me down.

Without a word, Mom got up and walked out of my room. I heard the side door open and close and I wondered if it was Janie going on to work. Would she go to work with that mark on her face?

I didn't wonder for long. After the things she'd said, I didn't even care. I flung my quilt aside and sat up. All of a sudden, I needed to get on my computer, to see what else was going on. But my laptop no longer graced my desktop. Mom must have taken it while I slept.

I threw my legs over the edge of the bed and stood, stumbling toward the dresser, the blood rushing from my head leaving me dizzy. I realized I hadn't eaten. That pulled me toward the kitchen. And there lay my phone, on the breakfast bar. Blue shadows striped it from the slanted window blinds behind the sink. Raindrops curled down the window. I dragged my feet. *Do I want to know, do I want to know what they're saying now?* My head said *no, leave it alone*, but that didn't matter, my emotions overruled my head and I snatched up my phone, unaware I'd been holding my breath. When I exhaled, my thumb immediately pressed the home key and I was in, scrolling through the most recent posts and messages.

Mom came in from the side porch and saw me with the phone. "Oh, honey, don't. You shouldn't—"

I knew she'd been outside, probably trying to catch Janie before she left, but that didn't matter either. My classmates were angry. They were as furious as Janie, but for different reasons. The parent phone tree had been utilized after all—why, I don't know—and it had worked fairly well.

According to the new texts, parents all over town were demanding to see what their kids were doing that caused the principal to contact them. Of course that didn't sit well with any of the kids. They all blamed me. Just like I knew they would. The automatic text tree that had been set up for use in case of emergency had been implemented for me. For my stupid painting and me.

My phone slipped from my numb fingers and clipped the edge of the bar before it hit the tile floor. I looked up at my mother. I wanted to be angry with her, but I couldn't. I just felt sad. She didn't cause it; just tried to fix it. In the back of my mind, hadn't I wanted to run to her when it first happened, when I got those first rude memes?

I bent down to retrieve my phone just as a new text came in. *Bing!* I touched the screen. THIS IS AWFUL. The new message was in all caps again, to get my attention, I suppose. ARE YOU OKAY? Once again, it came from a number I didn't recognize. I tried to scroll back to see if it was the same one from yesterday, but there were too many. Even though most had been deleted, there were still too many.

I glanced up at Mom, who had gone straight to the coffee pot. I threw caution to the wind and hit reply. *I'll be all right, I guess. Who is this, Will?* He was the only person I could think of who might care. We'd spent so much time together, sharing music, our dreams, our fears.

I could see the other person typing. "Will? The one who caused all this? Are you serious?"

The all caps were gone. That made me feel better. An all

caps person always seemed slightly unhinged to me. "Then who?" I wanted to ask if it was Kera, but that first text (Don't let the bastards get ya down) had seemed so *masculine* that I couldn't imagine otherwise.

The response came rushing back. "You don't know me. I just recently transferred here. But I saw your painting. I'm amazed."

I carried the phone to my room and sat, cross-legged, on my bed, trying to decide if it could be another joke. "Did you send me that other text, yesterday?"

"If you mean the Atwood quote, then yes. That was me."

I still wasn't convinced. It was what Will used to say. Would he be that cruel? To lead me on this way? For what purpose? Did he want to be friends without letting on to Kera? What was that other quote, the one about "oh what a tangled web we weave?"

Maybe I could catch him out somehow. Trip him up.

I wrote, "If you've only been here a few weeks, how did you know the painting was about Will?"

The person shot back. "Arrrggghhh. You're killing me! Everyone knows it's about Will and that chick, Kera."

Before I could respond, another came in. "The way she hangs on him makes me kinda sick. I'm not a prude or anything, but what's she trying to prove?"

I sent back a big-eyed Smiley. "I wondered that, too. Do you understand my painting, I mean do you know what it represents?" So much for trying to trick him. All of a sudden, I wanted to know what he thought.

"To answer your question, I sit with Bucky Tabor at lunch. He told me how you and Will dated all year and *she* was supposed to be your best friend. I understand the imagery. It's very powerful."

Bucky Tabor. I pictured the stout boy with the buzz cut hair and far-away eyes. He was the only kid I knew with Asperger's syndrome. No one bothered him, but no one really befriended him, either. He just sort of bopped along, talking to himself and smiling at things no one else understood.

I tried to recall a new kid sitting with Bucky, but since I'd been keeping my head down the past few days, I hadn't noticed much of anything. "Bucky, huh? What do y'all talk about?"

The person sent back a row of laughing Smileys. "Anything and everything. That kid knows a little bit about every topic. I asked him if he liked to read and he said only the internet."

"What's that mean?"

"That's what I asked. He said he just scrolled the news feeds and trending topics and looked up what he didn't understand."

"Wow." I let that sink in. It reminded me of—me. "So, who are you? And why did you scream at me in those first texts?"

This time the response did not come shooting back at me. I glanced through everything we'd said. It all seemed legit. What was taking him so long? If it was indeed a *him*.

At last it came. "I was afraid you would just delete my text without reading if I didn't get your attention. So I yelled at you."

Well, that didn't make much sense. "I almost deleted you *because* of the all caps. But to tell you the truth, I thought you were Will trying to make me feel better. That quote you sent? He said it all the time."

"OMG. *bangs head on desk* I almost screwed up without even knowing it. My name is Sam Edgerton. I live at 1526 South 3rd St. My Dad and I rented the house when he got transferred here from Dallas. As you can see, my number is

555-432-1008. I'm so, so sorry. Man. I can't believe I almost messed up without even knowing it!"

I waited. Could it be real? A new student? How could I not know this?

Another text came in. I clicked on it.

"It's me. Sam. Please don't delete me."

For one second, I debated on deleting anyhow. How could I be certain? Other texts were still coming in. Not as many—apparently some parents were taking note—but some were still coming. Thanks a lot, one read. Another person wrote, if you can't stand the heat—stay out of Art class. (The fact that someone from Art may have sent that one really upset me. Art had always been my refuge.)

Mom had already deleted my social media accounts from my phone. I wondered if she'd went into my laptop and deleted the accounts completely. She could have. All my passwords were stored on my computer. Since Dad and his affair, transparency had become her number one rule. Apparently Dad and Sharla-the-slut had been texting and sexting each other for months before he left us. If Mom had known his passwords, I wonder what would have happened. Could she have stopped it? Or would she have even tried?

At last, I added Sam to my contacts list. "Okay," I texted. "I've added you."

I set about deleting almost all my old contacts. When I came to Will's name, I hesitated, then I hit delete and moved on. When I finished, the only ones that remained were a few I couldn't decide about, plus my mom, my dad (why, I don't know), my sister (again, why, I don't know), and Uncle Aidan.

When I came to Uncle Aidan, I actually smiled. I thought

about calling him, getting his take on all this. Uncle Aidan could make light of anything. My dad said that was one of his problems. Didn't take anything seriously. Maybe that's how I should be. Take a cue from Mom's little brother, go back to school with a smile on my face and give everyone the finger—as if I could.

I went back through my list. When I came to Karma, I hesitated. Had she sent anything ugly? I couldn't recall. There'd been so many. Then I remembered how she'd seemed to talk to Shelly's group at lunch yesterday. How they had all glanced at me under their lashes. Maybe Karma was the one who started the pregnancy rumor. My thumb smashed DELETE on her entry.

How about Jenny and Steph? They were both in Art, too.

My finger skipped over their entries. I was pretty sure one of them had sent a nice message. If anything bad came in, I could always delete later. But for now, benefit of the doubt.

I came to Kera's entry. I'd taken her out of favorites, but I hadn't deleted her completely. There was nothing nice left between us now. Nothing but hate and anger on my part. I touched delete. It hurt to see her name disappear.

A loud clap of thunder brought me back to the present. I glanced at the window, surprised to see that night had fallen. Lightning splashed its strobe into the room. I looked down at the phone. One text waited. Sam.

At least he's polite, I thought. Waiting for me to respond. "Want coffee?"

I stared at the text.

Want coffee? What did that mean? How did he even know I liked coffee? Did he really think I'd meet him this late, not even knowing what he looked like? "Send me your profile pic." I started to hit send, and then wrote. "I don't even know you."

He wrote LOL, and then sent his picture.

I examined it carefully. His hair was longish, brown, a little messy. His eyes were sea blue. Lashes black. They outlined his eyes dramatically. I enlarged the picture. Was he wearing guyliner? If so, he was an expert.

"When was this taken?" I asked.

"Just now," he replied. "Here's my room."

He sent me a video of a cluttered room, bed unmade, clothes all over everything, a poster of some guy with a guitar on his wall, a closed MacBook on his desk, and then he reversed the camera to his face and gave me a huge grin. One of his front teeth was crooked, just slightly. "Hi, Benji." He waved comically, like a beauty queen.

I touched my tiny phone screen and enlarged his face. Hmm. Hello, Sam. Are you for real? Now, that I could see him, I did remember glimpsing him in the hallway once or twice. But I'd been so busy watching for Kera and Will that I had barely looked up.

"Hi," I texted. "Nice to see you." Smiley face.

"Your turn," he replied. "I already know what you look like, but I wouldn't mind a picture or video."

Something clunked into the pit of my stomach. He could do anything he wanted with a picture of me. Would he superimpose it over my painting? Put my face over Kera's or even over Will's? Of course they weren't facing us in my painting, but I could easily imagine him putting my face on the back of one of their heads. Just for fun.

Honesty? Or make an excuse? For the first time in my life, I stuck up for myself. If only I'd done that the day the monster had come over. If only I'd said, "No, you can't come in. You can't have a drink. You need to leave." And then slammed the door shut.

How would that have felt? Would he have left?

It didn't really matter now. I'd made a stupid little plan to give him the water he requested, and *hope* he would go away. It didn't work anymore than it had worked for me to jokingly go along with the tickling from Keenan rather than screaming *Stop!* loud enough for his mother to hear. I'm not sure that would have done any good in his case, the situation was too weird, but at least I would have tried. At least I might've prevented that last painful, humiliating pinch, and that cold shoulder from his sister.

At that very second, I made a pact with myself to always stand up for myself from now on, even if it hurt someone's feelings.

What if I'd been honest with Will and Kera? What if I'd jumped at the chance to go with him that night at the party, the way Kera had done? The way I'd really wanted to do. She certainly hadn't worried about hurting my feelings. Nor had he.

Would he and I be together instead of him and Kera? Would all of this mess be an alternate universe story? Why would I even want that? If he and Kera didn't care anything about me, if they could turn their backs on me as easily as they did, why would I still want either of them? Besides, we'd broken up because I wouldn't have sex with him on the screened porch day bed. Shouldn't that be my choice, instead of a requirement?

The questions loomed in my head. Something would have to be wrong with me to want to go back in time. To be with people who treated me like that.

The phone lay quietly in my hand. Whatever the principal had said in her announcement, or in the phone tree text, it had worked. No one texted. Could it be over?

I looked at Sam's picture again. At his crooked-toothed video grin. And I wanted to respond. To have a nice interaction with a guy who didn't want to kiss me, or tickle me, or hurt me. But I couldn't be certain. Not yet.

So I said I'd think about it. Then I said goodnight and shut off the phone before he could reply.

Eight

The Fifth Rung

Mom didn't come in my room again. That surprised me. I went in search of her and found her in the living room recliner. The TV had been muted. I couldn't believe how tired she looked in the glow of the black and white movie playing silently in the rain-dark room.

I stood watching as rain pelted the window behind her. Sometimes the power went out when it rained. Should I find the flashlight just in case? Things felt strange, in limbo. I couldn't imagine ever going to school again.

"Mom?"

She raised her head and looked at me. That's when I realized she was on the phone, listening to someone.

"Who is it?" I mouthed.

Either she couldn't understand me, or she chose to pretend she couldn't. She looked back at the TV and dismissed me completely.

That scared me. Who could she be talking to? I felt certain it was about my situation, but if so, why didn't she even look at me?

In the kitchen, I made a grilled cheese sandwich and a glass of chocolate milk, comfort food, and attempted to soothe my shattered nerves.

I sat at the breakfast bar again, and I thought of Sam. And I thought of school, and my painting, and Mr. Stanford, the Art teacher. What would become of my painting? Would it still be put in the school newspaper? Not now. Surely, not now.

The sandwich turned to dust in my mouth.

I gulped the cold chocolate milk and stared out the window at the night rain. The storm was almost gone, no more thunder, no more lightning, just sweet, sweet moisture. I walked to the kitchen window and opened it the way Mom had opened my bedroom window earlier. The smell soothed me even more than the food.

It was one of the last good things I remember from that night. The next thing I knew, we were all standing on the fifth rung on the ladder. Despair was just around the corner. There would be no turning back.

I did a cursory search of the house but didn't locate my computer. Mom had hidden it well. She would probably give it to me if I asked, but I didn't ask. I felt as if I'd already put her through too much. Caused too much trouble. Besides, every time I looked in; she was still on the phone. But she didn't seem to be talking much, just listening, like before.

Eventually, I went on to bed. The whole house felt empty, on the edge of a precipice ready to slide. Things were just off. I thought of turning on my phone; it was so hard not to, but I held myself steady. The thought of Sam, wondering what had happened, lured me. But I'd been burned too many times in the past few hours.

I turned on my old TV instead. Found the Investigation Discovery channel—people with problems a lot worse than mine—then crawled back into my little bed. I still had a nagging headache, but who wouldn't with all this going on?

That reminded me of my vow not to return to class, but seriously, life without school? Was there such a thing? I drifted off wondering what life would be like without a regular schedule of classes to attend.

I awoke to the sound of raised voices. Mom. Janie. Someone else. A man. What the hell? Was I dreaming? I lay still, listening, trying to decide what was real, and what was imaginary.

In the next few seconds, everything became clear.

My mom yelled, "Oliver!"

That's when I knew my dad was in the living room.

Still wearing the same pajamas from the day before, I climbed out of bed and stood just inside my bedroom doorway, waiting to see what would happen next. Why had she yelled at him? What was he doing here?

Over the squeal of tires on wet pavement, I heard Janie yell, "Good riddance!" I stepped into the living room just as Mom sank down on the couch.

"What's going on? Was that Dad?"

Janie ignored me. I felt like an intruder—or a kid. As if she'd suddenly become an adult and this was adult business. Not for kids like me.

Not knowing what else to do, I sat down beside Mom. Something had gone wrong. I didn't think it involved me, but what if it did? Dad never came over anymore. Not since Janie and I had made it clear we didn't want to be a part of his "new family."

"What's wrong?" I said at last. "I heard Dad's voice, right?"

Mom turned her face toward me. I had forgotten all about the bruise on my forehead. I'd washed my concealer off when

I went to bed. It had only been three days. Today would be the fourth.

Mom reached toward me in the light of the reading lamp. "What happened to your forehead?"

I immediately smoothed my bangs down. "Oh, I fell the other day."

Janie started to say something, but I jumped into the gap.

"But why was Dad here? I know I heard his voice; heard you yell his name—"

"He wants to come back," Janie said. "After all this time, he thinks he can just waltz back in."

Nothing could have shocked me more. I sat there with my mouth open, catching flies. Now I understood Mom's phone calls, all the listening. It had been Dad. No wonder my problems had suddenly taken a backseat.

I didn't know what to say. I remembered my pact. Honesty. "So, do you want him to come home?" I regretted the word home as soon as it slipped through my lips. "I mean back. Do you want him to come back?"

Mom smiled a sad, sad smile. I remembered wondering if I would have taken Will back when he asked me to go for a walk that night. Was that how Mom felt?

The rain had stopped. Without it, the world went melancholy. The hole Dad had left in our lives felt like an abyss. But now it had become an abyss filled with possibilities.

Janie faded into the background. I assumed she'd gone to her room, back to bed. Or had she even been to bed yet?

Mom still hadn't answered.

"What time is it?"

She glanced at her phone. "3:15 a.m. Way too late, that's for sure."

I thought of the imagery in my painting. Kera and Will. I thought Mom's time-telling might be a sort of omen. *Too late. Way too late.*

My painting seemed trivial now, in the dead of night. Especially compared to the fact that my dad might be coming back, might be coming home. "Did you tell him about me?"

Mom looked at me as if she had no clue.

"Did you tell him I wasn't going back to school?"

"I... Yes. I tried. He couldn't seem to comprehend." She sighed. "All he could talk about was how Sharla had thrown him out. How he'd made a mistake, how he suddenly realized how much he loved us." She patted my hand. "Maybe she found someone younger. Her own age, or something."

There may have been a trace of bitterness in her voice. Or it may have simply been fatigue. Still, there was that honesty thing. I had to know. Had to ask. "Do you want him to come back, Mom?"

Janie reappeared in the doorway. "No, she doesn't want him to come back and neither do I." Her voice wasn't bitter; it was venomous.

"I don't think it's your place to say." I made the statement quietly, taking the honesty thing a step too far, but Janie heard. She pounced on me.

"What would you care?" She shook her finger in my face like an angry schoolteacher. "You screw up everything anyway—"

Mom stood, wearily. "Janie I told you earlier—your sister didn't do anything to you. It was my fault. I'm the one who got the principal involved. Now, go on to bed." She pointed toward the bedroom. "I think we've had enough drama to last a lifetime."

Janie stood her ground. "You can't just send me to bed like a, like a *child*. I'm a grown woman. I pay my own way around here." She stood there with her hands on her hips. For a second, I was certain she would stomp her foot, too.

"Dear God, Janie," Mom said. "Not tonight. Let's do this another day—"

"You can't talk to Mom like that!" I interrupted. "She's got enough on her mind without your constant damn whining." There. I'd matched her ugliness and even thrown in a cuss word of my own. I was getting a little tired of being everyone's doormat. Especially in my own home.

Eyes blazing, Janie advanced on me from across the room. She looked like murder. I picked up the nearest thing I could find, a plastic bottle of vanilla scented hand lotion, and hefted its weight menacingly.

She took another step toward me. "What are you going to do, throw that at me?"

Until that very moment, I wasn't sure what I'd intended, but as soon as she turned on her heel, dismissing me just like she'd done earlier, I heaved it straight at the back of her head.

Maybe it was a cheap shot, but she deserved it.

The plastic bottle didn't hurt her. It grazed her thick blonde hair and sailed on past, smacking the opposite wall. Okay, it might have nicked her ear, but that's all.

"You little bitch!"

She landed on me scratching and clawing, a witch without her broom.

I didn't back down. I grabbed a hank of her blonde hair in my fist, snapping at her face with my teeth. For a moment, I lost all sense of time and place, and she was Paul. I did my best to smash her to the floor. Then her face melted into Keenan, and I yanked at that fistful of blonde hair, tearing it out before Mom could pull me away.

"I hate you!" She raked my arms with her nails before Mom could get us apart. "Why don't you just go off like Dad and never come back?!"

Tears of rage blinded me as I broke free and ran to my room. "I hate you, too," I screeched. "You're the one who should leave!" But even as I said it, I regretted it. I didn't mind hurting her physically, we'd fought like animals before, but of course I didn't really want her to leave. I just wanted her to stop being so awful. I couldn't understand her fury over one little picture. And I hated that she wanted me gone like Dad. Like our worthless excuse for a dad.

I awoke to the sound of someone sobbing. It wasn't me. I'd cried tears of rage, but those tears had finally run dry. My entire body felt as empty and brittle as an old Styrofoam cup. I glanced at the clock on my nightstand surprised to find I'd dozed off with my hands still balled into fists.

Apparently I'd slept almost two hours. My sheets and quilt were all tangled together. I debated whether I should get up and go find out who was crying now. It had to be Mom. Janie always cried in secret. Neither of us liked to cry in front of people. Dad had always teased us if we did.

Gathering my courage—after all, what could I do, other than say I'm sorry—I sat up and swung my legs over the side of the bed. All at once, I was sick of this room, sick of this house, sick of everything in my life.

I heard a man's voice. Dad?

Before I knew it I was out the door, running down the hall toward the living room, toward the sound of his voice.

But it wasn't Dad.

A policeman stood in the doorway. He appeared to be holding Mom up.

She was still sobbing.

Nine

Despair

"Mom?"

She didn't acknowledge me. Couldn't acknowledge me. Her head had fallen to one side and she appeared to be slithering to the floor as if oiled.

"Mom!" I screamed out her name and rushed to her side. The policeman had been joined by a policewoman. Together they half-carried, half-dragged her to the couch and laid her down. She wasn't unconscious, but her head lolled to the side and one of her eyes was open more than the other. A zombie face, not dead, not alive.

I sat on the floor in front of the couch and took her hand. I wanted to know what happened, but I didn't know what questions to ask. "Mommy?"

The policeman looked at his partner. "A cold cloth?"

The policewoman looked around. "Bathroom?"

I pointed down the hall. "What is it? Is she sick? Did she—did she have a stroke or something?" Oh, my, God. Did I cause her to have a *stroke*? "Did my sister call 911? Where is Janie?"

The policewoman returned before her partner could answer. She leaned over and pressed a wet washcloth to Mom's forehead. "Mrs. Stevens?"

I watched as if from a distance. The front door stood half open, a draft crept in, but it wasn't cold. Just cool. It reminded me of Paul. The day of Paul.

The policewoman shook Mom's shoulder, not hard, just a little. "Mrs. Stevens, wake up." She bathed Mom's face with the cloth again.

Her eyes opened slowly, both of them.

I squeezed her hand, probably harder than I should have. She looked at me. "Ben?"

"Mommy, what happened? Where's Janie?"

The policeman patted my shoulder. "Your Mom fainted when I gave her the bad news." He looked down at me as if judging what to say next, how much to say, perhaps.

Mom spoke, her voice little more than a rough whisper. "Your dad, Benji. It's your dad."

"I know. He was here earlier." My head swiveled toward the still open door, expecting to see him standing there, ashamed for causing all this. "Where is he now?"

But no one stood in the doorway. It's emptiness filled me with dread. I actually heard the dry rustle of my soul filling up with fear.

"Where is Dad?"

The female officer took me by the arm and pulled me onto the couch near Mom's knees. They'd only got her halfway up. Her feet were on the floor.

"Your father's gone." Mom reached for me, pulling me to her right there in front of the two strangers. "He's gone, baby." She pressed my head against her bony chest and burst into loud, ragged sobs again. With my ear against her chest, it sounded as if her insides were tearing loose.

The fear that had filled me turned to panic and I shot up,

dragging Mom's hand away. "What do you mean gone? He's *been* gone for years."

Mom couldn't talk. I looked at the two officers. They were clearly uneasy. The man kept looking toward the door, as if calculating his chance for escape.

"I'm sorry," the policewoman said. "Is there someone else we can call to be with you?"

"Where's my big sister, where's Janie?"

They glanced at each other.

I ran to the door to see if her car was in the drive. And there she sat, in the driver's seat. Even from this distance, even in the near-darkness of nothing but the porch light and a pale slice of pre-dawn moon, I could see her sitting there, hands covering her face. I couldn't hear her, but Janie appeared to be sobbing, too.

Once of the cops came up behind me.

"Tell me," I said without turning around. "What's happened to my dad?"

She took me by the shoulders. "Can we call your grandmother or grandfather? Would they come over?"

I shook my head. "They live in Oklahoma. I have an Uncle Aidan, though. We can call him." Sparing a quick glance at Mom, I turned and ran to my room for my phone. I pressed his name in my contact list and then realized I didn't know what to tell him.

He answered before I could get back to the living room. "Benji? What time is it? What's wrong?"

I gulped. Just hearing his voice caused my throat to close up. I shoved the phone at the policewoman. She took it and walked out onto the front porch, away from me.

But I could still hear her. I heard her say they'd found

him in his car. At first I thought he must've been in an accident—a bad wreck—but then she went on. What I heard next explained everything.

"Gunshot wound to the right temple. Self-inflicted."

I looked at Mom lying on the couch. Her sobs had subsided. Now she lay as still as stone. He'd just been here, begging to come back. Now—

I rushed out to Janie's car and yanked open the door. For one terrible second I was certain it would be locked. When it opened, she looked up with her red eyes and runny nose and opened her arms to me.

"Oh, Benji. Did they tell you?"

My own frantic tears mixed with hers and we fell to the ground outside her car door, sobbing and braying in the driveway. Our world, never perfect, had just come undone again. "We have to go in and see about Mom," I said. "Uncle Aidan is on his way."

"How can you even talk about them right now? Dad is gone. Don't you get it? He blew his brains out. We will *never* see him again."

As harsh as those words were, she then whispered something even worse in my ear. Something that turned my insides black. "It's your fault," she whispered. "If Mom hadn't been so upset by the mess you made at school she might have let him stay the night—now he never can."

I shoved away and examined her messy face. It wasn't a cruel joke. She wasn't trying to be funny or dramatic. From her expression I could tell she meant every word.

Scrambling to my feet, I took off running, my mind a slurry blank void filled with pain.

Still in my pajamas, I ran blindly, bare feet slapping the

wet sidewalk, moist air sheeting my skin like perspiration on a hot day. I ran past driveways, past parked cars, past children's plastic toys and past bikes that should have been put away but weren't. I ran until I came to the intersection and had to stop.

Bent over at the waist, gasping for air, I heard a commotion as a car swerved to the sidewalk and slammed on its brakes in a screeching slide. When I wiped my hair from my eyes, I saw a man fling open the driver's door. Kidnapper, I thought. But then I heard him call my name and I recognized Uncle Aidan's old green Roadrunner.

"Benji, what are you doing? Where are you—"

I flung myself into his arms just as a patrol car pulled in beside us. An officer stepped out, speaking into the microphone on her shoulder.

At first, I thought she was there for Uncle Aidan, because of his erratic driving, but then I realized it was the policewoman from my house. As she neared us, I heard her say, "10-4. I've got her." And that's when I knew she meant me.

"Benji." Uncle Aidan smashed me to his chest. The river of tears I thought had dried up came gushing out in a flood.

"Is it true?" I asked. "Is it really true?"

Uncle Aidan held me and steered me to the passenger side of his car. "It's all right," he told the officer. "I'm Aidan. I think you might be the one who called me."

The policewoman nodded. "I'll escort the two of you back to the house. Her mom is pretty upset."

I didn't want to go home. Not with Janie there. I never wanted to see her face again. "Do I have to?"

Uncle Aidan looked at me. "Why wouldn't you want to go home? Your mom is very worried."

No way I could tell him what Janie had said. I was too ashamed. Everything that happened could have been avoided if I just hadn't painted that stupid picture. It had turned out to be the key to Pandora's box. "I just want to be alone," I told him. "I don't want to talk to anyone."

My uncle hugged me tightly. "It's okay, little one. I'm here. We'll get through this together. Okay?"

I didn't say anything else. What difference would it make? I was just a kid. No one listens to kids unless they give them a visual reference, like a painting. Emphasis on the *pain*.

Ten

PILLS

Uncle Aidan pulled the Roadrunner into the driveway. In the space of a few minutes everything had changed. A brown filter had fallen down over everything. Sepia toned. I knew that word from Art. Everything looked sepia now. Janie was no longer sitting in her car. It sat empty, forlorn.

When he killed the engine, the front door flew open and Mom burst out, arms wide, and met me on the walk. "Baby girl, I'm so glad you're okay. Don't ever scare me that way again." The whole time she was scolding me, she was also kissing my face and hugging me to her. I barely felt it when she kissed the bruise on my forehead.

I looked over her shoulder at the two officers. Had they ever seen such a crazy family? Did they have to give this kind of news every day? If so, I truly pitied them. I wouldn't wish this on my worst enemy, not even Will and Kera.

Janie had already gone to her room before we went inside. At least I assumed she had; there was no sign of her anywhere. Uncle Aidan enveloped Mom in a giant bear hug. I got sandwiched in between them.

The policeman looked away. The woman officer came in behind us. "If you have any questions, now would be the time to ask them." She stuck her flashlight in its special holster and braced herself—hands on hips, feet shoulder-width apart—for the barrage.

Mom's voice was little more than a whisper. "Can we see him?"

I almost fainted. Uncle Aidan held me up.

"Tomorrow," the policeman said. He handed her a card. "Call this number in the morning to make certain it's okay." The look the two partners exchanged said more than words. "There'll have to be an autopsy, of course. But it's only standard practice in cases of suici—I mean, uh, in cases like this."

Mom nodded. Her eyes were those of a lemur, huge, round, startled. "Is there anything I need to do?" She sat on the arm of the couch and twisted her hands together in her lap. She needed a Kleenex, something to shred. "I feel like I should be doing something."

Aidan shook his head. "I'm sure his new wife will be the one to make all the arrangements, Liv."

At the sound of her nickname—or maybe the dose of reality from Uncle Aidan about the other family—Mom cratered. She dropped her head into her hands and began to sob again. Oliver and Olivia. I remembered Mom telling me how she used to write Oliver + Olivia 4Ever on her high school notebooks. How she would practice writing Mr. and Mrs. Oliver Stevens over and over again. How they'd eloped right after graduation and how he'd bought her yellow roses when Janie and I were born. Oliver and Olivia. Ollie and Liv.

I stood beside my mother, wrapping her in my little girl arms as best I could. *Be tough, tough like denim*, I thought. *If I can do it, so can you.* But of course I didn't say it aloud. Kids can't tell parents what to do or how to be. If we could, Dad would have listened to us when we begged him not to leave in the first place.

Now that Uncle Aidan had arrived, the two cops seemed to feel we were in good hands. They took their leave with whispered condolences and instructions to call them if we thought of anything we needed, or needed to know.

I had a lot of questions, like where was he found, who reported him, and most of all why. Why did he do it? But I had a pretty good idea it wasn't my place to ask those things. Especially the last one, the cops wouldn't know the answer to that one anyway unless, wait—

"Was there a note?" I asked the room at large.

No one answered.

Uncle Aidan went into the kitchen and within moments the smell of coffee wafted into the room. Soon he appeared with two cups, one for me and one for Mom. She wiped her eyes and moved to the other side of me, patting my hand as she did. "Thank you for coming, Aidan. I—I'll be all right now."

"I'm here as long as you need me." He glanced around. "Where's Jane?"

Mom shook her head. "She's in her room. She's very angry. Seems to think it's all my fault."

I cringed. *No. She thinks it's all* my *fault. Are you kidding?*

"You want to tell me what happened?"

Mom shot a glance at me and shook her head. "Later."

Aidan took the hint. He went back to the kitchen for his own cup of coffee. Mom set hers on the end table and lay back against the cushions. "I just can't believe it. I knew he was unstable, he told me he'd made a huge mistake, but I never thought he would do anything like this." She closed her eyes and sighed.

"Did he want to come home?"

She nodded. "He said he did, but how could I be sure? How could I trust him?"

I didn't say anything. It didn't sound like it was my fault. It didn't sound like it had anything to do with me.

Then Mom said, "I should never have called him. I should have left well enough alone."

The sepia tone turned back to black. The blackness enveloped me like a shroud. Janie was right. She'd told the truth. If Mom hadn't called him to talk about me, he'd still be alive.

I didn't run from the room this time. I took my white coffee—Uncle Aidan had filled half the cup with milk—and walked casually toward my room.

"You okay, baby?" Mom's voice seemed far away. Much farther away than across the room.

"Sure," I said. "I'll be all right. Just tired."

"I'll see you in the morning, then. Try to get some sleep."

I didn't answer. I couldn't.

Janie's side of our Jack-n-Jill bathroom was closed. I could hear her music playing "Fake Love," by Drake. Pretty appropriate tune. I put my ear to the door. I could barely hear her talking to someone in a low voice, probably Shawn. I wondered if they were on the phone or whether he was actually in her room somehow.

Anger had settled into my chest like a coal. It smoldered, but no longer burned. Now it just felt heavy and hot. I hadn't lied to Mom. I really was tired. Things were too confusing; nothing seemed to matter except the fact that this was my fault. I'd killed my dad. My own father. I looked into the mirror, pressed my fingertips to the faded bruise, hoping to feel the familiar lurch of pain that would tell me I was still here. But now I felt nothing. Nothing at all.

I opened the medicine chest. Mom had been prescribed sleeping pills and anti-anxiety pills after Dad had first left. But they weren't there now. All I found was a huge bottle of Tylenol, a box of Midol, and a small amber colored bottle of pills with Mom's name on them. Vicoprofen. I looked at the date on the bottle. These were getting old. The doctor prescribed them for her when she broke her ankle in her one and only skiing trip three years ago.

I shook the bottle. Pills rattled in the bottom of the small container.

These are pain pills. I wanted something to take away the pain.

Through the bedroom door I could hear Janie laughing with Shawn. I pounded my fist on the connecting door. It wasn't right for her to sound like any other normal day when our dad was lying in a ditch with his brains smeared all over the car window.

"Stop pounding on my door!"

I heard Shawn's voice say something. I still couldn't tell if he was live, or on Facetime, then she replied, "Stupid little twat. I wish she'd just off herself. Do what the old man did for God's sake."

I backed away from the door as if stung. The Vicoprofen bottle was child proof. I pushed down and twisted, then upended the bottle over my mouth. Tiny white pills fell in. A few slipped past my lips and hit the sink.

I dry swallowed as many as possible then grabbed a paper Dixie cup and shoved it under the faucet.

I tipped the cup over my mouth and let the water pour in. The pills went down.

I swallowed while watching my non-me face in the mirror,

I had a moment to wonder who I had become, who I'd always been. I just wanted this to be over—all over.

As the pills began to dissolve, I dropped the empty bottle and made my way back to my bed. Nothing mattered now. Everything would be all right. I'd go to sleep and never have to deal with Janie, or anyone, ever again.

Crawling onto the bed took more effort than it should have.

I'd thought it would take longer to begin.

The Death of Winnie the Pooh

Sometime later I woke up to Janie shouting my name, pounding on our connecting bathroom door. I opened my eyes. The air in the room was black. How can air be black? Then I realized I'd gone blind. I opened my mouth to scream but vomit shot out and ran back down my throat. Rolling onto my side sent an ice pick deep into my brain. Gagging, coughing, I tried to stand. My knees locked themselves to my chest, my entire body cramped into a tight fetal position.

Intense pain made me gasp. Solid pieces of vomitus lodged in my airway. I tried to call for help, choked instead.

Janie kept pounding. "Open this freakin' door or I'll break it down! *You don't own the whole freakin' house.*"

Moaning, I shoved my fingers down my throat, clawed something loose, tasted my own blood, tried again to stand, couldn't see. Why wouldn't she come around? My legs were locked. Retching, puking, my belly spewed more vile liquid onto my bed. I rolled onto the floor, hitting my face on the metal frame, landed in my own filth. My bowels let go.

"Ben! Benji! Wake up!" Someone was slapping my face. "Get me a cold cloth. Hurry!" That sounded like Uncle

Aidan. "No, the hell with it. Call 911. Janie! Where are you? Call 911 dammit!"

"Oh my God. What?" Mom's voice. "Benji!" She screamed and fell to the floor beside me, pulled up my head.

"Mom…" I couldn't tell if the word came out or stayed inside my head. "Mom. Help."

I heard scrabbling, felt an arm under my knees. My gut clenched; dry heaves shook me. "No," I tried to say. "Don't." But they did. They put me on the bed. I curled back into fetal, dry heaving.

"Vicoprofen," I heard Janie say. "The bottle is empty."

Janie? Go away. I hate you. I hate you.

"Look at this old bruise," I heard Uncle Aidan say. "Look at these scratches on her arms—look."

The next thing I knew, other hands. A stretcher, a Gurney, rolling, cool air, a hard bump. My belly clenched; my legs tightened into hooks again. The dry cramps doubled me up. My head imploded.

"Charcoal?" one voice asked. "Or gastric lavage?" Someone said something in reply. It sounded like a different language.

Then, "Benji. Hey, Benji!"

"Dehydrated," the first voice said.

Something stabbed the top of my hand.

The siren drowned out everything. I felt the door clunk shut.

I didn't wake again until the sun was high and the light had leaked back into the world.

The first thing I saw when I opened my eyes was my mom's face, the sun through the blinds slashing it to ribbons. Her eyes were closed, her head tilted back and sideways against a Naugahyde recliner. Hospital. Had to be.

I didn't want to wake her. If I could avoid doing that maybe I could go back to sleep and wake in a different place.

"Ben?"

I opened my eyes expecting to see Mom looming over me. I must've made some sound, some little noise.

"Benji."

Not Mom. A woman. Streaky brown hair piled up, speared with hair clips, bright ruby lips, dark eyes, piercing.

Thank God I wasn't blind anymore. *Thank you, God.*

I looked at her face. Looked at my Mom. Her eyes were open now. I stared at her. Why wouldn't she speak? Why did she keep looking past me like I wasn't there?

Wait. Was I dead, did I die? I must have. I wasn't in pain anymore. No cramps. No dry heaves, no ice pick in the brain, no more blindness. I must have gone on... I stared back at the brown haired woman. Angel?

She smiled and it both gladdened and frightened me at the same time. Maybe this was the gatekeeper. Maybe she would decide my fate. Heaven or Hell, which would it be? Wasn't suicide a mortal sin? I hadn't thought of that.

Mom spoke. "Hi, baby."

Shame filled me. I wasn't dead.

I couldn't look at her. My eye found the brown haired woman. Her smile still held. Was she real? I raised my hand to shade my eyes. My arm felt heavy, unnatural. An IV bristled from the crook of my elbow. A stiff board kept me from bending it.

"I'm sorry." My voice came out so ragged, rusty, so low, I knew no one could hear it.

The brown haired angel-woman took my hand. I tried to take it back. It was filthy from all the vomiting. She didn't seem to mind.

Mom came to the bed, took my other hand, slid her arm behind my neck and pulled me sideways into her chest. "It's all right, baby. Everything will be all right. Thank God, you're okay. You're okay." She hugged me tightly.

I never wanted her to let me go.

I closed my eyes and let the warmth of the sun coat my living face.

When Mom finally turned loose and dragged a straight-backed chair to my bedside, I felt immensely stronger.

"Benji, my name is Dr. Blue." Brown haired woman smiled a toothpaste smile again. "I know it's weird, a psychiatrist named Dr. Blue. Would you call that ironic or just a coincidence?"

My eyes followed her lips. There were so many words spilling from them I couldn't keep up. She must've seen the confusion on my face.

"You know? Because I'm trained to treat the blues?" She squeezed my hand. "Dr. Blue?"

I smiled. At least I think I did. But I couldn't be sure, and I couldn't seem to come up with a response. A psychiatrist. Of course. I'm crazy. I went crazy. I tried to die. Will they put me in a strait jacket?

"Am I in the state hospital?" That rusty voice again. I swallowed, but it didn't help. It felt as if the top and sides of my throat were all stuck together. My breath tasted like old meat. "I'm sorry." The words were directed at my mom, but

I couldn't look at her when I said them. How would we ever go forward from here? Everything had gone so wrong, so fast. "Will you always visit me?"

Mom still had hold of my hand. She stood again. Loomed over me.

I turned my head to the side. Away from her prying eyes.

"Honey, you're in the regular hospital. You won't be here that long. I'm not going anywhere. I'll be right here until they release you."

Release me? They were letting me go home? "But the mental hospital—"

Dr. Blue spoke up. "You will come and see me on an *outpatient* basis. We'll also do some group work."

Tears crept down my cheeks again. *Group work. Psychiatrists. Suicide. Dad.* I shook my head but the motion made me nauseous. I squeezed my eyes shut. "Can I sleep, please?"

Silence.

I could imagine the two of them looking at each other across my bed. *Not stupid*, I wanted to say. *Hurting. Not stupid.*

"Yes, you get some sleep." Mom patted me and I heard her chair screak as she moved it away from the bed. "I'll be right here."

Dr. Blue patted my other arm. "And I'll be back for our first session soon. I know you're exhausted, but the sooner we begin, the better."

A thought speared me from out of nowhere. My eyes flew open. "Dad's funeral?" I was fairly certain I'd only been in the hospital overnight, but what if I'd been unconscious longer than that?

Mom stopped at the door. Apparently she'd been about

to follow Dr. Blue into the hall. "Not for a couple of days. You'll be able to go, don't worry."

Able to go? *No! It's my fault he's dead. I don't want to go.* I hoped it would be over already. Autopsy. That's what someone said. He will have to have an autopsy. Or did I dream that? Who would have told me that? I'd barely learned of his death before I flipped out.

Then I remembered. One of the officers at the house had said it.

I imagined him on the cold steel table, my handsome, boyish father, the one who taught me to ride a bike, throw a Frisbee, belt out old kid's songs like "I've Been Working on the Railroad" as he pushed me on the swing in the backyard. The one who read me Winnie the Pooh and made me fall in love with reading. My dad. Lying there with a giant exit-wound hole in the side of his head and a Y shaped incision across his broad Dad-chest.

A moan escaped my lips.

I'd never lay my head on that chest again. Wouldn't hug him at graduation, wouldn't dance with him at my wedding—we might've done one of those crazy dances, took lessons for weeks, filmed it all, put it on YouTube—but I'll never get married anyhow. Besides, we weren't even speaking. Janie and I had stopped going over. Everything had gotten so twisted, so tangled up.

Suddenly, I wished there had been more Vicoprofen. Maybe if I'd had only a few more. If I hadn't let those few slip down the drain—

Mom rushed back to my side. But I couldn't open my eyes. Couldn't stop the tears. "It's all my fault," I whispered.

"Nothing is your fault." She pressed her hands to each side

of my face. "Ollie was depressed. He realized he'd made a mistake. Didn't know how to fix it. Her family didn't like him. He didn't like them. He wanted to go back in time, but I just couldn't. Sometimes you can't go back. That's all. Sometimes you can't go back."

What did that mean. Wanted to go back in time? Just like I'd thought about Will and Kera. He wanted us to be a family again, but Mom couldn't? "How long had it been, how long did he want to come back?"

Mom seemed to understand my garbled question. "Oh baby. It hadn't been that long. He'd been calling, but I couldn't seem to forgive him for throwing us away like he did. Maybe someday I could've, but he didn't give me time. I think. I think his problems were deeper than any of us realized."

Like me, I thought. *Just like me.*

Twelve

More to the Story

I turned over onto my side and tried to figure out how to make it all go away. Even Mom. Though she tried to make me feel better, it didn't work. I knew mental problems were hereditary, now I had proof.

When I woke, surprised to discover I'd slept another night away, the morning sun climbed across the room on a ladder of dust motes. For long minutes I followed their paths as they swirled and dipped, drifted and swayed, floating through the air as if to entertain.

Not wanting to talk to anyone, I avoided turning my head to see if Mom sat in her reclining chair. It occurred to me that Dr. Blue had not been back yesterday after all.

Dozing in and out, playing possum every time I thought I heard someone in the room, I managed to avoid reality until a nurse brought in a breakfast tray.

Applesauce, toast, and tea. Yum. "Just until your stomach heals." She smiled and handed me a small cup of white liquid. "You'll take this before every meal."

She acted like I should know what she meant. Stomach healed? Drink this chalky stuff before every meal?

I did what she said. The liquid did not taste bad, just thick. And suddenly, I was ravenous, the smell of the toast as good as a steak on the grill. How long since I'd eaten? Two days; three? I didn't bother to ask. I just ate, and drank. And went back to sleep. As I drifted away, it occurred to me that there might be something in my IV to make me sleep.

Just before I went completely under, Mom came in. Strange. I thought she'd been sitting in her recliner across the room. She walked directly to my side. "Did you eat?"

I nodded, drowsy.

She leaned over and kissed me. Her breath smelled of coffee and I figured she'd been to the cafeteria.

When I woke again, the two police officers stood at the foot of my bed. Oh my God. They were going to arrest me, take me in for questioning or something.

"Hey, there." The woman came around to my bedside. "How ya feeling?"

I focused on her nameplate. "Officer Tate?"

She grasped my fingers and gave them a tiny squeeze. "Yes, ma'am. Do you remember us?" She indicated her partner with a glance.

I nodded. Her partner smiled, but he remained too far away for me to read his nameplate. "Yes, I remember."

I didn't know the protocol here. Should I thank them for coming, thank them for their service, thank them for being alive? It seemed I should thank them for something.

Officer Tate pulled a small gift from her breast pocket. It was wrapped in bright pink tissue paper and tied with a white ribbon. "We know you took your father's death pretty hard. So we got you a little gift." She held out the pink package and when I took it, she grasped my hand for just a few seconds. "Honey," she whispered. "I've been there. My own dad died when I was just a kid. It hurts like hell."

I grabbed her fingers like lifelines. Tears immediately welled up and I rubbed them away with my free hand. "Thank you." My faint voice barely registered, but she heard. She leaned in and gave me a gentle hug, her dark uniform crisp against my cheek.

When she straightened, my eyes closed. I knew I should open them; I didn't want to be rude, but the emotions were too much to handle. I held the little package tightly. The heft of it made me think of metal.

"Well, what is it, honey?" Mom asked.

I opened my eyes and wiped away the single remaining tear my knuckles had missed. Carefully, I tore open the bright paper. Nestled inside lay a shiny silver heart on a fine chain.

"Check it out," Officer Tate said.

Inscribed on the front, in delicate script, were the words "Choose life." And on the back were the names Loris Tate and Tom Brindon.

So now I knew the other officer's name.

I clutched the necklace in its pink paper. This time I couldn't wipe the tears away fast enough.

Officer Brindon stepped around to my other side, leaned over and kissed the top of my head. His aftershave smelled like fresh ink. They must be on their way to work. I was suddenly conscious of my filthy hair.

Blindly, I reached for his huge, warm, hand. He wrapped my cold fingers in his. "I have a daughter your age. You call on me or Loris anytime you need us, you hear?"

Officer Tate. Loris. "I will," I whispered. "Thank you." Finally a reason to say it. "Thank you, both."

He slipped a business card into my hand and gave my fingers a final squeeze. "I mean it," he said. "Anytime."

I nodded.

Officer Tate leaned over and kissed my filthy head, too. "Take care, little one. We're here if you need us."

I'd never felt such unconditional love in my life. And it came from two strangers.

The room door opened and the smell of chicken noodle soup preceded the same bustling young woman from breakfast. She came in balancing a tray as if it were nothing. "Not toast this time," she sang. "Chicken noodle soup. Cure what ails you."

Everyone smiled and made way. The two officers exited without fanfare.

Mom pushed the bed button to sit me up straighter as the woman arranged the tray on the rolling table. It was only then that I noticed a small bouquet of flowers on the table. Mom had affixed the card so that the name was visible. "From Sam," it read. "So sorry about your dad. Hope you feel better soon."

My eyes almost popped out, but I couldn't say anything. The cheerful nurse's aide was busy fluffing my pillows and unwrapping my paper napkin. "There," she said, stepping back to admire her handiwork. "You *will* feel better after this." She winked. "I promise."

I couldn't not return that smile. I leaned forward and took a sip. The salty soup was like manna from Heaven. It was all I could do not to pick up the bowl and slurp it. "You're right." I took another sip. "Delicious."

She nodded. "See you tomorrow. Angie will be here for supper. You eat it all, now."

We laughed and the pretty round woman bustled back out the door. "What a sweet lady," Mom said. She unwrapped my bendy straw and stuck it in my tea glass. "You know she's Kera's aunt, right?"

I inhaled soup and almost choked to death. Mom pounded me on the back until I waved her away. "Not helping," I gagged. I gulped the good cold tea until the burning in my throat eased. "Sorry, it just went down the wrong hole. I'm okay now." I couldn't bring myself to tell her I'd never thought of other people knowing what I'd done. Shame flooded my senses again. I wondered if it was too early to call Officer Tate or Brindon. Could they help me with this? Help me figure out how not to wish myself back out of this mess?

I sipped the rest of the soup and renewed my vow not to ever show my face at school again.

"It wasn't just my dad." I sat in a blue chair. One of those smallish recliners with the nubby fabric. I liked the texture. It gave my fingers something to pick at while Dr. Blue picked at me with her questions.

"What do you mean, not just your dad?"

I watched her write notes in her little notebook. She'd asked if we could record the session and I'd told her I didn't care. But she still took notes, a word here, a few words there. "I just mean if I was going to kill myself over him, it would have been after he left Mom for that slut." I don't think I wanted to shock her, but maybe I wanted to test her somehow. See what she would say.

"You mean, when your parents split up?"

I shrugged. Picked at a few more nubs. "They didn't split up, not really. He wanted that younger woman. I found them screwing each other in her car right in our driveway. Even so, we didn't want him to leave. But he left anyway. We were nothing to him. Nothing."

She crossed her legs, glanced at the clock. "That must've hurt—"

"Hurt even worse when Janie and I had to go to his house and watch him acting so happy with his new little family. As if we'd never been a family. Mom would be at home crying herself to sleep at night—trying to do it quietly so we wouldn't hear—and then we'd go to Dad's house and be expected to grill out, play cards, watch movies. Things we used to do at *our* house." I tried to remember his new wife's name and I went blank. That scared me. Had the pills damaged my brain? This morning I couldn't even remember if I had brushed my teeth or not.

That made me wonder about Uncle Aidan and Janie. Had either of them been up to see me? Not that I wanted them to, no. That's not what I wanted at all. In fact, if I could crawl in a cave and live out the rest of my days alone that would make me happy. Still, you'd think I could remember if they'd been there or not.

Dr. Blue waited. "So, if it wasn't the news of your dad's death that sent you into such a downward spiral, what was it, the painting?"

That got my attention. I'd forgotten all about the stupid painting. Where was it, still at school? "Yeah, maybe. Seeing Kera and Will together after what I'd been through. It sure didn't help." My mind was on the painting. How it had felt to sketch it out, add the watercolor, make the heart pulse with dying life. I'd never had such a feeling of being completely out of myself while I worked. I'd like to see it again, see if it had as much power as it seemed. In fact, I'd like to do it again. Create that way, without the suffering first, of course.

"Your mom told me about it. But I'd like to hear your version. Parents don't usually know everything."

I lay my head back and closed my eyes, exhausted. The nurse's aide had come into my room around two o'clock and helped me to the bathroom where she sat me on a wide plastic chair and treated me to a shower. I didn't even have to remove my heart necklace, Mom assured me it was silver-plated and wouldn't turn my skin green if it got wet.

Sure enough, my hair was so filthy the aid had to help me scrub it. My arms were just too heavy to do it by myself. Then she dried me and dressed me in two fresh hospital gowns. The first one went on the normal way, with the opening in the back, and then she showed me how to put the other on backward, like a robe, opened to the front.

"Can't I just wear my own pajamas?" I'd whined. She shook her head. Sweet as she seemed, she still brooked no discussion. She didn't have time for arguments. Do it her way. Or else she'd do it for you.

By the time we were finished, I was completely wiped out. She had to lead me back to the bed and let me doze while she went and bathed someone else. Mom had left while I was in the shower. I think she told me where, but I couldn't remember what she'd said.

Within minutes I'd conked out again. I didn't wake until an orderly came to wheel me down to Dr. Blue's office on the first floor.

Now, sitting in the nubby blue chair, the doctor waited patiently for me to open my eyes and answer her question. But I'd forgotten what it was.

"I'm sorry," I began. "What did you want me to tell you?"

She frowned and made a little note.

"Are you having memory problems, Benji?"

Fear gripped my insides. Even though I'd never admitted it to anyone, my IQ was like my secret super-power. If I lost that, then I had nothing left. It had always been my Ace-in-the-hole as Dad would've said. I certainly wasn't gorgeous like blonde-haired, blue-eyed Janie.

I closed my eyes.

At the thought of my dad, all the anger and sadness came bursting through and just as before, I felt the tears leaking from my eyes even before the sobs closed up my throat.

I felt Dr. Blue's hand on mine. She pressed a box of tissues into my lap.

Opening my eyes was a mistake. The sobs came braying out as soon as I saw her kind, concerned face. I grabbed a wad of tissues and shoved them against my lips, and eyes.

"Scream, if you want," she said. "Sometimes it helps."

Scream? Seriously? In a hospital? Even if I wanted to, I couldn't. It would go against all my upbringing.

"Walls are soundproof," she continued. "I took a course in scream therapy way back in the day. I use it myself. Releases frustration and so many negative emotions."

I opened my mouth to tell her how I couldn't possibly do anything like that and the scream tore through me like a freight train. My hands gripped the sides of my head, my whole body shook, and the sounds that came out of my mouth were as horrific and guttural as any movie werewolf.

Dr. Blue shoved a small orange pillow into my lap next to the tissues and then sat back and let me fall apart.

I grabbed the pillow and buried my face into it while I screamed and screamed and screamed. After a few minutes I collapsed back in my seat and wished I'd never been born.

The doc patted my knee and got to her feet. From a small refrigerator, she pulled a bottle of cold water and brought it to me.

I twisted the cap off and gulped until it was gone.

"Need another?"

I shook my head and handed the empty back to her. She tossed it into a blue recycling can. I closed my eyes and hugged the orange pillow as if it were a long lost pet.

"I know how hard this is," she began. "And I know what we are doing goes against every grain in your body. But it must be done. Like lancing a wound. We have to get out all the hurt, all the anger, all the poison."

My eyes wanted to stay closed. Maybe if they stayed closed, she would give up and let me go back to my room. Back to my ridiculous scrap of life.

"Stand up, please," she said. "We need to do a moment of stretching to refocus our chi."

I don't know if she was surprised when I didn't ask what she meant. I'd read about chi and the Chinese belief of chi gung. "Are we going to learn how to stand for fifteen minutes?"

She gazed at me. "We'll start with only a couple minutes of learning to stand and listen. I want to incorporate a few of the swings. I don't do everything by the book, but I do the things that have helped me, and my patients." She stood, loose-limbed and droopy, and told me to do the same. "If you get too tired, let me know. You've been through a lot."

I nodded. At first I thought nothing would work and I would just give her a minute, then sit back down. But to my surprise, my legs began to tremble and my arms began to shiver and the more I tried to stop them, the looser I felt.

"Now, this," she swung her arms from side to side in large scooping arcs.

I followed her example and soon my trembling lessened and I began to feel stronger. After we did the same motion to the other side a few times, she instructed me to bend at the waist and let the blood flow to my head.

That was the one thing I couldn't do, whether because of the pills I'd taken or all the screaming I'd done, I did not know.

"It's okay," the doctor said. "We've done a lot. I think you'd better rest."

I sat back down in my little blue chair feeling like Goldilocks in the three bear's house. Tired. Broken. Confused.

"Want to tell me about that bruise on your forehead?"

I'd forgotten all about that. "Oh, when I took the pills, it was so awful, I got so sick I tried to go to the bathroom, fell down instead."

"Uh huh. I see *those* bruises. You actually have two of them, on your knees." She glanced at my bare legs when she said it. "I'm talking about the older bruise. The one that's almost but not quite gone."

My hand went to my forehead. It was still a little tender.

Dr. Blue leaned forward, her voice soft, kind. "You said seeing Kera and Will together after everything you'd been through is one of the things that tipped the scale that day. Maybe it even caused you to create the painting in the first place." She waited a moment. "This was before your father died, what did you mean, after all you'd been through?"

I shook my head gently, afraid to bring on the pain. "Nothing. There was nothing else. Just Kera. Just Will. Then the painting. Such a stupid, stupid thing."

The doctor looked down at her notepad and made a little

mark of some kind. She didn't push. She didn't demand to know the truth; nevertheless, I felt certain she knew there was more to the story.

Thirteen

Because I'm Crazy

When I got back to my room, delivered by the same orderly that had taken me down, a huge vase of flowers had arrived. Attached were two balloons, the first was emblazoned with GET WELL in shiny gold lettering, and the other had a big cat face on it.

The flowers were beautiful. The balloons were sparkly, happy. They made me so sad I wanted to ask the orderly to take them down and throw them away.

"Aren't they lovely?" Mom asked.

I was saved from having to reply by using every ounce of energy still in my possession to climb out of the wheelchair and onto the bed. And still the orderly had to do most of the work.

"Uncle Aidan and Janie sent them," Mom went on. "He's been up a couple of times, but you were asleep."

She didn't say if Janie had been up or not. I didn't want to know. I hoped she hadn't. I never wanted to see her again. But how would that happen? Unless maybe she eloped with that guy she she'd been dating, the one whose name I couldn't quite remember just now.

Not being able to remember the name of my sister's boy-friend made me remember something else. After I finally got comfortable in the bed—having gone through another ordeal in which the orderly helped me remove the outer gown—my eyes examined my rolling table. Sam's little bouquet sat in the shadow of the big one.

I wanted to examine the card, see if anything else could have been written on the other side, but I didn't want to ask anyone to hand it to me, and by the time I tried to figure out the reason why I didn't want to ask about it, I was dozing off again.

When I awoke, shadows blanketed the room and the TV played on low. Andy Griffith grinned and laughed and Opie and Barney grinned and laughed and I couldn't figure out what had happened on the show or in my life.

I'd awakened completely disoriented.

For a while I watched the muted show and savored the soothing smell of rain. It seemed as if it had been raining forever. But it was only that season, the one time of year our area of Texas was treated to actual moisture. Droplets crept down the dark windows and I saw that someone—Mom, probably—had opened one of them so we could enjoy the smell.

Reality slowly emerged from the soft gloom.

I'd tried to kill myself. Two days ago? Three? At the time, I'd really wanted to die, or at least cease to exist—although I didn't think I wanted that anymore—now I just felt numb. Numb, exhausted, and foolish. Where would I go from here?

I drifted back to sleep watching the shapes of the raindrops echoed across the white hospital blanket covering my bed. I wondered if my little Maggie-cat slept alone on my bed at home. Ordinarily she would be purring on my chest, or in the bend of my knees if I turned over. The idea that she might have moved to Janie's room made me angry and frightened all over again. Maggie was the one thing that belonged only to me.

In the corner of the room, Mom's soft snores were barely audible. I reached across the gap and pulled the little rolling table to my bed. My water glass appeared to be empty, but the plastic pitcher was full. I poured half a glass and drank it slowly. My throat felt shredded. All that screaming.

"You okay?" Mom's voice came out of the corner.

"Just thirsty." I took another drink. "My throat is sore." I didn't tell her why. I couldn't imagine ever telling anyone how I'd screamed my lungs out in the little room downstairs. It felt shameful, but what else was new? Shame was now my middle name.

"I'll be right back." I heard the creak of her chair, and then the room door opened onto the softly lit hallway.

I watched her stop, yawn, smooth her silhouette hair with one hand, and then without another word, she disappeared. I had no idea where she'd gone, but I took the opportunity to pick up the little round bouquet of flowers from Sam. The vase was a yellow Smiley icon, and it did bring a smile to my face. Purple and pink spring flowers filled it to the brim. The little card was blank on the back.

The door opened and mom reappeared. She didn't turn on the light, just made her way to my bedside by the glow of the TV.

"Thought some ice cream might help." She showed me two paper cups of vanilla with tiny plastic spoons built into the lids.

"Where'd you get them?"

"Snack room around the corner, just for patients and their families. Secret code to get in. I saw these in there yesterday."

I tore into mine as if I were five years old again. The coldness soothed my throat immediately. "Umm."

"Better?"

I took another bite, let the creamy coldness melt in my mouth. "Much better."

Mom set the other one on my table. "Just in case you need another."

I smiled. It felt good. "How's my little Maggie cat?"

Mom sat on the edge of my bed. "She's just fine, ready for you to get home."

"Has Janie been staying alone while you're up here?"

"No. Aidan has been there. He's been a lifesaver through all this."

The ice cream turned sour. "I'm sorry, Mom."

She laid her hand on my arm. "Nothing to be sorry about, Ben. I wish I'd told you how your dad had been calling me, saying he wanted to come back as if nothing had happened. Maybe then you wouldn't have—"

"Yeah." I didn't want to hear her say that maybe then I wouldn't have tried to check out. Kill myself. Kick the bucket.

"I just didn't want to involve you girls because I couldn't find it in my heart to simply forgive him and welcome him back the way he wanted."

"You—what?" The surprise escaped my mouth before I could stop it. "What do you mean?"

Mom inhaled sharply.

The sweet, rainy scent coming in the open window grew abruptly colder. I waited for her to respond. Before all this, I wouldn't have dreamed of questioning my mother or even my father, regardless of what they'd said or done. Now, all lines had been smudged, blurred, broken. I waited.

At last Mom muttered, "Yeah. He said he'd made a mistake. Just like that."

Okay, then. That's all I wanted to know. I lay back in my bed. "Can I ask you something else?"

Mom sniffled. "Ask me anything."

I guess she realized things had changed, too. "Are you sure I'm going to go home?"

"Of course you are. Why wouldn't you?"

The TV, our only source of light, hit a dark spot in the film. And I was glad. "Because," I whispered, "I'm crazy. Maybe I really should go to a crazy place." There. I'd said it. It had ripped my skin off, but I'd said it.

"Oh, Benji. No. You aren't crazy. We already had this conversation, didn't we?" Mom moved closer to me on the bed.

I was glad she didn't touch me. I felt raw, skinless. If she had touched me, I'm sure my insides would have spilled out onto the bed.

"Honey, you made a terrible mistake. I feel partly responsible. If I'd been more open with you, and with your sister, maybe you could have come to me instead of trying to get rid of those awful problems on your own. Will and Kera, the big deal over the painting, and then your dad."

I knew this was the time I should have told her all of it. I should have told her about Paul. And about Keenan. No. Not Keenan. I'm certain his sister is the one who made it seem so much worse than it actually was (*yeah, but what if she hadn't intervened from that top bunk, my subconscious wondered, could you have held him off alone? Or would it have gone on like Paul, with not one bruise but a dozen? And what about that hard, awful pinch? That wasn't playful, not at all. That was violent. That was a warning.*).

Mom sighed. "I've read that teens can't always control their rash impulses. That the frontal lobe isn't even fully developed—"

"But that doesn't apply to Dad, does it? Maybe I inherited whatever made him do that."

"No, no, no. I promise. That's not it." She reached out to touch me just as the dark part of the film passed and a bright silvery light filled the room.

"You look like an angel," I blurted. I suddenly got a memory-flash of Mom sitting in her recliner at home the night Dad committed suicide. She'd been listening to him on the phone with an old movie playing and rain darkening the window behind her head.

Mom grabbed me and hugged me. I didn't explode, nothing splashed out onto the blanket; I didn't even cringe, much. But I couldn't hug her back. I couldn't.

"Baby, we're going to be all right. You will come home with me tomorrow. Dr. Blue said so, remember? You'll continue to see her on a weekly basis, and maybe even some group therapy."

"Right. Group. She did mention that." But I couldn't imagine sitting in a room full of strangers. Out of her whole statement, that was the part that jumped out at me.

"Yes, group. Other kids who have gone through the same thing you have."

"You mean, other kids who tried to kill themselves? Or whose father blew *his* brains out?" My tone came out much harsher than I intended. I went from not wanting to hear it to wanting to spew it in the air like noxious gas.

Mom sat back. "Kids who have gone through traumas like we all have. Divorce. Suicide of a parent—"

"My own attempted suicide?"

"Yes," Mom admitted after a few moments. "Yours, too."

I thought it over. "If Dr. Blue thinks it's a good thing. I will try it. For some reason, I trust her." Now that I'd said it aloud, I realized it rang true. I did trust her.

At last, we ran out of words. I yawned. Mom yawned. "Do I have to go back to school?"

"I don't know. You still don't want to?"

"God, no. Never. You saw all the texts, all those memes and posts." My voice thickened. "So humiliating. I don't understand why people went so stupid about it all. I can only imagine what they're saying now. Now that I—"

Mom shook her head. "I don't think anyone knows except your friend, Sam. Whoever he is."

"What?" How did she know about Sam and how did he know about me? If my brain had been functioning properly, I would have realized he knew where I was since he sent the flowers.

"He called and texted when he couldn't get in touch with you." She smiled. "His messages were decent, kind. I hope you don't mind; I left them on your phone. He sounded like such a nice boy."

Did I mind? I had no idea. "So, you told him everything?"

"No, I only told him about your father and that you were taking a few days away from all social media and other communications."

That made no sense. "But he sent the flowers here so he must know—"

"Oh," Mom tapped her forehead. "He sent the flowers to the house, I brought them here. He doesn't know where you are."

Relief stole over me. I hadn't realized how much it worried me, wondering if Sam knew what I'd done. "Thanks, Mom. Ummm. Do you still have my phone?" I thought I might feel like looking at it. But I was afraid to ask if I had anything left to look at. Had Mom deleted them all?

"I left it at home," Mom answered bluntly. "Dr. Blue thought we should just leave it alone for awhile. I told her about the painting."

"It's okay." Another wave of relief. "I'm kinda glad I don't have to mess with it right now."

A nurse opened the door and came in then. "Time to get some vitals," she said.

Her tone was way too cheerful for this time of night, but I held my arm out obligingly. At least I no longer had an IV. They'd removed it before my session with Dr. Blue.

She had also set up a consultation with a neurologist to find out about my memory problems. I made up my mind to ask him (or her) if it would be permanent. I knew it would make college a lot harder, if the short-term loss stayed with me. Oh the other hand, I wasn't even sure I wanted to go to college anymore. Especially since I'd decided not to go back to high school.

Fourteen

Flesh Like Wood

Somehow, I fell asleep and slept soundly the rest of the night. The next morning, I ate toast and oatmeal for breakfast, and it tasted like dirt. But I was hungry. So hungry.

After breakfast the neurologist came and gave me a physical exam, which included things like *follow my finger, close your eyes and touch your nose*, and my favorite, *grip my hands and squeeze as hard as you can*. Then he smiled and said he thought I was fine, just fine, but he would send me down for a head CT just to cover all the bases.

In half an hour, the aid came and took me to radiology. After the CT, I was wheeled back to my room.

Mom was signing papers at the nurse's station for my upcoming release. Then a doctor I'd never seen before came in and told me to take it easy and to keep all my appointments with Dr. Blue.

He seemed quite young, what they called a hospitalist, and he didn't really meet my gaze. When he spoke, his eyes landed somewhere near that place on my upper lip that I'd always thought of as God's thumbprint. He acted almost embarrassed by what had landed me in the hospital. For the first time I wondered why I hadn't seen Dr. Saldana, my regular doctor. Had Mom been too embarrassed to call him?

After Mom signed the release papers, and we got instructions about what to do in case of belly pain or ear ringing, I got dressed in my old sweats and a red tee shirt Mom had brought from home. I was so glad to see my flipflops I yanked off the hateful yellow hospital grippy socks and tossed them in the garbage can. "When will we find out the results of the CT scan?"

Mom rolled her eyes. "Good question. Let me just run down to the nurse's station and ask."

When she came back, she was laughing. "Everything was fine," she said. "The hospitalist should have told us. The results are immediate—the doctor was right there when they did it. He saw no problems of any kind."

"So glad they told us." I laughed sarcastically, but in reality I was thrilled. If I was going to have to live, I at least wanted all my mental faculties. But I still didn't understand why my memory was so spotty.

The nurse wheeled me down to the car in a wheelchair with Sam's smiley-face flowers on my lap. Mom carried my balloon bouquet.

Uncle Aidan waited in the pick up/drop off lane in his Roadrunner. I felt either like royalty or like a ridiculous spectacle, I wasn't sure which. Mom said he'd been there for a while, and that he would stay with me while she went to a showing she had scheduled in the afternoon. I realized she had probably missed a lot of work because of me. I said as much to Uncle Aidan when he had me tucked in the passenger seat, ready to go.

"Not because of you, little one," he replied. "Because of *everything* that has happened." He pulled into traffic. "Your dad's funeral is a major stressor for her. She doesn't want to go and see everyone, but of course she feels she has to."

The afternoon sun had burned off almost all traces of the rain from the last few days. All that remained were a few stray puddles and muddy spots here and there. It hadn't burned away the clean scent though. "I wish it would stay like this forever."

Uncle Aidan looked around. "Like what?"

"The scent of rain," I said. "The cool scent of rain." I smiled. "It smells good. Like hope."

My uncle smiled and lit a cigarette. "Hope. Well, I wouldn't have called it that, but yeah, rain is absolutely the best scent in the world, except for coffee."

I laughed. Not a big laugh, just a little one. But it felt real. Not sarcastic. And that, coupled with the beautiful weather, made me feel better than I ever thought I would again.

"Will you be all right?" Uncle Aidan stabbed out his cigarette and tossed the remains out the window. "Nasty things," he said. "Don't you ever start with them. Kill ya, they will. Make you sick and then kill you."

"Don't worry about me, Yoda," I murmured. "I can't stand 'em." It was only much later that I realized how funny it was to be talking about things that would kill me when I'd barely got out of the hospital for attempting suicide. And don't even get me started on the fact that I was enjoying the clean smell of rain when Uncle A covered it with cigarette smoke, and then tossed the butt out the window. It was all I could do not to jump out and pick it up. I never realized he'd turned into a cigarette-smoking-black-sheep-litter-bug. He was sort of the opposite of my mom in every way. Hard to believe they were siblings.

But it didn't really bother me. He seemed nervous for some reason. Maybe the funeral stressed him out, too. Of course, it could just be me. Apparently attempting suicide was the best way to build an invisible wall around yourself. I could be the major stressor for everyone.

We turned the corner and pulled into a spot at the Sonic Drive-In. In addition to cigarettes and beer, Uncle Aidan had often said he couldn't pass a Sonic without it calling his name. "Want anything?" He pushed the red button to order.

"Diet Coke, please. And tell them to add a splash of vanilla."

He grinned and ordered my drink and his chicken nuggets. Then he turned toward me. "So, you think you'll be okay at the funeral? It's day after tomorrow, you know."

I tried to imagine *not* going to my father's funeral. "I'll have to be all right. I can't imagine sitting home while you and Mom and everyone else go." I still hadn't seen Janie. As a result, I'd taken to avoiding even saying her name. It seemed obvious she blamed me for Dad. She'd said it was my fault.

"Right, right. Grandma and Grampa will be in tonight."

"Will you be there?"

"Do you think I should?"

"I hope you will. How much do they know? I mean, do they know about me?"

My uncle shook his head. "Your Mom and I told them you were in the hospital because you were taking your dad's death so hard—in fact, that's the story most folks got. If they asked."

The scent of hope died on the breeze coming in our open windows. "Yeah. Pretty embarrassing, huh? Having a kid try to off herself?"

"I don't know what to say, Ben. It's new ground for me. I've done my best to avoid feeling things all these years, now it seems to be catching up with me." His jaw tightened. "After my own dad—mine and your mom's—drank himself to death, I thought I had to fill his shoes." He navigated a four-way stop sign. "I couldn't do it. Our mom had to get a second job. Never remarried. I often thought if she had, she might not have been on the road that night—coming home from the night shift—when she fell asleep and wrecked."

I bit my lip to hold back the tears; surprised at his honesty. Apparently my suicide attempt had given me a new doorway to adulthood, or at least a window. "I'm sorry. Mom doesn't talk about them much. I guess I didn't realize why she was on the road so late that night." It seemed I owed everyone an apology. And here I'd thought I was only hurting myself. For a moment I felt like a tiny thorn in the side of my sad, unhappy family.

Uncle A patted my knee and dug into his chicken nuggets. He had his own ways of coping. Now I understood why.

My first glimpse of the house reminded me of Dorothy when she first spied The Emerald City. I imagine my face looked like hers, the awe, the wonder, the fear, all rolled into one. It had only been a couple of days, but it seemed like years, a lifetime.

The pecan trees were green and full. Almost all the tassels were gone, drifted into drying mounds all over the yard. Sometimes we had to rake them up, but usually the West Texas wind would blow them down the street into oblivion. I guessed the recent rains had dampened them enough to hold them in place for a while. I knew if I looked into the canopy of the tall trees, the green baby pecans would be barely visible amongst the leaves.

I loved those trees. Dad had loved those trees. Dad had loved growing things of all kinds, roses, pecans, canna lilies—green lawns. Why hadn't he loved his growing daughters that way?

As always, we entered the house through the side door. The arabesque pattern of shadow swayed across the gray concrete porch. For the first time, I wondered if Paul knew what I'd done. I hadn't let my thoughts stray there, not even once. Oh, I'd wondered about Will and Kera, and the trolls who had spread my painting like Internet wildfire, but I'd pushed Paul so far into the basement of my mind that he hadn't had a chance to surface. Until now. Until the arabesque pattern of leaves.

Uncle Aidan unlocked the door—I guess Mom had given him a key, probably the one that had belonged to me—and ushered me inside. I suddenly recalled how I'd puked on every surface from my bed to the bathroom and beyond. Like Buzz in Toy Story, *To Infinity and Beyond!* Would Mom have cleaned it up? Would I have to?

"Your Mom is meeting us here with Subway sandwiches when she finishes showing the house on Maple."

I nodded. Uncle A seemed as fixated on food as my gnawing belly had been earlier. I didn't have a suitcase or anything but a plastic bag with my toothbrush and some incidentals like body lotion and shampoo. Until today, I'd worn hospital gowns.

It seemed odd, this closed, quiet house. But what did I

expect, a welcome-home-from-trying-to-kill-yourself party? Janie worked all day on Saturday, Mom had a showing, and Dad was dead. Had it really been only a week since Paul? Could that be possible?

A lump the size of a baseball grew in the back of my throat. Just Uncle Aidan and me. We traversed the silent house. "It's really quiet, isn't it?"

He nodded. "Like a tomb."

I didn't know if that was black humor or just subconscious thought leaking out. "Yeah." I caught myself tiptoeing across the dining room toward the hall. "From now on, I'm leaving a radio playing every time I go off somewhere." I almost said every time I try to kill myself, but I thought that would be a little too much dark humor, even for Uncle Aidan. For ten steps, I walked with my eyes closed, past the rug and the paneling where my stray hair may or may not have still been waving.

I opened my eyes and stuck my head inside my bedroom door. There lay my little Maggie, curled up like a furry apostrophe on my neatly made bed. My heart ached when I realized the room smelled clean. Almost as good as rain. "Maggie May. My little Mags." I lay beside her, careful not to startle, and she purred into my hand with a tiny stretch as if to say, *there you are, it's about time you got back*. That may have been the best welcome home I could've asked for.

Somehow I drifted away and didn't wake again until Mom came in to tell me she'd brought supper.

Grandma and Grampa Stevens arrived right after we ate. They were staying at a motel on the Interstate. I got the distinct impression they didn't know how to spilt their time between Sharla-the-slut and us. I'd never even considered the fact that my dad was their child.

I hugged them both. Grampa held on fiercely. "I love you, Ben," he said into my hair.

"Love you, too, Gramps. Glad you're here." And I truly was glad. It took me out of my own head. We shared this nightmare, whether we wanted to or not.

"Olivia," Grandma said. "I just don't know…" and that's as far as she got before she collapsed into the wingback chair nearest the door.

Mom knelt and wrapped her arms around her ex-mother-in-law. "I don't know, either, Patty. I really don't." And then they were sobbing and the two men were patting and I was standing outside the little scene like an observer in a Night-mare Christmas Store, looking at a sad, animated, snow globe.

Eventually it occurred to me to wonder why Janie wasn't home yet, but since no one mentioned her, I didn't either. I still hadn't seen her. Not since the night she'd told me everything was my fault.

Grampa Stevens sat on the couch. He'd aged a hundred years since I'd seen him last. They'd made a quick stop by our house on Christmas Eve bearing gifts for Janie and me and chocolates and a fuzzy sweater for Mom. I remember wondering if the sweater was to keep her warm since she no longer had a husband. It was so strange, having to share them along with my dad. Family no longer had the same pronunciation it once had. Nor the same spelling. Certainly not the same definition.

"He messed up." Grandma finally caught her breath. "If only he'd never left you and the girls. He had that hole in his middle. That one nothing could ever fill. Had it all his life, always searching for something better, something more."

That made Mom break down again. I couldn't even imagine

what she felt about that statement. But I knew what I felt, what I thought. I thought, *but Gram, you don't know the whole story. He was trying to make it right; he was trying to come back.* But I didn't blame Mom. No. That's not it. I understood betrayal pretty well after the past week. What if Will and I had been together all the years Mom and Dad had been, before he screwed it all up? Wow. What would my painting have been like then? And why did an image of Frida Kahlo pop into my head?

We didn't put up any pretenses after that.

Together, we piled into cars and drove to the funeral home for the first viewing. I rode with Uncle Aidan and Gram, and Gramps rode with Mom. The official visitation would take place tomorrow, Sunday. But the funeral home had called and said Dad was ready for private viewing.

They made it sound like he would be expecting us.

"What about Janie?"

Uncle Aidan glanced my way. His eyes were unreadable but his mouth turned down at the corners. "She called your mom and said she would pick up Shawn and meet us there."

Something fluttered in the pit of my stomach. A small bird, trapped. Shawn was large and loud and my sister probably wanted him there as a buffer. She wasn't much in the feels department, either. What had she told him? What might he say? Would he tell everyone why I'd been hospitalized?

Dad.

Oh my God.

My dad. In the coffin. His profile so young, brow smooth. Unlined.

I couldn't cross the room fast enough. "Daddy." I touched his hand and it felt like wood. Stiff. Not cold, but cool. Room temperature. Flesh like wood.

The edges of my vision went gray, then spotted black like polka dots, then finally, faraway stars. And I was gone. Uncle Aidan caught me when I fell. What if I had pulled the coffin down with me?

Fifteen

Strong Like Denim

The funeral director held smelling salts under my nose. The pungent odor jerked me awake, and I knew immediately what it was even though I'd never seen smelling salts in my life. No short-term memory loss today, folks. Today I should only be so lucky.

My eye strayed to the front of the visitation room again—they called this one Dignity East—and that almost struck me as funny. Too much like Disney East. But it wasn't funny now. Shit had suddenly got real. Even my own battle with the pills and the puke and the ice-pick headache was nothing compared to this.

I closed my eyes and asked Uncle Aidan to take me home. I felt bad for Grandma and Grampa Stevens, but I couldn't look at them. My eyes wouldn't go anywhere but back to my dad, and I couldn't look at him, either.

That was almost me. That was almost me in there. For a solid moment, as Aidan led me away, I considered my face in that casket. And I knew I would never do that again. Death was real.

We went to Sonic and then to the duck pond where we got out and sat on picnic tables the way we'd done when Janie and I were tiny. Uncle Aidan didn't say a word—silent as a tomb—until a little boy ran by with a loaf of bread, two ducks chasing him for a handout.

"I lost all respect for Oliver after he moved out that way. But seeing him like that." He ducked his head and I saw a dark spot appear on the concrete tabletop.

My eye looked for arabesque patterns, but we were under an awning and there were none. "That isn't really him," I said. "I felt of his hand. Thank God it didn't feel like him. I think it's easier to know that isn't really him."

Uncle Aidan hugged me and sobbed and somehow I wound up comforting him. My own eyes remained as dry as old wood.

"Do you think Mom is okay?"

Aidan nodded. "All my life, she's been the strong one. Aidan, thy middle name is Wimp." He laughed self-deprecatingly and wiped his eyes with the back of his hand.

The little boy's mother shot us a worried look that made me so self-conscious I asked Uncle Aidan if we could leave.

We didn't speak again. Too much reality had driven us inward.

At home, I ignored all the reminders of the past few days and went to change my clothes. The funeral home didn't have an odor, but it seemed something had permeated the cotton of my shirt.

In my room, there lay my favorite denim shorts all clean and neatly folded on my dresser. I grabbed them, wanted to throw them in the trash the way I'd done the yellow grippy socks in the hospital. But as soon as my fingers touched the well-worn fabric, I remembered where I'd got them.

The summer before Dad moved out, Six Flags Over Texas. A purple and yellow tank top and these shorts. They were like a talisman or at the very least a memento of the last good vacation we had together as a family. And then Paul came and tried to rip them off me. But they were strong. Tough. I caressed them and put them in my bottom drawer. *Maybe I'll be strong enough to wear them again someday.*

In the kitchen, Uncle Aidan leaned against the counter drinking from his tall Sonic cup with the lid off.

"You okay, baby girl?"

I nodded, on my way to the laundry room in search of my second favorite pair of shorts. "You don't have to stay." I looked over my shoulder. "I'm not going to hurt myself again. I promise."

He gulped his drink and spluttered. I wondered if he might have added something to his Sonic Coke. "You okay?" I stopped and waited.

"Yeah, just hard to get used to all this honesty."

I had no reply to that. I found my second favorite shorts folded on the dryer. But when I slipped them on, I was shocked to find I didn't even have to unzip them. When I went back through the kitchen, Uncle A still stood in the same spot. I walked closer to him and smelled the sweet, unmistakable odor of alcohol. Rum perhaps. I knew Mom kept that in the cabinet. *If it helps Uncle A cope, maybe I should do that, too.*

I smiled and continued on to my room where Maggie waited patiently on my bed. If she had moved, I couldn't tell it. We lay together until I fell asleep.

The next time I awoke, Mom lay beside me, too. She appeared to be sleeping but I couldn't hear her breathing. Maybe she was holding her breath.

It didn't matter. She was there. She didn't leave me. She didn't leave.

I got up and spread my old unicorn blanket over us.

Maggie got up and stretched, then she sauntered to the edge of the bed and leaped. She knew she would land on her feet; she always did.

From the living room I heard the sound of a basketball game on the tube. I imagined Uncle Aidan, sitting there in the twilight. Who else could it be?

Daddy? Could that be you?

I crept to the door, and there in his recliner, angled away from me toward the TV, a shape. Long legs stretched out, New Balance running shoes crossed at the ankle. Soft snores, probably rum-soaked.

Uncle Aidan.

I slid down to the floor in the hall. It seemed to be my favorite spot anymore. *Daddy. I need to see you one more time. Why did you leave without even telling me what to do? I don't know what to do. How to be. How to go on…*

Eventually my nose clogged completely closed from holding back the tears. I rose and went to the side door, peeked out the glass. Janie's car was not there.

Maggie needed her bowl filled. She weaved herself around and around my ankles as I stood. Her bowl was in the laundry room. Thank God for small things.

After I fed the Mags, I went to the bathroom and ran myself a lavender bubble bath. Even with Mom and Uncle Aidan here, asleep, the house still felt empty. I undressed and climbed in. Should I shave my legs? Would Mom freak if she came in and found me using a razor, or would she freak even more if I locked the door and didn't let her in?

I turned off the taps and lay back, trying to relax, trying to feel like I'd come home. So far, I still felt gone. The hospital felt more home than this. I took up the razor, the heavy one

Dad had left in the medicine cabinet he shared with Mom. When she threw it in the trash all those years ago, someone had got it out and brought it to our bathroom. Of course it was Janie. But as far as I knew, she'd never used it, just hid it behind our towels. I had found it and bought new double-edged blades.

Every time I used it I dried it and put it back.

The blade was still sharp. And if it wasn't, I had a brand new sleeve of them hidden behind the same stack of towels.

Mom mumbled something in my bed. I had closed the door, but I hadn't locked it. Maybe Maggie had jumped up there with Mom. She liked to sleep on my chest, maybe she was walking around on Mom, purring, kneading her claws the way she does when she's happy.

I dragged the razor up my leg against the growth. The way I'd always done. The way I'd known to do even though no one ever showed me. It had been well over a week since I'd last shaved. The hair was fine, but thick. I bore down a little too hard. A thin, red line appeared on my thigh.

My washcloth whished it away, but it welled up again and I let it. It was something to do. It made me feel.

I heard a car door slam outside.

Janie.

I quickly shaved the other leg—carefully this time—then stood and let the water out, hid my razor behind the towels, and stepped out onto the thick pink rug. Then I leaned over and clicked both locks so she couldn't accidentally come in.

In minutes I was fairly dry and wearing my second-favorite shorts again.

But it wasn't Janie.

It wasn't anyone at our house.

I tiptoed through Janie's room so I wouldn't wake Mom in mine. Janie's room felt cold, empty. I turned on the lamp beside her bed. It cast a pink glow over the bed. She'd laid a gypsy scarf across the lampshade. If she knew I had trespassed on her turf, she'd never forgive me. But apparently she wasn't ever going to do that anyway. I turned off the lamp and made my way to Mom's room. I wanted my phone. I felt like I could handle it.

But Mom had it well hidden. Or maybe she had turned it back in. Do they give refunds if you take one back? I gave up and took the small flashlight from the kitchen junk drawer. My old iPod still worked as far as I knew. But it was in the back of my closet. By now, the sun had set and the twilight had given way to full gloaming. I liked that old word. I'd read it in a book once. It seemed just right for the eve of my father's funeral.

"Honey," Mom's sleepy voice. "What time is it?"

I hadn't even had the chance to look for my iPod. I must've made some little noise. "It's around seven I think, or maybe eight. I don't know. It's dark outside."

She sat up and turned on my reading light. Maggie stretched. Sure enough, she'd been on Mom's chest. "Are you hungry?"

Didn't we just eat? Why did people automatically think of food every time they looked at me? "No, I'm really not. But I would like to have my phone, or at least my iPod."

That seemed to get Mom's attention. To my surprise she reached across my bed and pulled open the drawer on my nightstand. "Here's your phone." She handed it to me without complaint. "After I replied to Sam that first time, I put it away. Kept it turned off." Her eyes sought mine in the dim light of the reading lamp. "Come over here and sit with me while we look through it, together."

"Okay." Maybe that would be better than going it alone. How could something that had always brought me such joy now feel like a little time bomb ticking in the palm of my hand? "I deleted almost everyone from my contact list," I told her. "And I'm not getting back on Facebook or Instagram."

Mom scooted up in the bed, her back braced against my padded purple headboard. "I deleted those for you."

I already knew it, and as much as I felt the need to open those apps and see what my former friends were talking about, even more, I felt a strong sense of self-preservation. A need to protect my soft, social media belly.

Of course when I tried to turn it on, the thing was dead. I bit my tongue, I'd been about to say, just one more dead thing to add to the list—Uncle Aidan might have appreciated that—but I couldn't say it to Mom. Instead I just leaned over, dug out my charger and plugged it in.

The long thin cut on my thigh stung from all my screwing around in the bed and I wondered if I had opened it back up. I glanced down, surreptitiously, but I didn't see any blood. Why had I done that? What was wrong with me?

"Benji?"

I turned to my mother. She had a strange look on her face. How long had she been trying to get my attention? "What?"

"Where were you, just now?"

I shrugged. "Just didn't hear you. What did you say?"

"I said has your sister come in yet?"

Oh, something not about me. That's a nice change. "No, I don't think so."

Mom took my phone and turned it on. She handed it back

to me, but she made it obvious through her body language that she wasn't going to go away until she made certain the device wasn't lethal.

Sixteen

Me, Me, Me

The only message was from Sam. He hoped I liked the flowers. It didn't surprise me that there were no more messages, after Mom's visit with the principal, I felt certain everyone had deleted me as I had deleted them.

"So I guess Janie and Shawn went somewhere else after the funeral home?" I didn't really want to know where; I just hoped to put Mom's mind at ease. *They're probably at some seedy hotel or something,* I thought.

Mom jumped on that statement. "Did you see them at the funeral home? What did she say? Did she say where they were going?"

I shifted my weight on the bed. Had she forgotten how I left the funeral home practically comatose? "No, I didn't see them, I just assumed they arrived after Uncle Aidan took me home."

Mom stood and stretched the kinks out of her back, rolled her shoulders, ran her hands over her hair. "They didn't come," she said. "Didn't even call."

It was then that I noticed her phone in her pocket. As I watched, she pulled it out and tapped the screen. From my vantage point, I saw Janie's picture appear before Mom put the device to her ear.

"Call, me Janie. I'm not kidding. If you don't call or appear on the front porch in five minutes, I'm calling the police to make a missing person report." Her gaze swept across the top of my head. I got the feeling she didn't see me at all.

"When did you last see her?"

Uncle Aidan appeared in the doorway. "Still nothing?"

Mom shook her head. To me she said, "Not since this morning when she went to work."

Uncle Aidan said the eff word.

"And I didn't actually see her," Mom said. "I just talked to her on the phone. She said she was on the way to work, but I had just missed her. I dashed home from the hospital to grab a shower before my showing."

"But you were here, right?" I looked at Uncle Aidan.

"Asleep," he said. "She didn't even wake me before she left."

So basically no one had seen her since Friday night.

"She came in late on Friday night," he admitted. "I told her I was going on to bed." He scratched at the stubble on his chin, obviously thinking back. "For all I know, she went right back out again. Her car was gone when I got up this morning."

We all looked at my darkened bedroom window. She could have been gone for nearly 24 hours by this point. "But you've talked to her, right?"

Mom nodded. "This morning, I called her cell when she wasn't here. You know she opens the store on Saturday morning, always has. I didn't think anything about it."

"So she worked all day today—" I let the thought hang as I worked it out in my own head. "She probably just couldn't handle seeing Dad that way." The image of his profile in the coffin rose in my mind. "Maybe she's there now. With Shawn.

And that's why she doesn't answer. Maybe she just wanted to see him without all of us there." Why was I defending her? Because of the look on Mom's face, of course. How much more could one woman take? First her husband, then me, now Janie. I looked to Uncle Aidan. *Don't you fall apart,* I thought at him. *Mom needs you.*

But look at me, jumping the gun. Janie just hadn't come home from work, that's all. No big deal. It's not like she'd been gone all day. In fact, by the time she got off at four o'clock, grabbed supper, then got Shawn, yep. They were probably just now at the funeral home. If they stayed open that late, that is. And if she called ahead and made special arrangements.

I grabbed my phone off the bed and hurried to the side door, peeked outside. Her car wasn't in the driveway. I walked on out, being as quiet as possible, and looked up and down the street. The bright, sweet moon lit the length of our block. It bounced off the cars that were parked here and there at the other houses, but Janie's Ford was nowhere. It reminded me of an old black and white episode of *The Twilight Zone* in which the characters find themselves transported to a place where everything looks real but is really fake.

Our entire street looked fake, bathed in silvery-white moonlight, nothing moving, not even the sound of a car anywhere. I pulled up my contact list and hit the icon for Janie before I could lose my nerve. It went to voice mail. "Where are you, Janie?" I asked. "Mom is worried. Please give her a call."

Then a terrible idea smacked me in the head. If not for the fog that still permeated my brain, I might've considered it earlier. I opened my contacts list again, but didn't find what I wanted, opened Safari instead, typed in The Sweet Treat and got the phone number. They were open until ten o'clock on Friday and Saturday nights. But Janie didn't work that late when she had to open.

The phone rang a few times and then someone answered, "Sweet Treat, may I help you?"

"Hello?" I didn't recognize the voice of the person who answered.

"Hello-o-o. May I help you?" Obviously busy.

I could feature the girl standing there with the phone in one hand and an ice cream scooper in the other. "I'm looking for Janie Stevens," I said. "Did she work today?"

"Who, Janie? No. I think she called in sick or something—oh, no, that's not right." She took a short breath. "Her dad passed away. Stan opened up this morning. He worked all day."

Stan was the owner. Damn. Janie didn't even go to work today. Where was she when she talked to Mom this morning? Did she leave sometime last night without telling Uncle Aidan? "Okay, thank you." I hung up the phone and took one last glance down the weirdly empty street. A coldness came over me, it stole inside me like a mist I couldn't escape. It scared me. Made me feel like free fall, like free falling from a roller coaster.

I stood in the yard a few more moments, putting off my task. More than anything I wanted to pretend I hadn't called The Sweet Treat. I didn't want to go in and lay another burden on Mom's shoulders. Should I wait? How long before Mom or Uncle Aidan would think to call the shop?

Of course I couldn't wait. Janie might be eighteen, set to graduate in another month, but she wasn't really an adult, was she?

"Benji, you out here?"

"I'm here, Mom. Just looking for Janie's car." I turned and went back to the house. The moonlight cast the arabesque shadows on the side porch. I began to think it was some sort of omen. Every time I saw that pattern, something terrible happened.

Mom took one look at my face and plopped down in the same chair Grandma had sat in earlier. "Hey," I said. "Where are Grandma and Grampa?" I hadn't seen them since my collapse at the funeral home.

"They are staying at a motel," Mom said. "I tried to talk them into coming here, but with Uncle Aidan on the fold-out couch—"

"I would've taken the day bed on the porch," Uncle Aidan piped up. "Or the recliner, I've done a lot of dozing there the last couple of days."

That made me wonder, for a moment, about his job. He sold cars for a living. I assumed he was able to take off for a while. I hoped it didn't get him in trouble, baby-sitting me this way. I touched the heart necklace nestled against my throat. So many people trying to care for me. And for Mom. "They could've had my room," I said. But I was just stalling.

Finally, I bit the bullet. "I, um, I called The Sweet Treat to make sure Janie wasn't working a double or something." I let the little white lie sink in.

Mom looked to me. Her expression said, why didn't I think of that? But her voice admitted she already knew the answer. "She wasn't, I suppose, or she would've called."

I nodded. "Mom," I instinctively moved closer to Uncle Aidan before I spoke. "Janie didn't go to work at all today."

The stillness in the room echoed the stillness on the street. It felt like a waiting pause.

"But I talked to her. She was on her way to work." She clasped her hands together. "Why did she lie to me? Why won't she answer the phone now?" Her gaze sought that of her younger brother. "Where is she, where's my Janie?"

Uncle Aidan shrugged and jabbed his fingers into his rough hair. He'd always favored the bedhead look, but this was a little wild, even for him. "I think it's time we call Shawn, don't you?"

Mom nodded and handed over her phone. Uncle Aidan took it and quickly scrolled through her contacts. When he got to Shawn's name, he stabbed it with his blunt forefinger, and then put it on speaker. We all heard it ring and ring and ring until a recorded memo came on and said to leave a message at the sound of the—

And then a cartoon crash happened accompanied by Shawn's laughter in the background. "This is Janie's uncle," Aidan said. "Call me immediately. We are on our way to the Police Department to file a missing person report." His face was grim when he handed the phone back to Mom.

"Wait," he said, taking it back. "Do you have the number for Shawn's parents?" He began scrolling again.

Mom nodded. "It's there. Look under his last name, Powell."

Uncle Aidan must've found it, his finger struck the small screen and he put it on speaker again. Once more we were treated to a recorded voice telling us to leave a message. "This is Aidan Donahue, Janie's uncle. She hasn't come home since yesterday," he said. "We need to talk to Shawn right away. Please call Janie's mom at this number."

Within seconds, the phone rang. Mom was so startled she dropped it as Uncle Aidan was handing it back to her. "Dammit!" she cried.

Uncle Aidan grabbed the phone and answered it. "Yes?" His eyes were wide. "This is Janie's uncle." He listened intently for a few seconds. "Hold on, hold on one minute." He exhaled and turned to Mom. "She says Shawn told her he was going to the lake with a friend named, Jeremiah."

Mom grabbed the phone. "Mrs. Powell, Janie didn't go to work today—you know she always works on Saturday—and no one has seen her since early last night. Could you call Shawn and find out if she's with him? You know we just lost her father. He committed suicide." Her face paled when she said it, but she clenched her eyes shut and went on. "I'm sure she was upset, but I talked to her on text messaging this morning and she said she was on her way to work."

I don't know what Mrs. Powell said, but tears slipped out from under Mom's closed lids. "Yes, I'm very, very worried." She listened again. "Thank you. I appreciate it."

When she clicked END, she opened her eyes. "She's going to call Shawn and impress upon him how important it is that he call home—or us—immediately. She's also going to call Jeremiah's mom and find out if they're really at the lake house."

Uncle Aidan sat on the arm of the chair and put his arm around his sister. "That's good," he said. "That's good. I'm sure they're together."

Mom nodded, but her eyes stared at the door, unseeing.

I looked at my Mom through my young artist's eye. I couldn't feel that much for my sister—she'd hurt me too badly—but a question occurred to me like a bolt from the blue. Why were we suddenly struggling so, and why did everything suddenly seem so meaningful? Every tiny thing took on so much meaning, became so poignant.

Do people who struggle see things differently than those

who don't? Was this one of those stepping-stones on the path to enlightenment like I'd read about in our World History study of Buddhism? It had to mean something. If it didn't, where did that leave us, down in the dirt with the animals? Like roadkill?

And why did my mind keep coming back to that? I wasn't an atheist, or even an agnostic. I believed in a higher power, I always had, it's just that since Dad threw us away, I'd been questioning everything about my childhood. Especially the part where Dad taught us how if one just followed the right path, we'd all go to Heaven. Just remember the Golden Rule, he'd say every time we got in a scrape. *Do unto others as you'd have them do unto you.*

What was I supposed to think about that now?

What was I supposed to think about him?

Think that he's only human, my super-Mom had said when I asked her a mini-version of this question one day not long after Janie and I had come home, disgusted and hurt from one of our earliest weekend visits to his new "family."

Only human? If I'd been her I would have been killing mad. He threw her and us away for a younger woman. How was that following the Golden Rule? "Well, honey," Mom had said, and it was the last time she'd ever speak of it with me, "it's like church. If everyone in church was a saint, there'd be no need for salvation."

At the time I thought she was being cryptic to make me quit asking questions; now I think that's how she really felt. But I also knew how badly she hurt inside; I'd seen her on the back porch, crying. It made me respect her even more, to watch how she handled herself in the face of abject misery.

I looked at her sitting there with Uncle Aidan beside her.

I'd paint her with swashes of blue, just broad outline strokes blending into the background of the living room, the oddly silent street barely visible through the window behind them.

Her phone buzzed. Mom tapped the icon to answer it. But she didn't put it on speaker. I wished she had. Instead, she stood and paced. And listened. Her face grew still and her hand strayed to her chest, as if to massage her own heart. "I see. I—I don't know. I'm going to make a report, I think. I don't want to get Shawn in trouble, but I have to do something. I have to find my daughter."

I sat on the chair she'd just vacated. This didn't sound good. As much as I hated Janie before, now that feeling was all mixed up with something else—fear.

"Where is she?" I didn't wait for Mom to tell us.

She stood, big eyed, phone in hand. "Shawn doesn't answer either. Not a call, nor a text. It goes straight to voice mail. His mom said she left a message threatening to call the police, and still no response." Her voice shook. "She doesn't think Shawn went to the lake with his friend. She's waiting for his mom to call back."

My hand strayed to my own chest, and the necklace nestled there. "Let's call Officer Tate or Brindon."

Mom and Aidan both looked at me as if I'd lost it. I held up the heart charm the officers had given me at the hospital. "They said to call if I needed anything."

Without another word, Mom began to peck at her contact list, as if looking for their number.

"Wait." I ran to my room and dumped out the plastic bag I'd brought home from the hospital. Officer Brindon's card fell onto the bed. I grabbed it and ran back to the living room.

Mom called the number. Officer Brindon was off duty

but said he would come right over. Aidan couldn't believe it. He hinted that his past dealings with police officers had not been pleasant. "But those things all happened back in my drinking days. I don't do that anymore." He shot me a quick glance and I recalled the odor of rum last night.

"You'll like these officers," I said. "They gave me this." I held my heart out to him so he could read the inscriptions.

Mom headed toward the kitchen. "I'm going to make coffee."

We waited anxiously for the arrival of the cops. Mom set out coffee and a tray with sugar, cream, Coffee mate. She added spoons and napkins. And I thought of the fancy little honey spoons we'd picked up at Cracker Barrel restaurant last Christmas. If we'd had any left, they would probably be on the tray as well. It was around nine p.m. now.

What did she think was about to happen? Did she think Officers Tate and Brindon were going to bring reams of paper and print out missing person flyers on our small Hewlett Packard? Would she start going through pictures of Janie, maybe one of her and Shawn together?

When that thought crossed my mind, some little idea bulb burst in my head and I ran for Janie's room. If she came home now and caught me, I'd be dead just like I thought I'd wanted earlier, but it was a chance I'd have to take.

Where her laptop usually sat on her desk, there was only a clean rectangle of space. I tore through her largest desk drawer hoping she'd simply slipped it in there for safekeeping. I found nothing but a drift of papers and notebooks from school.

I glanced around the room, wondering where she could have hidden it, and then I slipped my hand in between her mattress and box spring because I'd seen her slide it in there once when she thought I wasn't looking. But it wasn't there, either.

Finally, I began to go through every drawer. When I came to her underwear drawer, I didn't find much underwear, but I did find something.

I found her diary.

Without thinking, I opened it. The first words transported me back to our little-girl-before-dad-left-elementary-school days, the days when I looked up to my big sister, when in my eyes she was second to none, not even my mom. Back then, if Janie said it, then it must be so.

Dear Diary, the first page read, *I had the best vacation ever. Dad took us to the Gulf. We rented a giant house right on the beach and stayed a whole week. Every morning Mommy and Daddy drank coffee on the wide porch while me and Ben played in the water and made sandcastles.*

When they got tired of watching us, they would take us into Port Aransas to eat lunch and go exploring. Once, Daddy took us deep sea fishing, but we didn't like that. Ben cried when they flopped the big fish on the deck and we watched it gasping for air. I wanted to cry, too, but big sisters aren't allowed. We have to be big and set a good example.

The next time Daddy went fishing, Mommy took us girls on a dolphin boat. We loved watching them play in the waves, at least until Benji got sick from eating too many hotdogs and we had to leave. But it turned out okay. We went back to the beach house and Mom sent us on a treasure hunt to see who could find the biggest uncracked shell. I won! The shell is in my treasure box with the sand dollar. I'll keep them forever, Diary, or at least until we go back next summer.

Goodbye for now, I have to go. Mommy's taking us school clothes shopping.

It took me a minute to read those few pages. It must have taken Janie a couple hours to write them. I remembered that vacation. But I didn't remember being such a pest. Was it always that way for my big sister? Did she always have to be the strong one, to look out for wimpy little me?

Though we begged, every summer, we never went back to that beach house. Daddy began spending more and more time fishing and hunting with his buddies. And other than the trip to Six Flags and one to The Alamo, we didn't have any more big family vacations.

I closed the little book with my finger in the pages to hold my place. This isn't what I'd hoped to find. I quickly paged through the rest of the diary, glancing only at the dates from time to time. We needed recent information, not fractured childhood memories. I sniffled and Uncle Aidan laid his hand on my shoulder. I had no idea how long he'd been standing behind me.

"I was looking for her computer. But this is all I found. Is it wrong, reading it just to try and learn where she might be?"

When he didn't respond, I glanced up. His eyes were filled with tears. He swallowed, hard. "I don't know. But it doesn't help us much."

I nodded and flipped toward the end of the book. Would she still be writing in it after all these years?

Dear Diary,

Janie's usually elegant cursive leaped out at me. It wasn't elegant here, just angry. I could see how hard she had pressed on the paper. The back of the page felt embossed.

The entry was dated last week, right after I'd made the painting and Mom had gone to school. Right after Janie had come home and told me how everyone had looked at her and pointed and laughed behind their hands. It was the day she said I'd ruined her life. The day I tried to take mine.

I can't believe what my stupid sister did. I wish she'd never been born!

Behind me, Uncle Aidan made a noise, but he didn't tell me to stop reading.

After the picture she painted went viral, everyone started pointing at us, laughing, even started making fun of Shawn and me, saying better watch out, she'll be painting your pictures next.

He didn't like it. Said he wants to break up. Take a little break is how he put it.

Diary, I can't lose him.

After Dad left, he was the only one who understood. I sure couldn't talk to Mom, especially not to Ben. Nothing ever seems to touch her.

This ISN'T HAPPENING, DIARY.

I WON'T LET IT.

I'll do whatever it takes, but I'm not going to lose Shawn.

Not now! I haven't even told him my news yet.

She didn't bother to sign the entry. And there were no more after that.

God. No wonder she hated me so.

I flipped backward through the ancient little book, but she hadn't been writing in it regularly, only now and then through the years. Before this entry, the last one had been when she first started dating Shawn. *It's true love,* she'd written. *I've found my soul mate.*

Uncle Aidan strode to the closet and jerked open the doors just as Mom wandered in from the kitchen. "What in the *world* are you doing?"

"She's run off, Liv. Run off with Shawn."

Mom looked at me for confirmation.

I held up the diary. "Shawn tried to break up with her over that ridiculous painting I made." I had to stop and breathe before I could go on. "The kids were so vocal about it, Mom. And Shawn couldn't handle the noise." I closed the diary. "Her last entry said she she'd do anything to keep him."

Confusion shuttered Mom's face. "But what does that mean? What could she possibly do that would change his mind? I mean if he's that damn shallow—"

I thought the same thing. If he's that shallow, why would she want him? Shades of my dad filtered through my consciousness. I figured Mom had the same, or similar, thoughts going through her head.

Before I could answer, or pose a theory, Uncle Aidan said, "I want to see the painting that caused all this. That must be some work of art." He stabbed a glance my way and I felt my flesh wither on my bones.

"I guess it's still at school, in my art class. I don't even know."

"Oh, hell." Uncle Aidan's words leaked out of his mouth like air out of a slashed tire. "Shouldn't she have a lot more clothing?"

Mom beat me to the closet and pulled the string for the light. "Oh, Janie. What have you done?"

There were several empty hangers. I peered over her shoulder at the top shelf of the closet. "Her overnight bag is gone."

They followed my line of sight to the blank space where something large should have rested amongst the chaos of purses and bags.

"That one with the roses and skulls," I said. "I wonder what else is missing?" I ran back to our shared bathroom, opened the large linen cabinet where we kept everything except linens. "Her makeup is all gone."

Mom appeared behind me. "All of it?"

I nodded and swung the cabinet door wide so she could see the empty shelf. If I hadn't been so wrapped up in my own self-pity, I might have noticed the missing makeup earlier. But all I could ever think about was *me, me, me.*

Seventeen

Get Married?

We all heard the doorbell, such an unusual sound this time of night. It had to be Officers Tate and Brindon. I hurried down the hallway and through the living room. I could see in the dining room where Mom had set out the good china cups and saucers. The dichotomy of the afternoon tea setting with the knowledge of the purpose for the cops' visit almost stopped me in my tracks.

I opened the door and they came right in and hugged me. Hugged me for God's sake. I hugged them back.

"Tell us what's going on," Officer Tate said.

I showed them to the dining table just as Mom and Uncle Aidan came in. Everyone said hello, and I could see Mom was about to offer coffee, but the officers were already pulling notebooks out, clearly waiting on me to speak. So I did.

"My sister, Janie, is eighteen. She's about to graduate, all set to go to Texas Tech in the fall." I don't know why I thought they should know that, but it seemed important to let them know she wasn't a low life, that she actually had plans. "Anyhow, she messaged Mom this morning and told her she was on her way to work. She works at The Sweet Treat—"

Officer Tate held up her hand, wrote a few more words, and then said, "Go ahead."

"She never went to work at all. And she won't answer the phone. She didn't come to the funeral home even after Mom texted and told her we were going to... to see my dad."

I had to stop for breath, and to make sure my voice wasn't going to crack open and embarrass me.

"Okay. Anything else?"

"We think she's with her boyfriend, Shawn Powell 'cause his Mom can't get a hold of him either. He told her he was going to the lake with a friend."

Officer Brindon spoke up then. "We can't open a missing person's report just yet. She's technically an adult. But tell us what car they are in, the name of his lake friend, and then give me a picture of the two of them if you have it."

"And of course I'll want cell phone numbers and social media details."

I must have looked stunned. One more thing I hadn't thought of.

Officer Tate smiled gently. "You'd be surprised how often runaways can't resist posting about their exploits on their favorite sites."

I grabbed my phone. "I'll show you all her accounts. We can look at them right now. Everything's happening so fast, I didn't even think to look—"

"We just now discovered her missing suitcase and clothing," Mom said.

Uncle Aidan added, "And her diary said her boyfriend wanted to break up with her—"

"Yeah," I interrupted. "She said she'd do anything to prevent that."

The officers looked at each other. "Sounds like they've run off together, all right. The question is, where, and how far?"

"Does she have a computer? Have you looked through it for clues?"

"She has a laptop, but it's gone, too," I said. "That's what I was looking for when I found the old diary."

"Well," Officer Brindon said, "at least she's with someone you know and not out on her own. Alone."

Mom's face grew paler and paler as he spoke. "You're right, of course. At least she hasn't been abducted or something. At least she's missing because she wants to be—" The dam burst and all the good china in the world could no longer staunch the flow of pain that emanated from her chest. She wailed and dropped her face into her hands. Uncle Aidan and I rushed over and wrapped her in our arms.

"She's been through so much," Uncle Aidan said, as if needing to make excuses for her lack of control.

"We know," Officer Tate said. "We understand." She stood; pencil poised over her little notebook. "Tell me Janie's phone number and that of her boyfriend, maybe I can leave a message that will convince them of the seriousness of their actions."

I told her Janie's number, the description of her car—Uncle Aidan told them the plate number—then I picked Mom's phone up off the table and scrolled through it until I found Shawn's number and gave them that one, too.

Just then the door opened and Grandma and Grampa Stevens walked in. "What has happened now?" Alarm colored Grampa's voice.

Uncle Aidan quickly filled them in on the details. They both sat down as if suddenly exhausted. "What can we do?" Grandma asked. "What should we do?" Grampa echoed.

"We can't do anything officially, yet," Officer Tate said. "They're both adults and it appears she left on her own. No foul play. But we *can* look into it unofficially; make sure there haven't been any accident reports or anything of that nature. Meanwhile, call all their friends, make sure they didn't simply go to the lake, and let me know if you hear from her."

The five of us sat and looked at the door after the officers let themselves out.

"Should we call Shawn's mom back?" I directed the question to Mom. But Uncle Aidan answered.

"Yes. Get the name of that friend. I'll drive out there to the lake if that's what it takes."

"I'll go with you." I waited on Mom to make the call but she sat like a statue.

I put the phone in her hand—since she didn't ask for it—and waited. Grandma got up and poured coffee for herself and Gramps.

The clock in the dining room chimed the half hour. "Nine thirty," Mom said. "If he wanted to break up, why would they run off together?"

I shrugged. Nothing that happened made sense to me anymore. I went and sat by Grampa. He looked as lost and lonely as I felt. My dad was his middle child. He had an older one, an uncle I'd never met—Easly—who had died in Afghanistan years earlier. And he had a younger daughter, Carmen, who had moved to Italy after marrying a military man. It worked out well, Grandma always said, since Grampa still had relatives in Sicily. I hope to meet her someday.

Grampa enveloped my hand in his rough palm. "The world's going to hell in a handbasket." His blue eyes were milky. "I loved your dad, but your Gran is right, he always had a hole in him no one could fill." He squeezed gently. "You take after him, you know."

My heart plunged. Did he know what I'd done? Is that what he meant?

He let go me and laid his gnarled, plumber's hand on my hair. "Same dark hair, same deep blue eyes. He was a beautiful child, too." A solitary tear made a slow trek down one side of his mouth. It disappeared in the deep smile brackets.

I took his hand off my head and brought it to my lips. "I love you, Gramps."

Grandma brought him another cup of coffee. She smiled softly. I couldn't tell if her cheeks were wet, but everyone knew she was the strong one in the family.

Mom poked a name on her contact list. Shawn's mother must've answered immediately. "We can't fill out a missing person report," Mom said. "They are considered adults." She paused. "Yes," she agreed. "My brother said he would drive up to the lake if—"

Her eyes widened. "Oh, you did?"

Even from the one-sided conversation, I could tell what his mom had said.

"I see." She closed her eyes. "Of course. And you call me, too. Anytime."

"Shawn didn't go to the lake, huh?"

Mom shook her head. "When his mom didn't answer, Shawn's mother called the other boy's dad. He didn't know anything about it. His son was right there, with him, watching something on Netflix."

Uncle Aidan said a bad word under his breath and plopped down on the couch. "I knew it," he said.

"What do you think—" Grandma started to ask.

She was interrupted by the jangle of Mom's phone. She

had turned the ringer all the way up. For a split second, no one moved.

From across the room I could see Janie's blonde head pop up on the iPhone screen. Mom smashed her thumb down on the icon so hard nothing happened. She took a deep breath and tried again. "Janie?"

We all heard the tiny voice.

I couldn't make out the words, but I knew it was my sister, and she sounded contrite. Officer Tate must've got in touch.

"Are you all right? Where are you? Are you with Shawn, why did you run off?" Mom pelted her with questions.

We all crowded around her and listened. Mom put it back on speaker.

Janie said she and Shawn were on their way home. They'd got all the way into New Mexico, headed to Las Vegas, when Officer Tate called her told her they were about to put out a BOLO for them.

"BOLO?" Mom asked.

"Be on the lookout," Uncle Aidan whispered.

"Who's that?" Janie's voice went up a notch. "Do you have me on speaker?"

Mom touched the speaker icon and made it go off. "Of course not. Uncle Aidan just heard me ask what a BOLO was." She frowned and stabbed the speaker icon, putting Janie back on. It felt like she was *saying there, take that*. But I could be assuming too much. Or putting my own thoughts onto her actions. I had grown extremely tired of my older sister trying to control everything. Maybe Mom had, too.

"We're falling apart here." Mom smoothed her hair, but didn't qualify her statement. "You need to be with your family." She straightened her spine. "We need you here with us." She listened for a moment. "Yes, I heard you. On the way to Vegas. What were you going to do, get married?"

We all heard Shawn's whispered disbelief in the background. "You *told* them?"

"We thought about it." Janie's voice sounded defiant. "We aren't kids, you know. And everything at school is ruined now. Ruined."

Mom put things in perspective. "Your father is dead. Your sister almost died. And your response is to run off with a boy who only hours ago wanted nothing to do with you? Who wanted to break up with you just when you needed him most?"

I felt my eyes bulge with surprise. My mom never criticized, and she'd also let the cat out of the bag, so she quickly rushed on. "We looked at your diary to see where you'd gone."

I thought Janie would explode, but for a moment I heard nothing but silence. Then she said, "Stupid, huh?"

Mom laughed a shaky little laugh. It sounded good. "Not as stupid as some of the things that have happened around here lately, but yeah. It's up there." She looked at me with an unreadable expression.

Was she scolding me for taking the pills? I almost wished she would. I wished she would scream at me or shake me, or tell me what an idiot I was—something. Talk about stupid. It could be our new family surname.

Eighteen

Like a Cinder Block Chained to my Waist

Mom hung up after Janie assured her she and Shawn would be home in a few hours. "And don't worry," Janie said. "He is calling his mom as soon as we hang up."

Grandma hugged Mom from behind her chair. "Thank God, they've been found. Maybe things can settle down a bit now." She patted Mom. "My son was so confused. I hope you girls don't let his problems shade the rest of your lives."

Mom squeezed her ex-mother-in-law's hand. "I think we will be all right, eventually. I miss him, though." She looked up at her brother who hovered over us all. "You know I never could stop loving the man I used to know."

Grandma couldn't say anything to that. I imagined her thinking how much she loved the little boy he used to be. She started toward my Gramps and we all saw her stagger, not much, just a little sidestep.

"Mom!" My mother jumped up to grab Grandma's elbow, but Grampa got there first.

"She's all right. Aren't you old girl?"

Grandma smiled, nodded. Her face was shiny wet now. Maybe the tears had blurred her vision, causing her to stumble.

"Take my room," I told my grandparents. "Grandma needs some rest. I'll sleep on the couch. I don't mind." I envisioned myself snug on the sofa with my unicorn throw on my legs and the remote control in my hand.

"We can't stay." Grampa ushered Grandma toward the door. "All our medicines are in our bags at the hotel." He patted my forearm as we all crowded around the front door. "Thank ya, though. Sweetheart." He stopped and looked right into my eyes. For a moment, his blue eyes looked deeper, less milky. "Are you okay, now?"

I knew what he meant. I felt so small. Everything my Grandparents had been through, losing two sons, now me. "I'm going to be okay, Gramps." I smiled. "I promise."

His grizzled old head bobbed up and down. "C'mon, Mama." He held Grandma under her elbow. "Let's get back to our room. Gonna be a day tomorrow."

When he said that, my heart broke. I swear it felt as if someone punched me in the chest. We were burying my daddy tomorrow. I'd never see his face again except in pictures. Or in my memory.

Together my grandparents shuffled out the door and down the sidewalk to their car. Mom grabbed Grandma's purse at the last second and ran it out to the car just as Gramps got her tucked into the passenger seat. "I love you two," I heard her say.

"We love you girls," Grandma replied.

And then they drove away.

I stepped outside and watched as their taillights bloomed red at the stop sign. It made me want to run after them, beg them to come back. Something felt so final. As if I were losing them along with my dad.

Uncle Aidan sat down on the porch. I sat down beside him. There were only two steps. Mom came back up the short sidewalk toward us. I scooted over and made room on the small front porch. She sat down, too. "Life sucks sometimes, doesn't it?"

I laughed. Mom hated that particular 's' word. I couldn't believe she'd just used it.

Uncle Aidan wrapped his arm around us from behind. "I don't know about y'all, but I need a burger."

Of all the things he could've said, that was one I least expected. "I want a milkshake," I said. "Sonic is open till eleven."

Uncle Aidan stood and pulled us up by our hands. "Start up the Green Hornet." He slapped the keys in my palm. "I'll lock up the house."

Mom turned toward the door. "I'll wait here." You two go ahead.

"C'mon, Sis," Uncle Aidan said. "We aren't taking no for an answer." He turned Mom away from the front door.

I linked my arm in hers and pulled her toward Uncle Aidan's Roadrunner waiting at the curb. I couldn't believe he'd told me to start it up. I turned loose of Mom's arm and ran to the driver's door. There was no clicker to open the door remotely. Uncle Aidan's key was huge and silver. It gave me a tremendous feeling of power to fit that giant key in the lock and actually feel the mechanism turn inside the door.

Before I started the engine, I leaned across the wide bench seat and popped the lock up on the passenger side.

Mom slid in and closed the door.

The giant white moon painted a silver stripe down the hood of the Green Hornet. I didn't think I'd ever seen anything so beautiful. I stuck the key in the ignition and realized I had no idea what to do next. I'd ridden with Uncle Aidan on numerous occasions, but I'd never seen him actually start the car. He usually picked me up with it already running.

I knew I had to push in the clutch. The gearshift was a stick on the floor with a round wooden ball on the top. The shift pattern was engraved on the ball. That part I had studied as we drove, but I didn't have a clue how to make the car start.

Uncle Aidan came bopping down the walk. "What's the holdup?" His voice sounded jovial. It carried to us on the night air like a voice on a phone line. I wondered if he'd been in the rum again.

Since the car didn't have power windows (or power anything), we had been able to roll down both of our windows while we waited.

"Are we out of go juice?" he asked as I jumped out to let him in the driver's seat. "Did I forget to fill up?"

I felt so silly. Like a little girl again. "No, Uncle Aidan. I just don't know how to start it with that thing." I pointed to the stick shift.

He grinned and his teeth reminded me of the Cheshire Cat on the old *Alice in Wonderland* cartoon. They glowed in the dark interior of the car. "Well," he said. "Here's what you do."

I'd crawled into the backseat when he got in, but now I hung over his shoulder and watched carefully. Without actually starting it, Uncle Aidan showed me how to hold down the clutch with my left foot while turning the key as I touched the gas pedal with my right foot. "But you have to make sure your gearshift is in Neutral." He demonstrated how to wiggle the shifter to make certain it was in neutral.

"There's so much to do," I said. "I don't think I could ever drive it."

He finally keyed the engine and it roared to life. "Glass-packs on the muffler," he said.

I didn't even ask what that meant. Uncle Aidan spent a lot of his time-off working on The Green Hornet and other cars like it. He sold new cars in the daytime, to pay the bills, he once said, but on his days off, he restored vintage cars for car shows. *It's my life,* he'd told me. *My passion.*

We took off down the street at a good pace. We didn't lay rubber, as he jokingly called it, but we didn't let any grass grow under out tires, either. When we hit the main road into town, the traffic picked up considerably. I felt like a teenager and a little kid all rolled into one.

We were on one of the main streets in town. I recognized a couple of cars from school. It was Saturday night. Kids were coming and going. Movies. Dates. House parties. Cruising.

For a few minutes, I completely forgot about my father lying in his new satin-lined bed at the funeral home. But when I did remember, it was because I realized that Uncle Aidan would probably be the one to teach me to drive now—oh, not The Green Hornet, I didn't think I could ever master that shifter— but maybe using Mom's Camry. No way Janie would ever let me drive her Focus. Would she even speak to me now? I felt certain she would know I was the one who had found her diary.

But on the heels of that awful thought, about all the things my dad would not be around to teach me, was the realization that even if he *were* still alive, he probably wouldn't be the one teaching me anyhow. He'd already left us for the new and improved family. Tossed us away like yesterday's news. Put us out beside the curb.

That didn't make me feel better, but it did allow me to enjoy my milkshake a little more. And when my favorite song came on Sonic radio through the open window, I even hummed along, just a bit. Not so anyone could hear.

It didn't feel right to have happiness creeping back in so soon, but my sister had been found and was coming home. As much as I hated her, (*She's such a twat! I wish she'd just disappear!*), I didn't want anything bad to happen to her. I didn't really want her gone the way she did me. Mostly because I didn't think Mom could take it if anything happened to Janie.

And really, Mom was all I had left besides Uncle Aidan and the grands. But they were old, and Uncle Aidan? He was... flighty, and he really liked his rum. Dad often said booze broke up both of Uncle Aidan's marriages. Then he would always say, "Thank God he never had kids. We'd probably be raising them, too." That was after Mom had allowed Uncle Aidan to crash on our couch for a few days in between wives.

After Dad left us for The Slut, I wrote him a letter. Too bad you had kids, I'd written. *Now I guess Uncle Aidan will have to raise us since you can't be bothered anymore.* But I never gave him the letter. It had just felt good to write it out. Janie wasn't the only one who kept a diary.

Looks like it came true, though. Maybe I'm clairvoyant like Johnny Smith in *The Dead Zone.*

That dampened my mood. Knowing what I'd written had come true. Now Uncle Aidan *was* staying with us, trying to take care of us. I guess some might call that karma. Others would say precognition. Most would say it's just life.

Uncle A asked me if I wanted to cruise the drag a few times with him and Mom. That made me laugh. "No thanks, I believe I'll pass on that one."

He gave me a crazy grin in the rearview mirror and we headed home with our burgers and shakes.

The pall had lifted, temporarily, at least. And then a news report came on the radio—no Sirius in the Hornet—telling that President Trump had just sent Cruise Missiles into Syria in response to a chemical weapons attack the Syrian president had allegedly carried out on his own people.

"What?" I leaned over the seat and turned up the volume. We'd been debating the refugee crisis in Civics class right before my own life had come apart at the seams. "When did all this happen?"

Uncle Aidan told me how he'd seen news reports on TV of the Syrian men, women, and children who had been gassed with some horrid nerve gas. "They're certain their own government did it. To keep the rebels in line. I saw an interview on PBS with a couple of doctors who work over there. They said this has happened over two hundred times in the last few years. Usually killing only a handful of people at a time so as not to draw the attention of the whole world." He shook his head. "Monstrous. The United Nations should have stepped in long ago."

I fell back in my seat, my milkshake sloshing over the edge of its cup. The world goes on, it doesn't stop because we have our little family problems. Dad couldn't handle real life—as a result, I couldn't handle it either—but what if we had someone bombing us like those poor people over there? Would we still be so quick to try and take our own lives, over such petty crap as we'd experienced? I mean, a painting for God's sake.

The thought overwhelmed me. Uncle Aidan told how the Syrian people had no fresh water because the wells had been bombed along with the hospitals, and even the schools. All to make them give in to the current ruler.

And here we were, tooling down the road in our fast car with our fast food and our shakes in their Styrofoam containers. We've never known real hunger or disease. Never had to run for cover in the middle of the night, or watched our loved ones gasping for breath like fish out of water. I'd seen video of nerve-gas damage. The foaming at the mouth as the victims' insides are acidized. The wonders of technology brought it all right into our classrooms, and right onto our phones. Of course I'd researched it even more after class. That' what I did, that IQ thing. I always wanted to know more.

This knowledge took me back down into the black depths of despair. It took me there like a cinder block around the waist of a mob hit thrown off a bridge. But this time, the black feelings were not self-pity for my own problems, this time the black emotions came out of pure guilt. Guilt that I had everything anyone could ever need, and yet I'd tried to throw it all away because of a few stupid words and pictures—*and Dad's ultimate betrayal*, my mind whispered.

My mind wouldn't slow down. The thoughts spiraled around and around like a Mobius strip in front of the A/C vent whirling and twirling and swirling without end.

I dropped my head into my hands.

This crazy world.

"Ben?" Mom touched my knee. "What is it, baby, headache?"

I sighed. We were back in front of the house. Uncle Aidan stood outside the car, white Sonic sack in hand, waiting on me to get it together.

"Yeah," I said. "A little bit." I squeezed her patting hand. "But trust me, I don't want any pain pills." I smiled to let her know I would be all right. "I just feel so bad for those people over there. Did the missiles help? Did President Trump do the right thing?"

"Only time will tell." She climbed out of the car. "I haven't kept up with it, you know, with all this going on."

"Right." Everyone has her own set of problems, her own priorities. But I couldn't help feeling some priorities were really skewed. Or maybe screwed was a better word. Screwed up. Totally.

Nineteen

Do I Want to Go?

I went in the house, turned on CNN, and watched report after report of the bombings and the nerve gas attack. The images of children dying right there on my screen were almost too much. My milkshake melted on the coffee table, unnoticed.

Uncle Aidan watched a few minutes. "I hope Trump bombs the hell out of them until they get the message. All those kids—that guy over there must be the devil." He went to the kitchen where I heard the clinking of glass against glass.

Was that the bottle of rum? Nah. He had Coke in a Styrofoam cup from Sonic. Wouldn't he just add the rum to that? And why was I wasting my time worrying about his drinking anyhow? Was it really any of my business?

"I'm going to bed, kid." He'd walked in behind me without my knowledge. "Don't watch too much of this. It's out of our control, know what I mean? We can hope for the best, but we can't obsess—"

"Oh, I know, Uncle A." I gave him what I hoped was a real smile. "I'll go to bed as soon as Mom's out of the shower."

He leaned down and hugged me.

I sniffed, but didn't smell alcohol.

Mom came in, a towel on her head. I glanced at the clock.

An hour had gone by while I switched from channel to channel, each video clip more disturbing than the last. The repeats of the chemical attack were horrific, and of course they replayed the ones from 2013, but after I'd sat for a moment, watching those and then watching real time video of our missiles bombing the Syrian airbase—even Russia posted video of the attacks—it all became so surreal I began to lose focus.

"Honey?" Mom sat beside me in her fluffy pink robe.

"It's awful, isn't it?" I could hardly tear my eyes from the screen.

"So horrible it's hard to grasp. But—"

I rolled my eyes. "I know, I know. Uncle Aidan already told me to turn it off and go to bed."

Mom didn't say anything, just reached for the remote. "We have our own trials to get through tomorrow and the next day." She glanced at my face. "Not like those poor people, no. But we have to face things nevertheless."

"Let our elected officials take care of this, you mean?"

She nodded.

"Oh my God." I put my hand to my mouth. "It just dawned on me. I'm in Uncle Aidan's bed. Where did he go?"

Mom laughed. "He's in the other bathroom shower, I think. He's easy to get along with, isn't he?"

I nodded. "You are lucky to have him for a brother."

Mom pulled me over against her shoulder. "Yes, I am. He's not perfect. Always got in trouble when we were growing up. But my sweet mama just said he'd outgrow it someday. Unconditional love, all the way." She smoothed my hair and that seemed to make her remember her own hair. Pulling off the towel, she ran her fingers through it to detangle as much as possible. It was only shoulder length, so it didn't take much.

Drops of coconut-scented moisture plopped on my arm from the ends of her hair. I recognized the scent of her favorite shampoo and conditioner.

"When daddy died from liver disease, Aidan was only fifteen. He went wild with grief. Began drinking, running with the wrong crowd... I tried to help. Mama did, too, but sometimes grief gets its claws in you and just won't let go."

I listened intently.

"Maybe if he'd been around for the nursing, like Mama and I were, he would've had an easier time letting go. It was awful, what my daddy endured those last few months of his life." She settled back into the couch a little deeper. "Aidan worked a lot. He worked more than he went to school. Tried to take over Daddy's responsibilities." She laughed at her memory. "But it also kept him away from home, that garage where he learned all about cars from Daddy's friend, Jim."

"He tried to help, huh?"

Mom nodded, her chin bumping the top of my head as she cuddled me. "He was a good man, too. Tried to keep Aidan occupied those last few years when daddy was drinking and then when he got so ill, so fast."

"Wish I'd known him," I said. "I would've loved him. Even if he did drink."

"Oh, baby. He would've have loved you, too."

We heard Uncle Aidan coming so Mom sat up. "It still hurts him to talk about our dad."

I looked at Uncle Aidan's freshly scrubbed face when he walked in. "You can have your bed now." I stood and picked up the folded blanket and pillow from the basket at the end of the couch. "I forgot you slept here."

He plopped down in the recliner and threw the feet up. "Or here, doesn't matter to me. Actually," he looked at me with a gleam in his eye. "While you were in the hospital, I slept with Maggie May."

I feigned shock. "In my bed?"

"Yeppers!"

"And Mags didn't even tell me, that little traitor." I laughed and started down the hall. "G'night, Mom. Uncle Aidan."

"Goodnight, sweetie. Love you."

"Love you, too, Mommy. And you, Uncle A."

Silence from the living room, then. "Sleep tight, little one." I blew him a palm-kiss even though I knew he couldn't see me.

Grief. Could that really account for Uncle Aidan's problems with alcohol, and relationships? If so, what had been his father's excuse for drinking? I'd read that might be hereditary, too. More questions to ponder. More questions without answers.

I took a quick bath, put on my fleecy pajamas, made sure Maggie had fresh food and water—she was so undemanding, so easy to forget—and then I crawled in bed with my phone. Mom hadn't said a word about me having it back. Of course I no longer had Facebook, or Twitter, or Snapchat. I didn't even have Instagram anymore.

I thought about looking up some of the apps Kera and I used to play around with like Yik Yak and Kik, even though I knew there would probably be stuff on there about me. I mean, most parents don't even know about those—and wouldn't know what they were if they did find them, especially ones like Line or Omegle or Whisper—so there's no way they could all be deleted.

But did I really want to go there again? Did I really want to see what the trolls were saying? If it was bad before my mom went to school, and I went to the hospital, what on earth would it be like now? Ten times worse, a hundred times. A thousand. There would be no brakes on it at all.

I pulled up the app store and typed in Whisper.

A message appeared on my screen that I was no longer allowed to peruse the App store without parental consent. Mom had put something called Web Blocker on my phone.

Great. Now I really felt like a little kid again, but not in a good way like before. I laid back, a huge weight falling off my shoulders. *I can't look. Mom took over. I can't see anything at all.*

I awoke the next morning with little Maggie on my chest and sunlight across my legs.

Rolling over, I reached for my phone to check the time, but it wasn't on the nightstand. Struggling out of the quilt and sheets, Maggie stretched and scolded me with a sideways look. Then she curled up in the warm spot I'd just vacated.

Careful not to disturb her furry majesty, I sorted through my bed in search of my phone. But I couldn't find it.

The bathroom called and I opened the door on my side. Janie's door was closed. I wondered if she'd ever got home. Judging by the slant of the sunlight striping my bed and the bathtub, it had to be after nine o'clock.

I took care of business, amazed that I'd forgotten about making the thin line on my thigh. It had already healed over and I felt no compulsion to reopen it. Things had been so calm with Janie gone.

Would they stay that way? I glanced at her door again. My insides curled up just like my little Mags had done, searching for a warm spot, searching for a safe place.

Back in my bedroom, I made up the bed, lifting Maggie, moving her, putting her back down. She cooperated fully, with only a tiny meow from time to time. I began to worry that maybe she was sick, but the last time I put her down—between my two pillows—I lay beside her and caressed her until she began to purr again.

It was good to have someone who needed me, who loved me unconditionally the way Mom said her mother had loved Uncle Aidan. The way she loved me.

I'd have to examine that later. After things got back to normal, if they ever did, but right now all I wanted was my phone. And a cinnamon roll.

The evocative smell led me to the kitchen by my nose.

"Morning." Mom stood at the breakfast bar smoothing icing on homemade rolls. "Remember how you used to call them cimmamon rolls?"

I nodded, stuffed one in my mouth. The warm, sweet icing dripped down my chin and I wiped it away, licked my fingers. "Have you seen my phone?" As I spoke, I realized I hadn't looked under the bed.

Mom shook her head. "I hope you don't freak when you find out I took all the social media stuff off, for now, at least. Maybe later, when things cool down—"

"It's okay." I stuffed another bite in my mouth, followed by a drink of the icy cold milk she'd just set before me. I didn't tell her I already knew.

The look of surprise on her face was classic. "You don't care?"

I shrugged. "I thought I would, but everyone was so mean. And it was a good picture. Maybe the best painting I'd ever done. I um, I'm really kind of pissed off now."

She frowned.

"Sorry. I know you hate that word, but it's true. How dare they? I mean, it was bad enough having to watch Ker and Will stroll all over campus, arm in arm, but then when I put my feelings on paper, well. Who gave them the right to plaster—"

"Is that what it was about?" Uncle Aidan helped himself to a couple of rolls on a paper napkin. He sat on a wooden stool beside me. "I had no idea what the picture was about. But I still say *day-um*, that must be some work of art. I'd like to see it."

I felt my face grow warm. "Thanks, I think."

He laughed and side-arm hugged me. "Your sister's still asleep. I just checked on her."

My sweet breakfast turned to a lump in my belly. Just the mention of Janie killed the half-decent mood. "What time did she make it home?"

"Four a.m." Mom said. "I told Aidan to wake me when she came in. I knew she wouldn't get past him lying there on the couch."

I cleaned up my mess, washed out my glass, went back to my room to look under my bed.

"The official visitation is at six tonight," Mom called after me. "If you want to go, that is."

I couldn't believe she was giving me an option. Did I want to go? I'd have to think about it. I'd said goodbye last night. Plus, I'd already seen Grandma and Grampa Stevens. Who else could I possibly want to visit? No one from school would come. And if they did, I wouldn't want to see them. Not at all.

Sure enough when I got down on my hands and knees, I saw my phone under the edge of the bed. I touched the screen and my little green message icon showed a number one beside it. Someone had sent me a text.

Twenty

The Note

I touched the icon immediately. I had a feeling I knew who had sent it.

"Hi," the message read. "I hope you're doing okay. Call me anytime you want."

Sam had attached a picture of himself sporting a wide, silly grin.

Did I want to talk to him? What if he asked me about my pills? I'd start to blubber. I didn't want that, but I figured everyone at school knew about it. Especially since Kera's aunt had been my nurse. I didn't want Sam to see me as weak. I didn't want that.

I opened my closet and looked at all my clothes. If I did go see my dad one more time, what would I wear? I thought of his profile over the edge of the casket. It was the first thing I'd seen when I walked into the Dignity East Parlor. Did I want to see that again before the funeral? It seemed so drawn out. This burial thing. Maybe I should just wait until the funeral tomorrow, say my final goodbye then. In front of a bunch of people. In front of his new, preferred family—the ones who maybe hadn't worked out after all.

I took out my black pants, and my navy blue shirt with the asymmetrical neckline, the clothes I'd worn to the Honor

Roll Awards assembly. I hung the two pieces on my closet door and dragged my black church shoes out of the back of the closet. I'll wear the silver heart from Officers Tate and Brindon, and maybe the charm bracelet Mom and Dad had given me for Christmas a few years ago. It had musical notes and paintbrush charms on it. I think it was the last gift Dad had given me that didn't seem forced. Mom had probably picked it out.

Looking at my clothes hanging there made my mouth go dry. I lay back down on the bed with Maggie and wished I could go back to sleep and never wake up. But I didn't mean it anymore. I just wanted to go to sleep and not wake up until this was all over. Sleep for twenty years like Rip van Winkle. Wake up as an adult with all this behind me. With my future all set and figured out. With my heart glued back together, whole.

I dozed. Came awake to the sound of the doorbell on the front door that was seeing more use than it had in years. Probably Shawn or Grandma and Grampa Stevens.

I waited, poking songs on my playlists, writing my thoughts in my Notes app. Starting note after note to my dad. Thinking maybe I should write one on paper to put in the coffin with him. Wondering when it would hit me that he wasn't just at the slut's house anymore.

Then my room door opened and Mom came in all white faced and starey-eyed. She held a sheet of paper in her hand. Had she somehow read my thoughts and brought me something to write on?

And that's when I noticed stains on the corner of the page.

I sat up.

Mom perched on the edge of my bed. One remaining stripe

of sunlight lay across her lap. She glanced at the clothes hanging on my closet door. "I need to talk to you." She held up the paper.

"What is that?" Panic stained my voice just like something stained the paper. "Is that—is that blood?"

Mom nodded. She couldn't talk. She pressed the rumpled page to her breast. "I didn't kill him," she sobbed. "I didn't kill him after all."

"Mama?" Alarm bells went off in my brain. What was she talking about?

She wiped her nose, glanced down at the page still smashed to her breast. "I thought he shot himself because I wouldn't let him come back..." Her voice went away while she composed herself. "But a detective just came to the door, said they had concluded their investigation and found no evidence of foul play."

Wow. I knew they were investigating, but I thought it was routine. An unattended death sort of thing. Foul play made it sound different, *criminal*. "So he brought you that?" I nodded toward the paper she held.

Mom pulled it away from her body and looked down at it. "Yes." Her voice came out low, breathy. "His last words. Telling us why—"

I reached for the letter. I reached for it blindly, but Mom held on a moment longer. "You'll be shocked," she said. "I'm just warning you—"

"Be shocked about what?" Janie stood in my doorway rubbing the sleep from her eyes. She had on flannel shorts and a long sleeved tee. Gorgeous, as usual. If I didn't hate her, I would've told her so.

Mom patted my bed. "Come in, Janie. You need to hear this, too."

By this time, my curiosity felt like a spring inside me. If she didn't tell us soon I might leap over and snatch the letter away from her.

"Your dad left a suicide note." She sniffled, wiped her nose. Uncle Aidan came to the door, coffee in one hand, the other pressed up against the frame in such a casual pose it seemed intentional.

"Want me to read it out?"

Mom nodded, handed it to him, gathered Janie and me to her breast like a mother hen with her chicks.

"Livvie." Uncle Aidan placed his coffee cup on my dresser and cleared his throat. The paper trembled slightly. He grasped it with both hands, no longer concerned about looking cool. "I'm sorry for everything. Tell the girls I messed up. Tell them I love them more than anything in this world. Them and you, Liv. I was stupid and selfish. Thought I wanted a different life. I took money from the company. A lot of money. The boss found out, told me to pay it back or he's turning me in. I can't pay it back, Liv. It's all gone. I came to tell you, but I was too ashamed. I can't go to prison. I can't."

Uncle Aidan fell onto my desk chair, all the breath knocked out of him by my dad's words. He kept a tight grip on the paper but his eyes seemed unfocussed. "It's like a bad movie."

My own mind kept going back to the word stupid. He used it like I used it. It was our shared word. I scraped my memory to see if we'd always shared that word, but I couldn't recall.

Janie's sobs echoed Mom's. "Is that blood? Is that Dad's blood on that paper?"

Uncle Aidan touched the questionable stain. "I don't know."

Janie leaned across the bed and pulled it from his grasp. "It is. It's—" She ran her thumb over the corner of the page.

"I can't believe it's his blood." I knew that sounded lame. "I can't believe he did this."

Janie said, "Why not? It seems to be a family trait." She avoided my gaze but her aim was true. Her words went straight into me like a dagger.

Mom looked like she might slap her again. "You should be ashamed, Janie. Shame on you. I don't know what is wrong with you. Acting like such a... a..." I thought she would say "such a bitch," but she finished with, "Such a *beast*."

Thanks, Mom. That's really telling her. "It's okay, Mom, it's only my heart she just cut out." I got up and walked across to the bathroom door. I made certain not to slam it behind me. From the linen closet I grabbed the razor blades and opened one, not caring that Mom and the others were right outside the door.

My dad was a thief. A stupid, selfish thief. But at least he did it to himself. At least it wasn't my fault; it wasn't even about the painting or about me at all. It wasn't even about Mom. Had he always been this way? Is that why Janie has such a horrid mean streak? Did we both inherit something strange in his DNA? Or maybe we didn't inherit something, like, maybe something was missing.

I sat on the edge of the tub and laid the sharp thin razor blade against my skin. I'd read that that serious folks made the cut vertically, not horizontally. I pressed down. Should I just slash? Wait. Get in the tub. Less mess. I stood up to step over inside. The blade slipped, hit the bottom, slid toward the drain. I leaned over, made a grab for it. My necklace fell out of my tee shirt. The heavy sliver heart slapped the side of the porcelain tub with a loud *clank*.

"Ben? Everything okay?" Mom's voice.

Someone twisted the doorknob. I had it locked.

I picked up the razor blade from the bottom of the tub and my necklace hit the side again. I grabbed the heart to shut it up. The words *Choose Life*, stared up at me from my palm.

Uncle Aidan knocked on the door none too gently. "Benji? Did you fall?"

I squeezed the blade too hard. It sliced into the thin web of skin between my finger and thumb. I threw it into the trash and yanked open the door. "I'm okay!" My voice shook. I could feel blood filling my palm. I prayed it wouldn't drip onto the white tile before I could get rid of him.

"What was all that noise?" His eyes darted around the small room, looking for trouble.

I rolled my eyes. I didn't mean to; I loved my Uncle Aidan more than anything. "I dropped something in the tub."

He actually leaned over and looked into the tub from across the room. "I don't see anything . . ."

I laughed. "I got it out already." Even to my ears it sounded kind of forced. "When I leaned over, my necklace whacked the side of the tub." I looked him in the eye to make him believe me. But my heart sputtered in my chest. Could he hear it?

He looked me in the eye, too.

All I saw there was love. And maybe a touch of suspicion.

"Okay, sweetie. I just thought you fell down or fainted or something."

"Thanks, Uncle Aidan," I whispered. "It *was* quite a shock, wasn't it?"

He turned away. "Quite a shock indeed." Under his breath, I heard him say, "And he always treated *me* like the criminal—"

That part was very true. I recalled all those arguments

between Mom and Dad about Uncle Aidan's lifestyle. But before I could give it any more thought, I caught the heat of someone else's eyes boring a hole through me.

Janie let her gaze travel from my hand to the floor.

The blood from my palm had dripped onto the pristine tile. The three drops were even redder than the pulsing heart in the painting that had started her hating me.

Twenty-One

WE CAN HANDLE IT

I clenched my hand to stop the bleeding and slowly closed the door. If she said anything to Mom, I felt certain I would know immediately. But there came no admonition, no scolding, no shocked Mom-voice yelling through the door.

I wiped the blood up with a wad of paper and flushed it down the toilet. The bleeding had nearly stopped but it started up again when I ran it under cold water. I soaped it enjoying the sting, and thought how proud Mom would be to know I had cleaned it thoroughly. I patted it dry with more paper—being so careful not to get blood on the hand towel beside the sink—and held pressure on it until the tiny slit dried up. Every time I opened my hand it wanted to start bleeding again.

A Band-Aid from the medicine chest would do the trick.

All these little things kept me from thinking about the note. My dad had taken money from his job. Somewhere along the line, he'd turned into a criminal. An actual just-like-you-see-on-TV criminal. My dad. And that's why he killed himself. It wasn't because of me or Mom or even Sharla-the-slut. It was because he'd done something so bad he was going to go to jail.

I opened the door to my room, relieved to find it as empty as I felt.

My phone lay on the nightstand.

Sam's message waited.

Before I could chicken out, I picked it up typed, "My life is ridiculous."

He didn't come back immediately, but by the time I'd tugged on my shorts and tank, remade my bed and tidied things up—to keep from having to go into the living room— he had responded.

"Want to talk?"

Did I want to talk? I looked at his goofy grin, the one he'd taken earlier so I could use it for my contact, and I wondered. Could I trust him? Or would he splash my words across the universe the way others had done with my art?

From the other side of the door, Uncle Aidan called out, "I'm going to my place for clothes, anyone feel like riding along?"

Saved by the bell. I quickly texted, "Going with my uncle for a bit. Talk later?"

He sent a thumbs-up emoji and I breathed a sigh of relief and tucked the phone in my back pocket.

Janie's closed bedroom door felt like a statement, but I passed it and went to the kitchen to check on Mom. The kitchen was spotless; Mom wasn't there.

"She went to lie down," Uncle Aidan said.

I stopped. I could easily imagine her on her bed in the fetal position, curled around that bloody letter. "I'd better stay here."

"Let's give her some space." He opened the side door. The Roadrunner waited at the curb.

"Is she okay?" Dad, her ex-husband, her high school boy-friend, the love of her life, a criminal, a cheater, a suicide. God. My problems seemed pretty small in comparison.

"She's the strongest person I know."

It seemed like he'd said that before. With their shared history, it seemed like a lot. "But let me just tell her we're going." I paused in front of her door. "Mom?" I knocked timidly.

Throat clearing, clothes rustling. "Ben? Come on in, honey."

I opened the door a crack and there sat my Mommy, her face as rumpled as the bedspread. I ran to her, sat on the bed beside her.

She read my mind.

"I'm okay." She smiled a little. "I *wouldn't* be okay if I didn't have you girls, and Uncle Aidan."

He stood in the doorway in that one-arm-stretched-up-grasping-the-door-frame pose that I'd earlier thought was practiced. So he could look cool. Now I realized, he just was cool. Really cool guys showed up. Stuck around, even through tough times.

"We'll be okay." I looked into her smeary face. "Won't we?"

She grasped the point of my chin with her thumb and forefinger. "We'll be fine. We are strong. Tough. We have each other and that will never change. Even Janie will see that, some day."

I looked down at the letter in her hand.

She smoothed it, and then folded it neatly. "I'm putting this away. But anytime you need to reread it, let me know. I will never keep secrets from you, okay?"

My eyes were swimming. The stains on that paper. Those stains—"Hey," she forced me to look at her again. "It's life. It's not pretty, but we can handle it. We can. I promise."

Uncle Aidan turned away, cleared his throat, wiped his face. "I'll be in the car."

"Thanks, Mom. Mommy." I hugged her.

She tucked the folded letter in her robe pocket. "I'm going to get dressed. You go, help your uncle."

"Okay." I dashed out the side door, down the sidewalk to the loud car, wrenched open the door. "Can we go to Sonic? I'm dying for a diet vanilla Coke."

"Let's ride." Uncle Aidan slipped the shifter into first. "Now, pay attention. I'm going to expect you to drive me to my doctor's appointments someday—when I get too old and decrepit."

I rolled down the window and dried my face in the slipstream. The air smelled like honeysuckle. "Okay," I said. "If you teach me to drive the Harley, too."

He threw his head back and laughed. "You bet. As soon as we get one."

The day felt unnaturally bright, the sun on my bare knees magnified by the Roadrunner's wide windshield. I watched Uncle Aidan drive. It seemed to give him great joy. The way I sometimes felt sketching and painting.

Twenty-Two

THE VISITATION

Uncle A lived a few miles away in a small apartment complex with a pool. In the summer, we loved visiting so we could swim in the pool. He had only lived there for two years, since moving back from California, where he'd been a truck driver, but suddenly I couldn't wait to go swimming again.

His apartment on the second floor looked out over the pool area. "This is almost like living at the beach," I said.

"Yeah... not quite." He looked around as he opened the door. "We need to take a vacation to the beach this year. I loved surfing."

"Did you like living in California?"

"I loved it," he said. "Until Dad passed away, then it was too stressful for Mom."

"Did she really die of a broken heart?"

He nodded. "Maybe. That, and a boatload of stress trying to take care of me and your Mom. I mean, we were already teenagers, but still. She just didn't deal with things very well."

I walked to the large picture window overlooking the pool. "I guess some of us don't."

"Believe me, I was really glad your Mom and Dad let me come and stay with them after she died. Your Dad wasn't always thrilled, though. I guess I was still a little wild." He chuckled. "He only had to bail me out once, though."

"From jail?"

He grinned. "Too many speeding tickets. Lost my license. Got caught with beer in the car."

"Uncle Aidan!"

"Yeah, like I said. A little wild. Don't do like I do; just do like I say."

I raised my eyebrows. "And that would be?"

"Don't drink and drive."

"Oh," I laughed. "That's simple. I wouldn't do that anyway."

"I'll remember you said that."

I plucked a dirty shirt off the couch and threw it at his head. "Thank you," he said. "After you pick up the rest of the clothes we'll take 'em down to the laundry room."

Crazy man. Sometimes he seemed more like my big brother than my uncle. But what the heck? I went ahead and picked up the rest of the clothes and put them in a basket. I could hear Uncle Aidan in the shower.

In the livingroom/diningroom/kitchen combination, I clicked on my favorite playlist and stuck my phone in a deep coffee mug. Janie had shown me that trick to magnify my speaker back when she still liked me.

I picked up and put away everything I could find out of place. Then I put away the dishes from the dishwasher. Could this be a new habit in the making—cleaning to kill time? It beat the alternative, which was thinking about ways to hurt myself, such as cutting with a razor. I tested the small wound in the space between my right thumb and forefinger. It was extremely sore.

Maybe soreness was a good thing. It reminded me of what

I did not *intend* to do again. Mom was right. We didn't cause Dad's death. Now, if only I could figure out a way to erase what had happened at school. But I had no hope of that.

I didn't even think about Paul, or Keenan. Although they were part of the fabric of my existence now, I never considered them to be the catalyst for anything.

"I'm walking down to the pool," I called through the bathroom door.

"Be out in a few," he replied.

I grabbed my phone and headed for the door. On the way out, I spied a notepad and pen on Uncle Aidan's desk. I tore off a couple sheets of paper and made my way down the stairs to the deserted pool. The unlocked gate and crystal clear water beckoned me. Only a few weeks before the official start of summer. I wondered why this pool wasn't covered. Were residents already swimming on warm days?

Maybe Uncle Aidan would let me swim every day. Without Will and Kera, or even my big sister, I couldn't imagine what I would do otherwise. Before this, I'd thought I might get a part time job at The Sweet Treat. But not now. No way. I could only imagine the faces of kids I might have known in school if they came in and saw me working—Paul, Sergio, Kera—even the thought of being that close to Janie made me want to run and hide.

I sat in a lounge chair and put the notepaper on my knee. "Dear Dad," I wrote. "I miss you." And then I couldn't write anymore because the tears fell onto the paper and my fingers clutched the pen and pressed down and made a hole in the page that went straight through to my skin.

After half an hour, Uncle Aidan's voice floated down from above. "You need anything from up here, kiddo?"

I squinted upward to where he leaned out over the balcony railing. To my great surprise, I'd filled both sides of the paper with tiny, tiny script. "Nah, I'm okay." I signed my letter and stuck the pen in my pocket.

In another minute, Uncle A stood beside me on the pool apron in tan slacks and a button down chambray shirt. "You look nice," I said. "I guess I'd better go back and change, too." I stood and picked up my phone.

He put his arm around my shoulders.

"I'm worried, Uncle Aidan."

"About the visitation?"

I nodded. "I don't know if I can do it."

He led me to the Green Hornet. "You can, and you will. We'll all do it together. Don't worry, Grandma and Grampa Stevens will be there. Me, your Mom—"

"Janie."

He opened the car door for me. "Janie."

"Maybe I should stay home."

He waited by the door, holding it open until I explained.

"What if she starts yelling at me or says something awful like she always does?"

"Ben—"

"What if she humiliates me right there in front of every-one? She hates me."

He shut the door and went around to the driver's side. "I'll be there." He stuck the key in the ignition, checked the gearshift, engaged the clutch. "I won't let anything bad happen. I promise." He started the engine and pressed the gas. The Green Hornet roared to life and cut off any response I might have made.

That was good, because I'd been about to say something

like *Yeah, you've done a great job keeping things at bay so far*—but that would've just been ugly, as Mom would say. And why would I ever be ugly to Uncle Aidan? Or anyone else for that matter? Like my Gran tried to teach us, if you do something knowing it's wrong, you can never claim it was just a mistake. And if you keep doing it, then it becomes a habit. Or an addiction. I rubbed my hand over the faint scratches on my arm. They weren't deep. Thank God Janie couldn't have long nails at her job.

I thought about the cut on my thigh, and the one in the webbing of my hand. Both had been accidents, but the fact that I kept thinking about opening them up, or making another—what did that mean?

"Don't worry so much, little one," Uncle Aidan said. "Let the adults do some of the worrying for awhile. You just go back to being a kid."

Thanks. I'll do that. I'll just pretend none of this ever happened. Right.

I rolled down the window and tried to recapture the feeling of warmth I'd had earlier, on the way to his apartment, but it was gone. We were heading the opposite direction now, away from the sun.

Mom seemed a nervous wreck when we got there. She was dressed in black pants and a white blouse. She always said when in doubt wear black and white. Sometimes, I wish I didn't remember every single thing everyone said.

"It will only take me a minute to change." I hurried to my room and closed the door, stripped off my shorts and tank and slipped into my own black pants just like Mom. Did I choose those because of what Mom said all these years? I buttoned the waist and the pants slid back down my hips a couple inches.

Shock knocked all thought from my head as I stepped out of my pants and twisted the waistband down to examine the size, certain I must've got Janie's or even an old pair of Mom's by mistake.

But they were mine. The same pair I'd worn to the Honor Roll ceremony last semester.

With a feeling of dread, I turned to the full-length mirror on the inside of my closet door.

My reflection. Skeletal. My hipbones like knobs above the waistband of my too-low pants.

I lifted my tank over my head and held my breath. Every rib stood out. My collarbones were wings stretching out from either side of my neck. My shoulders were bony and my stretchy knit bra cups wrinkled where they should have been full.

When did this happen? Then it occurred to me. *When did I last eat?* Cinnamon rolls that morning. There. I *had* eaten. And I had the Sonic coke. Er, diet Coke. Before that, I couldn't recall.

"Ready, Ben?" Mom stood right outside my door.

I pulled the pants up, grabbed a belt from my closet, and yanked my blouse off the hanger, struggling to put it on in case she opened the door. "Coming!" I stabbed my feet into my black church shoes and dashed to my dresser to drag a brush through my wavy hair.

Mom no longer stood outside the door when I opened it.

"She went on to the car," Uncle Aidan said. "We thought we'd all arrive together, but I told her you would ride with me. I didn't think you'd want to be stuck in the back seat with Janie."

I hugged him, hard. "Thank you."

He opened the side door. "They're waiting. We'll follow them."

He didn't ask me if I was okay. "You look nice," he said.

I smiled, but my stomach churned. My hand strayed to the heart necklace. I held it all the way to the funeral home.

Grandma and Grampa Stevens were already there. They sat in chairs near the coffin where I could see Dad's profile again.

A spray of white flowers covered the foot of the casket. Greenery trailed from beneath it. Easels of hothouse flowers—carnations, chrysanthemums, daisies, and roses—lined the room. More baskets full of ivy and other plants I couldn't name sat on the floor and on the long trestle table. I didn't even know if we had sent any. Things had been so confused. I wanted to look at the tiny cards showing on some of them, but the overpowering odor kept me at bay. The whole room smelled artificial, like the inside of a giant freezer.

Janie walked forward. I'd kept my distance from her as we all trooped into the building. I forgot she hadn't seen him before now. She ignored everyone and went straight to Dad. All the air went out of the small parlor. The late afternoon sunlight fed the frosted-glass window, but even the dust motes seemed to have disappeared.

I went to Grampa's chair, stood behind it, my palm on his shoulder. Grandma reached over and laid her blue-veined hand on top of mine. I saw Janie stretch out her fingers toward Dad, as if to touch him. Then she drew back and simply stood, staring down. Something had changed her mind.

Tears welled up in my eyes, started their slow trek toward

my chin. Grampa offered a clean, folded hanky. His initials were embroidered on it in red.

Mom and Uncle Aidan went to Janie, one on either side. She collapsed against Mom, her hand covering her mouth. People began to file in. First, Sharla-the-slut and her boy, Alvin-the-chipmunk.

Sharla looked like she had stepped out of a dress store window. I hated every perfect hair on her head. But I felt sorry for the boy. He looked stunned, out of place. Without thinking of repercussions, I went to him, put my arm around him, pulled him to sit beside me on a small sofa. "Hey, Alvin, how you doing?"

He gazed at my face as if he didn't know me. Then recognition dawned. He relaxed into my side and we sat back into the cushions and let everyone flow around us. An 8 x 10 photo of my dad sat on a table. An official looking gentleman in a dark suit picked up a remote control and clicked it toward a medium sized flat screen mounted on the wall above the picture. Soft music flowed into the room. *Precious Memories* followed *Amazing Graze* followed by *In the Garden* followed by one I didn't know. I had to wonder who had requested all the hymns. Dad hadn't been a big church-goer. But maybe that had changed after he left us. Before he became a thief.

A basket full of tiny packages of Kleenex tissues appeared on the table as if by magic. Everyone who walked by picked up a package.

Alvin stared at the pictures that began to stream past on the video. Most of the pictures were from the last two years. There were only a couple of Janie and me, one of Mom. I figured Gran and Gramps were responsible for getting those in there. Mom hadn't been asked to contribute anything.

It occurred to me that my grandparents were probably responsible for the selection of hymns as well.

Sharla finally took Janie's place near the coffin, and she motioned for Alvin to join her. "Say bye to your Daddy," she said.

My gut cramped and I went back to stand by my grandparents.

In a few moments, Mom and Uncle Aidan joined me. Some of dad's old high school buddies stopped by and gave their condolences to Mom, along with a handful of people from her work, and one or two from his. I wondered if they were all aware of what he'd done? The rest of the people were friends and relatives of Sharla.

"I'm going out for some fresh air," Mom said. "This room is too small."

I agreed. But I didn't want to leave Gran and Gramps. The funny thing about family, blood family, some of us will feel connected no matter who severs the legal ties. "Y'all go ahead." I glanced at my grandparents sitting in their little island of loneliness. "I can't leave them yet."

Uncle Aidan patted my back. "You remember what I said about letting adults do the worrying, right?"

I nodded. "But sometimes, they don't." Then I saw Gran's little brother, Junior, come in. He nodded at us but made a beeline for his big sister. "I think it will be okay, now." Junior's wife, Heddie, came in, too. She always trailed a little behind. I recalled that from the family get-togethers we'd had over the years. They were like Jack Spratt and his fat wife. He was lean and moved like escaping a fire; she was big, soft, comfortable. She moved like a slow wave coming to shore from a long distance.

"Everything will be okay, now. Reinforcements have arrived."

Mom smiled and went for Aunt Heddie. I heard her murmur, "I'm so glad you're here."

Uncle J (we'd never called him Uncle Junior, it just didn't sound right) didn't leave his sister's side. The look he shot toward Sharla should have melted her on the spot. But it didn't.

Now Mom wasn't in such a hurry to leave.

I meandered over to the guestbook that stood on a stand beside the door. Two pages had already been filled with names. I took up the pen and wrote my name on the bottom of the last page. I knew it was childish even as I did it, but I didn't care. It was a spur of the moment thing, like my painting. That's how I felt. Like the end. Like forgotten. Like the last one. Like no one.

It reminded me of my letter. Should I put it in now, or tomorrow at the actual funeral? I wanted to send it with him, wherever he was going. And I didn't want anyone else to see it. Could I make myself slip it under the pillow, somewhere that no one would see it and pull it back out?

Better save it for tomorrow.

I turned the pages on the guestbook back to the front, ran my finger down the names. I saw Janie go past me, out the door toward the parking lot. I didn't care. As long as she never spoke to me again, I didn't care what she did or where she went.

Most of the names in the book were foreign to me except for the relatives and two of dad's old buddies who used to come over on Sundays and watch football and eat barbecue and potato salad with us. Their own kids always seemed a little younger. I didn't see any of the kids here, just their dads.

Then my finger came to a halt.

Sam Edgerton.

The name sat on one whole line, alone. No parent name accompanied it.

I turned around quickly, looking for that face, that grin. But I did not see Sam Edgerton in the room. How could I have missed him?

Twenty-Three

Contemplating All the Ways to Live

I almost died when Mr. Stanford walked in, accompanied by Ms. Kestrel and Mrs. Peterson. I never even thought about them showing up, but there they were. Mr. Stanford saw me first. He said something to the other two teachers who stopped a couple steps away.

Mr. Stanford enveloped me in a gentle hug. I hadn't seen him since the day of the painting. "How are you getting along, Benji?"

I nodded, my throat so tight I could barely breathe.

"I'm so sorry about your dad and about the painting, too." He looked at the floor. "I mean, about all the hoopla with the painting. The painting itself was amazing, I don't know when I've had another student with so much—"

Just then, Uncle Aidan sauntered over and introduced himself.

Mr. Stanford shook his hand. "I was just telling Benji how wonderful her painting was and how I—"

Mrs. Peterson signed the book and stepped in between Mr. Stanford and me. Uncle Aidan took Mr. Stanford by the elbow and moved him a few steps away, just enough so that I could no longer her what they were saying.

"—so sorry," Mrs. Peterson said. "We all miss you so much."

"And we hope you'll be returning to school soon," Ms. Kestrel finished. "I really miss your insights into our novels. World Lit just isn't the same without you."

I looked around for Uncle Aidan, hoping he'd rescue me again, but he was still engaged in conversation with my art teacher. Their dialogue seemed much more animated than it had a moment earlier.

"Benji?" Dr. Blue stood just to the right of Mrs. Peterson. It's like they all met up outside and said, *Let's ambush Benji now.*

"Hello—" I turned to her, then to my two teachers. I knew I should introduce them, but what should I say, "Meet my psychiatrist? My shrink? My head doctor?"

She beat me to the punch. "Hi, my name is Ofelia Blue." They all shook hands.

My shoulders slumped as the tension drained away. I forgot I could trust her. That one session in the hospital had been so surreal, it seemed like a complete dream to me now.

The two teachers repeated how much they missed me, and how they would create packets of makeup work for me to start on.

"I'll stop by and pick those up on Tuesday," Uncle Aidan said. "I need to go by the Art Department, too."

Dr. Blue examined my face. I hope it didn't show the shock I felt. Why would my uncle need to go to the Art Department? Then it dawned on me. Mr. Stanford probably told him to come and pick up the painting. Too much of a distraction, I'll bet.

I didn't know where Mr. Stanford went, but apparently my uncle had been hovering, watching over me. Even though I didn't want any makeup work, since I wouldn't be going back there, I did think it was nice of him to offer to get it.

Immense relief washed over me when the trio moved on to pay respects to my mom and grandparents. "I'll see you at the funeral tomorrow." Dr. Blue squeezed my fingers and actually pecked me on the cheek before moving away. The teachers both said they had to go to school thus the reason for coming by tonight. I also caught sight of Janie's homeroom teacher, but I didn't see Janie anymore. She had never come back in from outside.

"Thanks for saving me," I whispered to Uncle Aidan. "What's up with Mr. Stanford?"

Before he could answer, Officer Tate appeared. She wasn't in uniform, but she still seemed uncomfortable.

My fingers immediately sought my heart necklace. Should I tell her how it saved me from doing something stupid when the razor fell in the tub?

She walked right over and grabbed me in a full-body-press hug. "Just came by to lend our support," she said. "Officer Brindon got called in for overtime, but he said to tell you we're here if you need us."

I held up my silver heart. "This gives me strength." I smiled and tucked it back into my blouse. "I hope I can repay you guys someday."

"Just doing our job." She smiled. "Gotta go to work soon, you stay strong." She murmured the last part so everyone didn't hear.

She made her way to my mom and said a few words to her. Mom grasped her hand in both of hers and shook it warmly. Then Grandma Stevens did the same.

All of a sudden, I needed a chair. All my strength seemed to drain away.

"I don't know about you," Uncle Aidan took my elbow. "But I'm exhausted." He steered me toward the large foyer that connected all the small parlors. "We can wait for your mom here." He pointed to a comfy looking sofa, one of several. "Or we can go out and get some fresh air."

We both looked out the darkened windows. The parking lot was huge, bordered by green strips of lawn and planted here and there with blooming Indian Hawthorne bushes. Very simple, soothing.

Janie stood with her back to the windows, across the narrow driveway to the parking lot. Shawn faced her. We could see his face, but not hers. We couldn't hear them at all, but we didn't need to hear their words to figure out they were arguing.

Janie's back was rigid. The one hand on her hip reminded me of Mom when she was in the process of reading one of us the riot act. I expected her to start shaking her finger in his face at any moment—the way she'd done me at home.

"Wonder what the problem is," Uncle Aidan said.

I shrugged. "Maybe they really went off and got married. They look like an old married couple."

He laughed, and then covered it by coughing into his fist. "I hope they don't continue down that path. Your Mom talked to her, but I don't know if Janie really listened."

Janie turned around then, as if she'd sensed us talking about her. Shawn stuck his hands in his front pockets and watched her stalk toward the funeral home. At the last second, she veered off toward the parked cars.

"Wonder if I should check on her?"

I shrugged again. "You got me. All I know is she doesn't want me around." I crossed my legs and pulled out my phone, prepared to wait. I wouldn't allow myself to think about Dad lying in that room, surrounded by people I barely knew, especially Sharla-the-slut and her extended family. Her parents and siblings had arrived. They took up nearly the whole room. No place left for us, his original family.

Tears pricked my eyes, but they were tears of anger, or maybe frustration, rather than sadness. Why couldn't he have simply stayed with us? What did we not have that he'd needed? I felt that if he'd stayed with Mom, with us, he wouldn't have got in trouble—naïve, perhaps. But that's how it felt.

Uncle Aidan stood by the window. I assumed he was keeping an eye on my sister. Mom and the grands wandered out, together, and I stood and went to my grandfather. He seemed even more bent, even older than a few minutes ago, his steps even more hesitant. I took him by the arm. "Let's go home, Gramps."

"Yeah. My boy isn't here anyway." He wiped his eyes with his hanky. "Ain't been here for a long time." He walked beside me. "I didn't raise him to be... what he became." Wiped his leaky eyes again. "Didn't raise him to be a criminal. Turn his back on his family—us, your mom, you girls."

"I know, Gramps. He changed somehow." I tried to think of when he'd begun to change, and it always came back to Sharla. But could he really have been that easily swayed? Or did I just want someone to blame?

We walked slowly across the foyer toward the door. Some of Sharla's people had drifted out here, too. They pretended we were invisible. An idea for a new watercolor popped into my head. See through people, old and young alike, making their way toward a door.

"Was he on drugs?" Grampa asked.

The question took me by surprise.

"I don't think so." But then I thought about it. He really had changed. And then he'd stolen all that money. It sure sounded like a drug thing. Or some kind of addiction.

"Never knew him to take drugs," Gramps went on. "But he did like to gamble now and then." He faltered. I steadied him. "Reckon it was gambling? A gambling debt of some sort?"

"Gosh. I don't know. He liked betting on football games with his buddies. He liked going to Vegas, so I don't know. Maybe?" I understood Grampa needed to find a reason. Some reason his teachings had all gone astray.

"Yeah. Maybe." He stopped directly in the doorway, turned half-around to the room at large. "Maybe I'll ask that thing. His new wife." He jerked his head toward the parlor where we'd left Sharla still holding court.

Oh my God. No. Not a good idea. "Maybe later." I tugged on his arm. Not too hard. Didn't want him to fall. "Mom and Gran are already outside. We'd better get on home."

He made a noise in his throat, but at least he began to move again. In a moment we were outside on the sidewalk.

The night felt soft, waiting. The stars were obscenely beautiful. Shouldn't something be different? Shouldn't something be—changed? How could my father be gone and everything else remain the same?

Grampa said something too low for me to hear.

"What, Gramps?"

"You got food at your house?" His old voice came out crackly, but strong.

I laughed, just a little. "We've got enough food for an army."

When Uncle Aidan and I had returned from his apartment,

we found the counters covered with food from neighbors and friends from Mom's work. There were several casseroles and at least two buckets of fried chicken.

From behind my bedroom door, I'd heard Mom mutter, "Now where will I put this?" as she tried to fit another meal into the fridge or freezer.

I sort of wished we still went to church, so the funeral would've been there, with Reverend Jenson. But since Dad left us, we'd slowly stopped going. Mostly it was just Mom's work—she almost always had Sunday showings—but I thought some of it was Mom just not wanting to face the people she and Dad used to pal around with. We talked about going back, we talked about finding a new church, but so far, we hadn't done either one.

When Uncle Aidan saw us coming down the sidewalk, he broke away from the family unit near Grampa's car and hurried over. Without a word, he took Grampa's other elbow, but Gramps shook us both off. "I'm all right." He visibly straightened his spine. "Just a little slow."

Uncle Aidan grinned at me over the old man's head.

"We're going to our house for supper," I said.

"Sounds like a plan. You riding back with me?"

I shook my head. "I'll ride with Gran and Gramps this time." For some reason, I needed to be close to them.

Gramps pulled his keys from his pocket and started his Chrysler remotely, grinning as he did. Gran startled, just a tiny bit, and looked our way. I got the feeling it wasn't the first time he'd done that to her.

"See you at home." I told Mom the plan and she hugged me and clicked the remote to open her own car nearby.

I opened the door for Gran, made sure she was comfortable

in the passenger seat, and then I climbed into the back of my grandparent's car and waited on Gramps to take us home.

From the corner of my eye, I saw Janie climb into the passenger seat of The Green Hornet. Poor Uncle Aidan. Another kid to babysit. I vowed to get my act together and try to be more of a help than a hindrance. Knowing I never had to return to school made me feel a little stronger.

We all followed Mom's car as she exited the parking lot. We had a mini-convoy. My grandparents didn't say much, just remarked on how tired they were. And I knew that my earlier thought about nothing having changed was completely wrong. I could hear in their voices how Dad's death had affected them. "Parents aren't supposed to outlive their children," I'd overheard Gran tell someone at the visitation. "It's not the way things are supposed to be."

When we arrived home, I was glad someone had possessed the foresight to leave the porch light on even though it hadn't been dark when we left.

The kitchen light was on, too.

By the time I got the grands into the house, Mom had the oven preheating and a green enchilada casserole out of the fridge, waiting to be heated. I washed my hands and gathered tortilla chips, salsa, paper plates, and napkins and took it all to the table. Gran filled glasses with iced tea. Grampa took one and sipped gratefully. I liked the fact that he sat in Dad's old place at the head of the table. Over the last couple of years, Mom, Janie, and I had all taken turns trying it out—never speaking about it, just doing it—but it had never felt right.

Eventually it had become the chair that caught backpacks, purses, and carryalls. Anything we wanted nearby, but didn't want to put away.

Janie and Uncle Aidan still sat in his car at the curb. I'd caught a glimpse of her face in the streetlight through the passenger window and it appeared to be wet with tears.

He came in just as we pulled the casserole and began to dish it up. "Janie will be in after a while." His tone told us not to ask questions.

We sat down to eat and Gran took my hand and looked at each person until everyone had joined hands around the table. "Lord," she murmured. "Bless this food and bless our loved ones and please, let me see my son again someday."

After everyone muttered Amen, it was very difficult to get anything past the lump in my throat. Fortunately, the iced tea numbed it enough that I managed to get a few bites down.

When I stood to take my plate to the kitchen, Mom said, "Ben. I wish you'd eat more than that." She looked at my baggy pants. "You've lost a few pounds."

Remembering my vow to be a help not a hindrance, I dutifully sat back down and ate two more bites along with a few more chips. I think my immediate compliance shocked Mom into silence. She didn't utter another word.

After everyone had eaten—Mom even brought out brownies someone had made—and we'd cleaned up the kitchen, the grands said their goodbyes and informed us they would come over tomorrow to ride with us to the funeral. Gran didn't say so, but I got the impression she wanted a bit of moral—and physical—support in case Gramps got down.

"I'm going back to my place," Uncle Aidan said. "I'll just follow y'all if you don't mind."

Gran looked relieved.

By bedtime, the three of us had the house to ourselves for the first time in over a week. At least I assumed it was the three of us. Janie hadn't actually emerged from her room yet.

As if reading my mind, Mom went to her door and knocked. "Jane? We saved you a plate. Are you going to come and eat?"

I heard Janie turn the knob but I didn't stick around to see if she came out or not. I just took the opportunity to go through my own room to our shared bathroom. I didn't have to wash my hair, but I did want a soak in the tub.

Making sure her side of the bathroom was locked from the inside, I stripped off my baggy clothes and pinned up my hair. I smeared Noxema all over my face and cleaned it with a warm washcloth while my bathtub filled.

For the first time in days, I felt like a real person again.

After my bath, I went straight to my bed and crawled in. I pulled the quilt up to my chin and tried not to feel alone. I thought about texting Sam, but I just wanted to go to sleep, get up tomorrow, get the day over with, and try to figure out how to go forward with my life. Truthfully, I wanted to retreat to childhood when my Mom and Dad were still together, and they could fix any hurt with a kiss and a Band-Aid.

But I knew those days were gone for good. A tiny pocket of darkness existed in the back corner of my mind. It contained that little voice that kept telling me it would be a whole lot easier if I didn't have to deal with all this. If I just went out and started walking until I came to the train tracks on South Grant Street. I knew I would never try pills again. The pain from them was something I would never, ever forget.

There are other ways to avoid dealing with life. It seemed my brain had been compiling a list for a while now. The title of the list might be: All the Ways to Check Out For Good.

But I didn't really want to do that, not anymore.

I amended the title of my list. Gave it a subtitle:

All the Ways to Check Out and Why Each One is a Bad Idea.

I jiggled the list in my mind. All the options either got a label of too painful, too uncertain (I sure didn't want to wind up a vegetable), or too difficult to pull off.

And on the heels of it all, I simply could not imagine another ride to the hospital and all that entailed. If I ever do it again—WHICH I WON'T—it will be something quick and sure. *Like Dad*, my subconscious whispered. *Is that what you mean?*

My mind wouldn't stop whirling. Did all these thoughts resurface just because I wanted to avoid my father's funeral? Hadn't I got through the worst of it today?

No, the little black cloud of despair wasn't just because of my father. It was because my entire world had changed. It had started with Will and Kera and the painting. My father hadn't even known about that—he'd taken his own way out before even hearing about my problems. He'd taken his own *selfish* way out.

Did I *really* want to be like him?

I threw back my quilt and fell to my knees beside my bed. I gave up trying to maintain an appearance of strength. Tears and snot soaked my quilt as I allowed myself to visualize my mother being told I'd stepped in front of a train. She'd collapsed at the door when Officers Tate and Brindon brought her the news of my father, she might actually die if I did the same thing.

My hand grabbed for my silver heart. "Dear God," I began.

It had been a long time since I'd prayed, but I needed someone to talk to about all this. And Reverend Jenson said God was always there if we needed him.

I'm sure it was coincidence that a strong beam of moon-light lanced my folded hands as I prayed. I'm sure it was my imagination that my cool silver heart grew as warm as toast between my clasped palms.

When the heart became too hot to hold, I raised my head to see where the bright warmth originated. I knew it had to somehow be the work of the moonlight coming through the gap in the curtains.

But for once they were completely closed.

I dropped my head into my hands and contemplated the possibilities of the universe. *Are you there, God? It's Me, Margaret* was an old favorite book from my childhood. It had actually been my mom's book when she was a kid.

Now, it made so much sense.

Are you there, God? It's me, Benji. Please, will you help me change my thoughts? I don't want to keep contemplating all the ways to die; surely there must be some way for me to start contemplating all the ways to live.

To my surprise, my tears stopped. The heart cooled. I let it fall back into its customary place on my chest. I wiped my face on the edge of my quilt and I was reminded of the day Mom gave it to me. *My Grandma Donahue made it,* she'd said. *She would have wanted you to have it. You would have been her first grandchild.*

I'd felt special then, but now, I felt more than that. I felt connected. The coral blocks of the quilt were embroidered with doves.

In the strong moonlight, the doves came alive. When I lifted the quilt to climb back in bed, the doves fluttered their wings.

I didn't fall asleep so much as I gave up and let it take me down. *There is more,* I thought. *There is more to my life than this tiny little kernel of pain inside my chest. Maybe the doves are God's way of telling me to open my wings, try to learn how to fly.*

Twenty-Four

The Funeral

The day dawned cloudy and gray. I didn't realize more rain was expected. It seemed appropriate though. I had a black dress that came with a black and white diagonally striped waterfall sweater. It would be cozy. When I wanted to seep within myself, I could wrap the loose sweater around me and hide.

I pulled my hair around to the side and let it fall forward, echoing the waterfall ripple of the sweater. I didn't bother with makeup. I didn't want mascara tracking down my cheeks.

My short black boots and tiny shoulder bag completed my outfit. The bag was almost a joke. It barely had enough room for my cell phone and the small packet of tissues from the visitation last night, but it had a long, thin strap I could hang on my shoulder or slip over my head, hang it diagonally across my body like a shield. That was the important part.

In the kitchen, Mom had set out cereal boxes and bowls. Her way of saying, *You're on your own for breakfast*. It was okay. I didn't want much of anything anyway. The hour flew by and then Uncle Aidan arrived with Grandma and Grampa Stevens in tow. I was amazed at the way he had taken them under his wing. Especially since my dad had always talked so badly about him when he wasn't around. Either my dad had been a real ass, or Uncle Aidan was doing his own kind of personal makeover to try and move forward with us.

I didn't have time to wonder. Before long Mom emerged from her room wearing her best pearl gray dress and heels. She kissed my cheek and went straight to Janie's room. She brought Janie out dressed in a purple mini-dress and flats. Mom didn't say a word but her lips were clenched into a thin hard line. I got the feeling Janie's outfit was some sort of statement, but for the life of me I couldn't figure out just what she meant to relate. Dad wouldn't be there to see it. Was she trying to embarrass me the way I'd embarrassed her with my art? *No,* my subconscious said. *Everything is not about you, remember?*

Uncle Aidan to the rescue.

He dug around in the closet until he came up with a long dark sweater-jacket. "Better wear this." He draped it around Janie's shoulders. It actually belonged to Mom, but Janie could wear it. She was eighteen now. Almost grown. "It's turned downright chilly," Uncle A continued. Then he reached into the closet and brought out a couple of umbrellas. "We'll keep these in the car, too, just in case."

Dear God, I thought. *Thank you for Uncle Aidan.*

He looked up at me and smiled a strange little smile, as if he'd overheard my tiny prayer of thanks. I smiled back at him.

"You riding with me?"

I nodded. Without a word, Janie walked out to Mom's car and got in the passenger side. Gran and Gramps got in the back seat, and that only left Mom to lock up. "I'll get it, Liv." Uncle Aidan took the key from her hand and locked the door. I got in his passenger seat and looked back at the house recalling, for the first time in days, the awful attack that started the whole downhill slide. My fingers went to my forehead, but there was no more bruise, no more pain. Now that it was behind me, I was glad I'd never told anyone.

The ride to the funeral home was quiet. Uncle Aidan seemed subdued and I had no idea what to say. I didn't even know what to feel. Anger still bubbled beneath my skin.

The director met us at the door and whisked us all to the family room. Sharla and her family sat on one side of the room, we sat on the other. My grandmother took the director out into the hallway for a private conversation. When they returned, he went to Sharla and told her something that made her face go the color of old strawberry jam. She shot us a look and my grandmother lifted her chin and looked down her nose at her. Sharla quickly averted her eyes.

In a few moments, the director came to us and had us form a line. My grandparents were at the head of the line followed by my mother, Janie, and me. Uncle Aidan, Uncle Junior, and Aunt Heddie brought up the rear.

Sharla's family came next. The director kept them a few steps behind us. As we walked slowly down the wide lush hall toward the chapel, I became aware of the strains of *Amazing Grace*, one of the same hymns that had been playing at the visitation the night before. It was followed by another hymn and another. I had the stupid idea my gran was determined to save his soul during the funeral. I could hear sniffling from the crowd of people already seated in the pews.

Trying to ignore the eyes looking at us in sympathy, I clutched my shoulder bag-shield and forced myself to focus on one more step and one more step and one more step with my gaze fastened to the backs of Janie's black flats in front of me.

I made it a point not to look at the open casket in the front of the chapel.

Funeral flowers filled the room. Once again, the artificial odor overpowered me. The director took us to the first row of the family section. We barely filled it.

I became aware of Sharla's family filing into the pew behind us. They took up two or three pews and then it was time. Reverend Jenson caught my eye and smiled. He sat behind and to the side of a pastor whose name completely escaped me. I know he'd been introduced to us back in the family room, but now, I had no idea who he was.

The man read Dad's obituary. I looked down at the memorial program in my hand. I don't even know how it got there. The pastor said Dad was taken from us too soon. He never said Dad chose to leave. He glossed it over with words and platitudes and bits of scripture he thought would soothe. Then he yielded the pulpit to Reverend Jenson who read the following poem:

Do Not Stand At My Grave And Weep
Do not stand at my grave and weep,
I am not there, I do not sleep.
I am a thousand winds that blow.
I am the diamond glint on snow.
I am the sunlight on ripened grain.
I am the gentle autumn rain.
When you wake in the morning hush,
I am the swift, uplifting rush
Of quiet birds in circling flight.
I am the soft starlight at night.
Do not stand at my grave and weep.
I am not there, I do not sleep.

Mary Frye (1932)

During the poem, read by the kindly voice of the pastor I'd grown up listening to—until Dad left us for Sharla-the-slut—that's when my tears began to flow.

Mom took my hand. She sat in between Janie and me.

I know my mom cried; I heard her sniffling. I know my gran cried, but it was soft. I know my grandpa cried, I heard him honk his nose a time or two. I don't know if Janie cried—I ignored her. This was all the hurt I could handle at the moment. I don't know about Uncle Aidan, either. If I looked at him, I feared I would break down completely.

And then it was over.

The unknown-pastor got back up and asked if anyone had anything they wanted to say about my dad. I wanted to stand up and tell how he used to love us. How he used to read me bedtime stories and make up all the funny voices for Tigger, and Pooh, and little tiny Roo, but I knew I couldn't do that. I couldn't say anything at all without blubbering and making a fool of myself.

One of his high school buddies stood and told a funny story about a football game way back when. No one else had anything to say. That hurt almost as much as his death.

Another hymn began to play as the funeral director led row after row of mourners toward the casket. Most came and offered us words of sympathy, but not all of them. Some bypassed us and went to Sharla and her family.

Dr. Blue came. She hugged us all, one by one. Officers Tate and Brindol came, too. They shook hands and hugged as they deemed appropriate. I may have held onto them a bit longer than I intended. If I could, I would have followed them out, skipped the graveside service altogether. But I didn't.

They released me with promises to keep in touch.

Our high school principal, Mrs. Gloss, was also there. Her black heels didn't click on the carpet, but I'd heard them so many times in the tile hallways at school that I thought I could hear them anyway. She hugged Janie and me fiercely. I thought my ribs would crack. I hugged her back, but in my mind I thought, *I'll never see you again. Do you know that yet?*

Several kids from school came by and said, *Sorry, sorry, so sorry for your loss.* Jen and Steph came with Karma. They hung back a little, barely touching our hands.

I avoided looking at any of them. I knew they probably came just to get out of going to school. Mom thanked them for coming, but I didn't for a moment think any of them were sincere. Maybe that was just some part of me trying to protect myself.

Then it was time for us to go up to the coffin for the last time.

We stood together, our meager little row, and slowly made our way. And then I remembered my letter. I'd left it at home. I gazed at Dad's face and tried to whisper goodbye, but my parched throat wouldn't cooperate. I laid my hand on his wooden chest and sobbed instead.

Uncle Aidan led me away.

Mom, Janie, and the grands were already outside on the covered sidewalk, standing near the long, black limousine. It would be a short ride to the cemetery behind the chapel.

After Sharla's family said their goodbyes, she came out wailing. *Center of attention*, I thought cruelly.

We watched as the pallbearers exited with the coffin on their shoulders. They slid it into the back of the hearse and then we prepared to enter the limousine behind it.

As I bent to get into the backseat, cold drops of rain plopped on the back of my exposed neck. Uncle Aidan gently closed the door behind me and ran to The Green Hornet parked in front of the funeral home. He returned with the two umbrellas. One of them had Dora the Explorer on it. One more thing from my childhood—or was it Janie's? We'd once shared everything. It was hard to remember.

At the graveside, the funeral had chairs in rows beneath a green and white striped awning. Stands of flowers on easels and in baskets wilted in the growing drizzle. The smell of the rain comforted me, but at the same time I knew that forever after that scent would remind me of this dividing day. The day that would from now on divide my life into scenes of before Dad, and after Dad.

As we stepped out of the limo, the director held a large black umbrella over our heads. Uncle Aidan's face reddened and he tucked Dora and our other umbrella back into the limo, out of sight.

Due to the rain, only a handful of people came to the graveside.

Once again, we were seated in the front row, near the casket. After a short prayer, and another hymn, the pastor had us step forward and toss roses onto the lowering coffin.

When I turned around, there stood Sam Edgerton just outside the protection of the awning. His long wavy hair was crazy with moisture, but his sky blue eyes were as kind as they seemed on my phone. They stared straight at me.

All of the messages inviting me to call, or text, came rushing back. I was surprised he came. I'd been ignoring him, completely.

He walked toward me, out of the rain, into the drier area where I still stood after tossing my rose. He swiped his unruly hair off his forehead with one hand, but his eyes never left my face. It felt as if he were keeping me in place by sheer force of will. He wore a dark jacket with a striped tie.

"Hi," I said.

He took my hand, the one not holding the tattered Kleenex. "I'm sorry," he said. "My brother did the same thing. That's why we moved here."

"Are you kidding me?"

He didn't say, "Why would anyone kid about a thing like that?" But I thought it all the same. And I felt ashamed.

It occurred to me how much I didn't know about this boy. The fact that he wasn't mad that I hadn't returned his messages said more to me than any words ever could.

Mom, Uncle A, and the grands had started toward the limo, looking back for me. "I have to go."

Sam nodded, let go of my hand.

Where our skin parted the air felt empty, cold. I didn't think it was the weather. "I'm so sorry about your brother." I didn't know what else to say. "Thank you for being here."

He smiled. "Text me. If you want."

I smiled back. It felt good.

In the limo, Janie cried softly. I hadn't seen Shawn at the service at all. That must really hurt, to go out with someone for that long—to almost marry them—and then to have them break up with you at your father's viewing. At least I assumed they'd broken up last night.

Maybe I should paint her a picture, I thought. Maybe I should splash it all over the world—*guys are creeps*—it could be a scaly monster in a ball cap. He could be dripping good intentions like—oh, what was I thinking? Why did I always want to create something emotional? Hadn't it gotten me in enough trouble?

The limo took us back to the funeral home. Most of the other cars were gone except for Sharla's family. They were in a second limo behind us.

The rain came down in beaten silver sheets now. I'd tried to see where Sam went back at the graveside, but the rain had grown too heavy. For all I knew he had vanished in the mist.

Uncle Aidan finally got to use one of our umbrellas to run to the Green Hornet. If he noticed that he'd chosen Dora, it didn't seem to bother him.

The limo driver escorted my grandparents to Mom's car with one of the large black ones.

We went directly home. The rain let up long enough for us to get into the house, and then it came down as if poured from a giant bucket. *A real gully washer,* Dad would have said.

It felt cleansing, but it also felt as if we were all trapped inside a bubble of hurt. Mom had invited Dad's old friends to the house for food, but due to the weather—I assumed—only the folks from her office showed up.

After we'd eaten some lunch, a baked spaghetti casserole this time, Mom and I went with Uncle Aidan to take my grandparents back to their room. Even Janie came along. Gran and Gramps said they were tired but had some photos to give us.

In their hotel room, we sat on the two chairs and on the king sized bed. The photos were from an album they'd brought with them. The pictures went all the way back to when my dad was a little boy. I recognized some of them from the video at the visitation. With the rain coming down intermittently, this somehow seemed even sadder than the funeral itself.

Gramps announced he was going to take a bath and get

ready for bed. He'd always been blunt so we knew it was time for us to leave.

"Please don't be strangers," Gran said, hugging us each in turn. "It isn't that far to Oklahoma."

"I'll come up as soon as I get my license," I blurted. "It won't be that long." I turned around just as Mom rolled her eyes and shook her head. It made me feel like such an idiot. I was going on 15. It *would* be a while. But I loved my gran. I wanted to ease her pain however I could.

Gran patted me. "I know you will sweetheart. I know you will." She also hugged Janie, but they didn't exchange any promises. Janie was stiff with everyone. I didn't want to think about her.

On the way home, I rode shotgun in The Green Hornet. My phone vibrated as a new text popped up. It was from Sam.

"Wow," it read. "I wasn't going to bug you, but who drives that sweet Roadrunner?"

I laughed and held it up to show Uncle Aidan.

"It's my uncle," I typed. "He restores old cars for fun."

The response came immediately. "I've got a '69 Camaro I'm fixing up."

I showed that to my uncle as well.

"No way," he said. "What's the original color?"

Smiling, I texted Sam the question. He sent back a picture of a metallic blue car that was almost more rust than paint. I held it up for Uncle A to see.

"*Nice.* Tell him if he needs any help just let me know. I'd like to get my hands on that."

I wrote the words and pressed send.

Sam sent back a row of Smiley's with great big WOW eyes. "Seriously?"

"Definitely," I replied.

He sent his wide-smiling face and I showed that to Uncle Aidan, too.

"Hey, that's the kid you were talking to at the gravesite, right?"

I nodded. "His name's Sam. They just moved here from Dallas a couple months ago." I fiddled with the edge of my sweater. "He seems really nice. Not like most of the kids at school."

"Yeah?" My uncle pretended nonchalance. "Your Art teacher said there'd been some big deal about that painting you made." He put on his blinker to turn onto our street. "You ever gonna tell me about it?"

"Nah." I shook my head mortified that Mr. Stanford had even mentioned it. "Just a big misunderstanding. It's all over now."

I thought Uncle Aidan wanted to say something more, but my fingers were flying over my phone's keypad. Sam had just told me his favorite band was Kings of Leon. I couldn't let that go untouched. Then I told him I liked singer-songwriters like Ed Sheeran and Miranda Lambert.

I wasn't about to tell him I even liked Chris Stapleton, the bluegrass wailer that had suddenly appeared on all the awards shows and country radio. I thought I might just keep that tidbit of information to myself for a while.

At home, I got out of the car and made my way into the house. For once, I didn't even stop to notice the shapes of the leaves on the wet cement.

Sam and I texted for another hour until his Dad called him to come to dinner. By this time, I'd changed into my old shorts. They were loose, too, but not like my black pants.

Mom came and told me she was going to lie down for a while but there were plenty of cold cuts, chips, and fried chicken if I got hungry. As if we hadn't just eaten a couple hours earlier.

Uncle Aidan came in, too. He said he had to go home for a while and that if we were okay he would spend the night in his own home again.

We assured him we would be fine.

Mom went on to her room, so I took over the couch and the TV. I flipped through the channels looking for a movie, but I couldn't recall my favorite channel numbers. We watched Netflix a lot—that must be why they weren't programmed in my brain anymore.

I finally settled on a documentary about how the universe works. I couldn't watch it very long, though. The flashing lights of the stars and galaxies whirling through the universe made my head feel strange.

Before I knew it, fingers of sunlight were poking through the slats of the window blinds and the TV had been turned off. Someone had placed a fuzzy plaid throw across my legs. The thing usually lay on the back of the couch.

I must have been even more exhausted than I realized. I flashed back on the upside down days and nights in the hospital and vowed to myself not to go through that again. I felt better today, except for a nagging ache behind my eyes. I thought about taking some Tylenol, but since my overdose, I hadn't wanted to take any medicine.

Mom walked in wearing her pink robe and scratching her head. "Hair spray got wet in the rain yesterday. So *itchy*."

I laughed. I'd never worn hairspray in my life. My style was wavy and simple or pulled back in a ponytail or braid. Dullsville all the way.

"Did you sleep on the couch?" Mom looked surprised.

"Well, yeah, I fell asleep watching a documentary." I smoothed my throw down over my lap. If Mom hadn't put it there, then it had to be Janie. But why would she? Had the trouble with Shawn made her more sympathetic to my feelings?

"Did Uncle A come back last night?" I tried to keep my tone casual.

Mom had moved around behind the kitchen island to make coffee. "No, why?"

"No reason, I just thought he might've got lonely."

Mom laughed out loud. "He's got two girls practically fighting over him at his work."

"You're *kidding*. At the car lot?"

Nodding, Mom finished filling the coffee filter and pushed the button to turn on the machine. She took a seat on a barstool and leaned her elbows on the granite surface. "One is a loan officer, and the other is a salesperson like him."

"Oh, my gosh, Uncle Aidan."

"Well, I don't know why we are surprised, I mean look at him. Look how he took care of us during all this. He put his whole life on hold for us, didn't he?"

I stood and wrapped my blanket around my hips. "He sure did. I don't know if I could have got through it without him."

Mom laid her hand on the granite, palm up. "Are you feeling better now? Stronger?"

"I am." I laid my hand in hers. "I know I'll never be that stupid again. Thanks for not making me feel even worse."

"Thanks for not taking away my little girl," she replied. "I would never forgive myself if anything happened to you. Please, if you ever need to talk, come to me, okay?"

"About anything?"

"Anything at all, I promise. Nothing too small; nothing too large. Trust me when I tell you we've probably all been in your shoes." She smiled and squeezed my fingers gently.

Twenty-Five

Cognitive Malfunction

After we discussed my plans for the day, researching home schooling options, Mom said she was going to go into the office for a while. "But you promise me you will stay off social media. You can use the internet to research, but that's all. Okay?"

"Mo-o-m." I couldn't resist, I rolled my eyes just like she'd done when I said I'd be driving soon. "You deleted all my accounts, remember?"

She harrumphed. "I know you. If you want it, you'll find a way. Just promise me you won't. It can't be good for anyone."

"Surely that painting is all in the past." I chewed my lip and got up to pour myself a cup of milk with a splash of coffee.

"Just promise me, okay?"

I promised. "But Mom?"

She looked at me.

"Is Janie going to be here all day, too?" There it was. She said I could talk to her about anything.

"As far as I know, she isn't going to school or work. Not today, probably not tomorrow either."

I yawned. "I hope I don't have to throw another bottle of lotion at her head." I tried to make the statement sound light, comical, but of course Mom wasn't fooled.

"Don't you dare," she replied. "Just call if you need me. I'll come right home."

At least she didn't say, *Oh, that'll never happen.* Maybe she knew it wasn't all my fault. Maybe she saw how the tyrant really was.

I watched Mom leave with trepidation. But I pushed aside the feeling of unease and flipped open my laptop. It only took a few minutes to find what I wanted and then the scene outside the window wouldn't be ignored.

The weather that early in the morning felt perfect, damp and cool from yesterday's rain. I slipped on my Skechers—I'd slept in my shorts and tee shirt—and walked down the street. The morning air really was a revelation. Usually I'd be in class by now, sitting shoulder to shoulder with other kids trying to wake up.

Our street was more active than I realized. Cars backing out of drives, Mrs. Carol on the corner walking across the yard in her robe, cup of coffee in one hand, cigarette dangling from one corner of her lip, intent on picking up her newspaper without spilling her coffee. She reminded me of a dinosaur with the wide frilly collar on her robe like a Stegosaurus, slightly hump-backed, smoking a cancer stick, reading a dead tree.

Judgmental much? My subconscious surprised me, made me laugh at myself. But it was a very short mood. By the time I'd reached the corner, the notion hit me that my dad was out there in the cemetery in the cold hard ground. That he'd never enjoy a beautiful morning like this, ever again.

But he chose it, I told myself. Just like I almost chose it, too. I nearly wound up there right beside him. Mom could have had a double funeral—

My gut cramped, bent me over as if in memory of that horrific overdose night. I braced myself against the roughly pitted silver finish of the stop sign pole and took a deep, steadying breath. A slice of pain settled across the top of my head, slid down inside my face, and I realized I hadn't eaten since the after-funeral lunch yesterday. Had I drunk anything? Maybe this was dehydration, but the air felt cool, and I'd only gone a block.

I decided to turn back.

The sidewalk behind me didn't look familiar. Had I turned a corner without even thinking about it? I looked up at the street sign. Sixth and Ave K. How did I get here? This was four blocks from my house on Third and Ave G, and it meant I'd turned a corner as well. *Jeez.*

I started back home; the cool damp air quickly burned away in the Texas sun. Should have worn my sunglasses, my ball cap, something. But I hadn't intended to go this far. I hadn't intended to go far at all, just around my own block. Had I blacked out? I didn't even remember crossing one street, much less three. And I didn't even have my phone.

Slightly terrified, I walked all the way down Ave K until I got to Third Street, then I turned the wrong direction to get to my house. But I didn't get far before I realized what I'd done, and then I turned around and went back.

Janie stood in the driveway, one hand shading her eyes, watching me. When I got closer, she stepped back inside the house without a word. Maybe she'd heard the phone ring or something. Maybe it was my phone. Maybe that's why she'd been out there. It sure seemed like she was looking for me.

The inside of the house was cool, the dimness a balm for my sunstruck eyes. Janie had her door closed. I headed to the kitchen for water, maybe some cereal. Mom burst through the back door just as I entered from the kitchen side.

"Ben!" She seemed surprised to see me. "Are you all right?"

How'd she know? Did Janie call her?

"I'm okay." I felt like an idiot. "I went for a walk, the air felt so good—but I... I sort of went further than I intended."

"You didn't take your phone." She came to me, put the inside of her wrist against my forehead. "Your face is so red—"

"Yeah, it got kind of hot, in a hurry. I just meant to go around the block." My head felt mushy, like an overripe melon.

Mom put her two fingers under my chin and made me look her in the eye. I thought she might be checking my pupils.

"I'm okay." I gave her a thin smile. "Did Janie call you? Make you come home?"

"She couldn't find you," Mom said. "Searched the whole house, found your phone. You never go anywhere without your phone."

Probably laughing her ass off behind that bedroom door, I thought as I gulped cool water from the fridge door.

"Go slow," Mom said.

The cramps hit me again. A cold sliver of steel went into my right eye from the top of my head.

"Or you'll get sick."

I ran for the bathroom, barely got there in time to puke up all the water I'd just guzzled. *Oh my God. What an idiot.* Back to my bed, curled into a ball, knees to my chest again. Mom with a cool washcloth for my head.

"Here," she gave me two crackers and a cup of tepid tea. "This will help. Once, when I was a kid back in the Stone Age, I thought I'd chop cotton over near Lamesa. A lot of my friends earned their summer money that way—"

She shook the washcloth out to cool it off again, folded it length-wise, laid it back on my forehead. "—we didn't really chop the cotton, it was picked by cotton picking machines, you know, and sometimes migrant laborers for the smaller fields, those old cotton bolls and all that, but us kids chopped the weeds in between the rows."

She chuckled. "I didn't last half a day. Sun got to me. I gulped water back at the trailer, got sick just like you, started throwing up. Miserable. I never went back. I would have, maybe, but I was so embarrassed that I couldn't make myself."

I smiled. Ate another cracker. Sipped the tea. "Mom?"

"Yes?" She pulled another cracker from the waxed paper sleeve.

"This feels better. Thanks. I just wanted to get outside. The weather was so nice—"

"But?"

I closed my eyes, readjusted the barely-cool cloth. "But I went farther and even turned a corner and—and I didn't even know it."

I kept my eyes closed. I didn't want to see the expression on her face. Didn't want to think I might have ruined my brain with my stupid suicide attempt. My brain. My best asset. I wasn't pretty and blonde like Janie. I didn't have the storm-cloud eyes like Mom. Didn't even have height, or curves, or anything special.

My name should have been Jane instead of my sister. Plain Jane. Except for the brain.

I giggled. Felt like a fool. I can't walk around the block but I can rap. Maybe that'll be my new calling. Rapping and rhyming. I opened my eyes to find Mom staring at me with an expression of near-horror. Probably thinks I'm cracking up. "Sorry," I said. "I just can't believe I got lost going around the friggin' block."

She laughed. It sounded a little forced. "The neurologist said you might have moments of fog. Those were his exact words. Moments of fog. He told me the reason, something to do with ibuprofen toxicity—"

I held up my hand. "Is that because the Vicoprofen has ibuprofen?"

She nodded. "Ibuprofen mixed with hydrocodone."

No wonder it had taken effect so fast. "I really messed up, didn't I?" The air in the room felt thick, cloying. My voice wouldn't come out. Finally, I said, "Is it permanent?"

Mom plucked my hand out of the air. "It will get better. The doctor said the brain is so pliable. It will learn to reprogram—"

"Oh my God. Like a stroke victim, having to relearn?"

"Not nearly that bad." Mom shook her head, kept her grasp on my hand. "Just a bit of cognitive malfunc—"

"No! Don't say that. Don't say cognitive and malfunction in the same sentence." Tears sprang to my eyes, surprising me. Stupid tears. I'd thought the dehydration would have prevented this. Maybe it wasn't dehydration after all. Not in that moist, cool air. Maybe I'd damaged my liver or something along with my brain. Maybe I'd always suffer these cramps and headaches, from now on.

Mom kept her grip on my hand. "You made a mistake. It's not permanent. It hasn't been long. Things will get back to normal. You'll see." She leaned over and kissed the top of my head. "Don't be so hard on yourself, Ben. Today was the first time it happened, right?"

I let go Mom's hand and rolled over on my side. "Yes. That's what makes it so scary. Why did it happen today and not yesterday, or the day before?" I hiccupped. Took a deep breath.

"There haven't been any other symptoms? None?"

I thought back over the last couple of days. There had been a couple of moments, hadn't there? A couple of headaches?

Pushing the fear away, I said, "Our school has something called The Homebound Program. A teacher comes to the house. I can work at my own pace if I qualify."

Mom squeezed my shoulder. "That's what we will do, then. I'll call them right now. Can I bring you a little soup? When is the last time you ate?"

A bit of my old evil nature popped into my mouth. "Umm. Just now. Crackers and tea."

"Oh, you." Mom pushed my shoulder as she stood. "I'll bring you some chicken noodle soup."

I grinned into my pillow. "Thanks, Mom. I'm sorry you had to come home. Do you have any showings today?"

"Yes, I have one in a couple of hours. I was just in the office catching up on paperwork." From the corner of my eye I saw her pick up my tea mug and the waxed paper sleeve of crackers. "But never worry about that, sweetie. If you need me, you call me. You hear? Anytime."

I nodded, pressing the side of my face into the pillow. I could hear the cracker paper crackle softly as she twisted it closed.

"Leave the crackers?"

"Of course."

"And Mom?"

She waited.

"Could I have iced tea this time?"

"You got it, kiddo."

I felt like a kiddo. A tiny little kiddo taking advantage of a slight illness to be waited on hand and foot. That was the last thing I remembered thinking as I dozed. When I woke, my soup bowl sat on the nightstand beside a half-sleeve of crackers and a tall glass of tea that probably once contained ice. It was all melted now.

Looking around for my phone, I found a paper note stuck under my soup bowl. "I've gone to my showing. Didn't have the heart to wake you. Hope you feel better. Love, Mom."

I glanced at the window. The light seemed far away. It was clearly afternoon. I'd slept for hours.

The inside of my mouth felt like my fleece pajama pants. I sipped the sweet tea. Not bad. Suddenly I was ravenous, hunger like a beast awakening in my belly.

I sipped the cold soup, ate the cold noodles, crunched the buttery crackers, and wondered if I would toss it all up in ten minutes. But I couldn't seem to stop until I saw the bottom of my bowl.

This wasn't normal. Mom said I would get back to normal soon. I sure hoped she was right, whatever normal might be.

Twenty-Six

Tough as Denim

I leaned back against my pillows and willed my food to stay down.

My phone buzzed with a text from Mom. "Sorry sweetie, I completely forgot you have an appointment with Dr. Blue in twenty minutes. Get ready, I'm on my way to pick you up."

Oh, no. I stood, expecting to be shaky, but so far so good. In the bathroom, I turned on the water in the tub. My silver heart fell down and slapped the porcelain like it did before. It made me smile. *Keep reminding me,* I said to myself. *Please do.*

I took a quick bath and pulled on clean blue jeans and a plain black tee. My hair wasn't too dirty, but I would have to wash it tomorrow. Just as Mom opened the side door and yelled, "Are you ready?" I stepped into my shoes.

"Brushing my teeth," I yelled back. Wow. I felt strange. Above the floor. I rinsed and spit, headed for the side door. I remembered to unlock both sides of the bathroom. I hadn't heard a thing from Janie's side of the door. Maybe she was asleep. *Or dead,* my evil mind thought. But somehow, thinking—wishing—someone dead just wasn't funny anymore.

I came into the hallway just as Mom closed Janie's door. "She's asleep. I left her a note."

We walked out to the car. I was so nervous. Would she

make me scream again? I thought I'd got that all out but who knew?

Going to the hospital seemed like a step backward. "Be sure to ask her about getting lost this morning," Mom said, her voice soft. "I'm sure it's nothing, but still. Can't hurt to ask."

I nodded. What if my brain damage was permanent? What if it got worse and worse instead of better and better? What if cells were dying off, atrophying, as we spoke?

Mom walked me into the building, helped me find Dr. Blue's office. I couldn't remember much about the hospital. Today it felt like a maze.

"I'm going to the Starbuck's across the street," Mom said. "I'll be waiting right here when you are done." She indicated a grouping of hospital chairs in the wide foyer.

I nodded. Being inside the hospital felt strange. Her office had no receptionist, but her door was open and in seconds, there she stood.

With a brief greeting for my mom, Dr. Blue took my elbow and ushered me inside the somewhat familiar office.

"How are you feeling since the funeral yesterday?"

I sat on the nubby blue chair and thought about it. I could say anything. I could lie. I could try to hide the truth, but why? To help me, she needed to know everything. "To be honest, I feel relieved."

She didn't write it down. She didn't look away as if embarrassed. She didn't smile or not smile. I felt comfortable going further. "It was all too much. Me, my crap at school, my sister, and then my dad. I felt so bad for Mom, and for my grandparents."

"Did you not feel bad for yourself? For Ben?" Her tone still sounded neutral, but her words were pointed.

The afternoon sun illuminated the windows even though the blinds were closed. I tried to focus. "Me?"

She waited.

"Ummm. Yeah. I felt bad for me. I... I guess that's why I took the pills." I looked at the window. Measured its length, height, approximate area just guessing at the dimensions. *Waiting room math*, I thought. *Shrink math. Stalling-for-time-math.* "Of course I felt bad." My fingers went to the place of the old bruise.

"Tell me about that." Her voice sounded conversational.

I looked up, or rather out. I had been looking inward even while I did math in my head. "About what? Taking the pills?"

Dr. Blue stared at my fingers massaging the place where I'd banged my head on the floor. "Before the pills. Tell me about the bruise on your forehead."

What? There was no bruise. I tried to formulate a response, but nothing came. "What bruise?"

She leaned back in her chair. Tapped her iPad screen. "The bruise I noted on your forehead the first time I saw you after you were brought to the hospital." She watched me. "The one I asked you about before. You said you fell down."

I'd forgotten about that. Truth? Or not?

I looked into her eyes, searching for that feeling of trust I'd felt earlier. Her eyes were soft, brown, deep black pupils, direct gaze. No wrinkled forehead, no tapping of pen or pencil against teeth. No agitation, no hurry. Most importantly, no judgement.

"I will tell you if you swear it's in confidence. If you swear you won't ask for names, or anything. I don't want to press charges or even tell anyone. It's over. It could have happened, but it didn't."

She nodded. "Strict doctor-patient confidence." She held up a three-fingered Girl Scout salute. "I swear."

I laughed. But it was just nerves. Would it be okay? Would it be okay to remember, to allow myself to recall the details? To actually tell? I closed my eyes to shut out the illuminated window. Looked inward again. "A boy came to my house. Mom was at work. Janie was at work. I opened the door. Knew him, barely. He tried to—he pushed his way in. Pushed me down, made me hit my head." I laughed under my breath. Incongruous sound of mirth. I tried to explain. "The UPS man came, rang the doorbell. Saved me. I was saved by the UPS man."

My God. I'd said it all. I opened my mouth and out it spilled, like salt from an unscrewed shaker.

Now the good doctor smiled. "Feel better? More relief?"

I nodded. Why was she handing me the box of Kleenex? Oh. Tears. Streaming down my face. When did that start, where'd they come from? I mopped at them with a wad of tissue.

"Did he rape you?"

The question took me by surprise. Maybe it was supposed to. I shook my head. "Denim. Tough denim and the UPS man. That's what saved me."

She looked puzzled.

"My shorts were too strong. He tried. Tried to rip them off, but they were too strong. Then the UPS man—it could have been a woman, I don't know—rang the doorbell. Three rings. Three packages." I sat perfectly still, trying to recall what had been in those three packages. "He jumped up and ran out." Left me there to deal. The packages contained Mom's new business cards and a couple of books she'd ordered. Save by the written word. I wiped my eyes, blew my nose, walked around the office, tossed the wadded mess of tissue in the trashcan near my blue chair.

"You've had a hell of a time, Ben. I'm not surprised you tried to find a way out."

I stopped wandering, sat back down. "I got lost this morning. Wanted to walk around the block—it was so pretty after the rain, smelled so good—but I turned the wrong direction. Went further than I intended." I pulled another Kleenex from the box. "Scared me." I looked into her eyes again. "Do I have brain damage? Did I hurt my brain when I took all those pills?"

Dr. Blue shook her head. "Very doubtful. You may have had some confusion at first, but not after all this time. Ibuprofen is much harder on your stomach and digestive system than it is on your brain." She thought for a moment. "Don't get me wrong, everyone is different. Bodies react differently. But I would be more worried about that bruise, that head injury." She looked back in her iPad again. "What day did the attack happen?"

"The day before I made the painting. No. Two days before. It happened on Saturday. I went to school on Monday, saw Kera with Will, and it seemed—. It sort of seemed like I blamed them somehow. Like, if I'd still been with Will, it wouldn't have happened. The other one wouldn't have shown up at my house. Wouldn't have dared." More stupid tears dripped off the end of my nose. I'd just put into words something I hadn't even known. I blamed Will for not being there to protect me. I blamed Kera for not letting him.

Dr. Blue showed me a calendar. "Right here?" She tapped the Saturday I'd just mentioned.

"Yes."

"Did you go to sleep afterward? After it happened?"

I thought back. "Yes, I think so. I know all I wanted to do was go to sleep and pretend it hadn't happened."

"And did you feel dizzy at all?"

Concussion. She's thinking I had a concussion. "Yeah," I said. "I did. You think I had a concussion?"

She nodded. "A mild one, probably. Was there nausea, did you throw up?"

I shook my head. "I only got a little sick feeling if I touched the bruise. It was a mushy lump." I remembered always hearing if it swelled outward, that was a good thing. I said as much to the doctor.

"As a general rule, any injury that causes a bruise—a hematoma—will swell and yes, it's better for head injuries to swell out, away from the brain, but any trauma to the head can cause a concussion. Even a mild one can have lasting effects."

Wow. When she put it that way, it sounded possible.

"Does it bother you to read or watch TV?"

I thought back to the night I fell asleep watching old movies. "A little. I thought it was just because I was so tired. The headache, you know."

"I do know." She laid the iPad aside. "I had a mild concussion when I was a teen. Soccer injury. Made it hard for me to read my school assignments for weeks."

"Did you get confused, get lost like I did?"

"Not really." She looked thoughtful. "But I've had lots of patients who experience what you just described—and it's usually due to emotional trauma plus whatever drug they took." She let that sink in. "You had a triple shot—drugs, head injury, and emotional trauma." Leaning forward to pat my hand, she continued. "It will take a little time to heal. Maybe even more than a little." She sat back in her chair. "Besides, you had a CT scan in the hospital. It didn't show anything abnormal. You're in the clear."

That confused me a little. If I'd suffered enough head trauma to still be causing me problems, wouldn't something show up on the scan? I would have to ask her later. Just now, it was too much to think about.

"Thanks." I didn't know what else to say. "Can I ask you something else?"

"Sure. Anything."

"Do you have a lot of patients like me?"

"Who've tried suicide? Yes. Way too many. Especially in your age group." She clenched her jaw, and then spoke again. "It's almost an epidemic. Can I ask *you* something?"

I laughed. "Of course. Anything."

"Had you ever thought of suicide before this?" She gave me that direct stare again. "I'm actually compiling data for a paper on the subject. But if you don't want to answer—"

"I never did. Never. Not once. It was just like. Like a… what's that expression? Like a perfect storm. First, Will and Kera—I haven't even told you how they initially betrayed me—then the guy at the house, then the backlash over my stupid little painting, then my dad. And Janie. I also had a horrible fight with Janie." God. How had I forgotten that?

"What was the fight about?"

I heard a gentle series of guitar strings strummed, like a wave. I recognized the tone from my own iPhone sounds menu. I figured it meant our time was up. But the doc just touched her iPad to make it stop. "The fight?"

"It was—I mean she said—" I swallowed. This was too hard. "What did she say?"

I dropped my head. "She said it was all my fault that dad shot himself. That I should just disappear like he did."

"So that's what you tried to do." She stood and came to my chair, knelt beside me. "You poor kid. Thank God it's behind you now." She smoothed my hair, handed me more tissues. "You can let it go. It's over. You made it. You're strong. Very strong. Tough as denim."

"How do you know?" I blubbered. "How do you know I'm strong? How do you know I won't do it again the next time something goes wrong? I–I picked up a razor the other day."

She shook her head gently. "We've got more work to do, that's true. But I know you now. I'm your doctor. You *are* strong. Too strong to let anyone ever hurt you that way again. From now on, you'll guard your heart. I'll teach you how."

She stood and held out her hands.

I took them and let her pull me to my feet.

"It is going to be okay. I promise." She hugged me, briefly, firmly. "You call me anytime. And you talk to your Mom, or your Uncle Aidan. Don't talk to Janie. I think she has some things she needs to work through, too. In fact, I'm going to suggest family therapy to your Mom."

"Family?"

She gave me a more professional, side arm hug. "Just a couple of sessions, maybe three. I think it will help."

I dropped another wad of tissue into the wastepaper basket and then started for the door, hesitated. "Dr. Blue, do you believe in God?"

For the first time, she appeared genuinely surprised. "Why, yes, I do. How about you?"

I touched the silver heart at my throat. "I think so." I smiled. "I think I'm beginning to." I recalled how the heart necklace had kept me from cutting my wrists with the razor blade. "Next session, I'll tell you why."

"I'll make a note of that. Hold you to it." She stopped just short of the door. "Now, there's something I want you to take with you from this session." She tucked a little card into my hand. It read *You can't control everything around you—or even how others treat you—but you can control how you react. And that's how you take back your power.*

I nodded, and then I opened the door and walked back to the foyer and there sat Mom, right where she said she'd be.

/ Twenty-Seven

ALL ROADS LEAD TO HEAVEN

She seemed as if she wanted to ask how it went with Dr. Blue, but she managed to control herself.

"It went well," I said, taking pity on her. "We decided I just fell apart a little and she's teaching me how to keep it from happening again." I favored her with a smile. I wanted to let her know I was okay. That soon we'd all have peace again.

"How about pizza?" She steered us out of the parking lot onto the wide boulevard leading back toward town. Cotton Avenue was my favorite street in our small city. Wide, tree lined, faced with large two and three-story homes from the early 1900s when the town was founded, the street had been named after the industry which had brought the whole area to life.

The four lanes narrowed to two as we neared the center of town. Around the old-fashioned courthouse square, the streets still wore their original cobblestones. The Pizza Palace squatted on the corner of the square like a relic from the past. It had begun life as a music store in the early fifties, but like so many stores of that era, it had closed up shop long ago.

The new owners of the building kept much of the décor when they restored it. Vinyl records, sheet music, old posters, even guitars and other musical instruments lined the walls and hung from the ceiling. A massive antique Rock-Ola Juke Box dominated one corner. The owner was constantly on the lookout for 45rpm records to stock it with. As a result, most of the music it played was pre-1980.

I adored the Pizza Palace. There was also a retro game room in the back with free-standing arcade games like Pac Man, Ms. Pac Man, also regular games like foosball, and air hockey.

Of course, I hadn't been there in a few weeks, but during the day it was mostly moms and kids anyway. The only exception was around school lunchtime when seniors were allowed to leave campus. Lots of them made the Palace a popular lunch spot.

Being two o' clock, I figured we were safe. To my dismay, as soon as we were parked, Mom whipped out her cell and called Janie to come and meet us. She tried to call Uncle Aidan, too, but he didn't answer.

"He's at work today, isn't he?" I asked.

"I'm sure he is." Mom agreed. "But you know in that kind of business he doesn't always have a regular lunch hour. If he's in the middle of a sale, he will wait until later."

That made sense. I thought of what she said about the women fighting over him at work, and figured he'd rather lunch with one of them anyway. In the back of my mind was the idea that maybe someday I'd get lucky enough to have a relationship with a nice guy like Uncle Aidan.

"So, is Janie coming?" I tried to make my tone casual, but I really didn't know if I could sit across a table from her or not.

Mom held the door open for me. They were the original ten-foot-tall doors, cherry red with immense treble clefs carved right into the wood. "She'll be here," Mom said. "After all, this is going to be our lupper."

I smiled at that. It was our old joke word for a meal after lunch but before supper. We'd decided if folks could have brunch—which falls after breakfast but before lunch—then we could definitely have lupper.

A chalkboard sign said to sit anywhere, so of course we chose a booth near the jukebox. I dug around until I found quarters—one play per coin—and Mom told me to play B-17. I laughed because of course that was something else from our past. It was a silly song called "Guitarzan" by a guy named Ray Stevens. The song used to always make us giggle.

I punched the numbers for that one and two more—"Runaway" by someone named Dion (I secretly loved that song), and one called "Kathy's Clown" by The Everly Brothers. Those two songs always made me want to sing along.

They didn't make me giggle, like "Guitarzan," but they usually made me feel good. Singing almost always did. That's why I'd stuck with Choir since sixth grade. If not for Will being a member, I would really miss it. That, and Art. And Geometry. Oh, and even Literature, sometimes. I guess I really liked school after all. Before all this, I mean.

I hoped the music could work its magic today, but I really didn't have much hope. Just knowing Janie was on her way made me feel a little nauseous.

Back at the table, I picked up the squat glass jar of grated Parmesan cheese and shook some onto a napkin. Like a little kid, I usually licked the tip of my finger and dabbed it onto the cheesy-mound. Not today. For some reason, the dry cheese had suddenly taken on the sour odor of vomit.

I folded the napkin into a neat little square and shoved it behind the condiment rack so I couldn't smell it anymore.

Mom and I sat and waited. She said she'd been in touch

with the Homebound teacher and they were going to meet with all my other teachers and gather lessons to get me through the end of the year. She said they were certain I'd be ready to return next year.

I was saved from commenting on that—I couldn't imagine ever walking those halls again, no matter how much I missed it—when the door opened and the slanting rays of the afternoon sun silhouetted Janie. It lit up her blonde hair but hid her pretty face. As she crossed the room to our booth, I was a little shocked to see how tired she looked. Her eyes were red, and her hair lay in greasy strips against her cheeks.

I thought she would sit opposite me, but Mom had placed her large purse on the bench beside her and didn't offer to move it. Janie looked at me. Her face appeared naked, pained, her eyes haunted. I immediately scooted to the far side of the bench, up against the wall.

Janie slid in beside me. She placed her own bag in between us.

I didn't say anything. She looked so awful.

She picked up the menu, although I felt certain she knew it by heart, like I did. "Have y'all ordered yet?"

Mom motioned to the waitress. "We waited for you."

Susie, a middle-aged woman who had worked there since the dawn of time ambled over, pencil stuck behind her ear. "Hey, girls, what'll it be today? No, don't tell me." She pulled her pencil and aimed it at me. "Pepperoni, Diet Coke, salad bar." She aimed at Janie. "Hawaiian, Root Beer, no salad bar." Then she turned to Mom, but we were already giggling. Janie always got cheese with salad bar and Dr. Pepper.

"What's so funny?" Susie looked at us with an innocent expression on her face, and then turned back to Mom. She actually licked the tip of her pencil, an exaggerated motion.

"Now, you, Mom, I know what you always get... pickled pigs feet and sassafras tea." She yanked out her order book and began to scribble furiously.

By this time we were holding our sides and wiping at our eyes. I hadn't laughed so hard in—I couldn't remember when.

"Oh, Suse," Mom patted the waitress on the arm. "You crack me up. Even back in high school, you were always the one."

Susie turned, flipped her blonde-going-gray ponytail at us, and marched back to the counter. With a smile, she called our usual—correct—orders in to the cook in the back. Then she set about making our drinks.

We knew the drill. Leaving our purses on the seats, we all filed up to the salad bar. Janie took a plate off the stack, hesitated, and then handed me one, too. Such a small gesture, but it felt like a huge step. One small step for man, one giant leap for mankind, or rather, sisterhood.

Back at the table, things remained quiet except for the clink of our forks against our plates. Finally, Mom said, "When are you going back to school, Janie? I know you've got a lot of prom and graduation preparations to ma—"

Janie's fork hit the plate so hard I thought it had cracked. "Seriously, Mother? You want me to prepare for prom now? When we barely buried Dad and Shawn just dropped me like a hot potato?" She turned her hard gaze on our mother.

"Oh, honey, I didn't—"

"It's okay, Mom." She smashed the word mom down on the table along with her napkin. "I thought I could handle this," she gestured at our food, at me. "But obviously, I can't." She slammed her hip against the table in her hurry to get away.

"Sissy, come back—" I don't know what made me dredge up that old childhood nickname. The one I'd called her until we were both in grade school and she threatened to drown me if I didn't give it up.

She whirled around, murder on her face. "Don't call me that. Don't you ever call me that again. This is *still* your fault. You and that painting, you and Dad, now you and Shawn. It's because of you no one wants anything to do with me. Thanks to you, I won't even get to go to my Senior Prom." She opened the door to the parking lot and I heard her hiss, "Thanks. Thanks a lot, *Sissy*."

The door slowly closed behind her on its silent pneumatic hinge. I wanted to shrink into my seat. There were only a couple of other people in the restaurant, but they were witnesses. They—along with Mom's high school friend, our waitress—witnessed everything.

Mom stared at the closing door. The entire room waited in a vacuum of shock and disbelief. How could anyone be so cruel? And in public? "I can't believe I did that." Mom sounded broken.

"You?" I couldn't believe she blamed herself. "You didn't do anything. My God. We can't even have—"

Just then, the pizza arrived. "I went ahead and put Janie's in a box." The waitress smiled in commiseration.

Mom thanked her and received a pat in return. "I shouldn't have mentioned prom." She shook her head and toyed with a slice of pepperoni. "How could I forget she and Shawn were on the outs?"

Only Mom would say *on the outs*. "Mom, it isn't your fault." I glanced around the room. The other customers had gone back to their meals. Janie was such a bitch. I couldn't believe Mom let her get away with that behavior in public. "How can you stand for her to act that way? It makes me crazy."

Mom pulled a small book out of her purse. "When your dad left me for Sharla—"

The slut, I said under my breath.

"—I pretty much fell apart. I had some really black days." She stopped and opened her little book.

I recalled the times I'd found her crying on the screened porch.

"Anyhow," she wiped at her cheeks as if testing to see if they were wet. As if crying had become so second nature she could no longer tell except by feel. "I didn't know where to turn. My parents were both dead, so I turned to Uncle Aidan. Of course he was going through his own stuff." She laid the small book on the table with her index finger holding open a certain place. "He was going to AA."

"Alcoholics Anonymous?" I couldn't keep the surprise from my voice.

Mom nodded. "He introduced me to the man in charge of the meetings. His name is Father Flanagan, of all things." She smiled when she said it, as if at an inside joke. "He's a Catholic priest." She opened the book. On the black cover, stamped in gold, were the words, *Daily Devotionals for Modern Life*. "He encouraged me to use this." She held up the little book.

"Use it?"

She nodded and turned it around so I could read the passage she'd been holding open.

I do not need to figure everything out. You already know the best plan for my life. Show me Your supernatural power. Teach me how to walk by faith and pray breakthrough prayers. I choose to have faith in Your ability to break through every obstacle in my life.

Dear Lord, My God, teach me this lesson every day. In Your name, I pray.

I looked up at my Mom, still holding open the little book. The first part of the prayer was from the book, probably from The Bible. But the last line, that was Mom's own handwriting. I would have recognized it anywhere.

"When?"

"I've been going to Mass once or twice a week since your dad moved out." She shrugged as if caught in a lie. "I had to do something. I couldn't fall apart. I had you and Janie depending on me. I think that's what love is all about—being there."

I pulled the little book from her hands. Almost every page had some note or notation in Mom's slanting script. "Why didn't you tell us?"

She lowered her eyes. An elderly woman dropped some quarters in the Rock-Ola. Elvis began to croon "Love Me Tender." Mom smiled.

"I wanted to tell you so many times, but you were content going to church with Kera most weekends."

"Yeah." I thought about that. One more thing I'd lost when I lost her.

"I've been praying about it. About when would be the right time to tell you. And your sister, of course." She paused as if thinking about Janie and church. "St. Mary's is a little different from First Baptist. Not better, just different. You'll see."

Wow. Maybe her prayers *had been* answered. Somewhere it says He works in mysterious ways, right? And all spiritual roads lead to Heaven?

"Now that I've got you back, I have to trust Him where Janie is concerned." She sighed and I picked up my pizza. Knowing my mom trusted God with the reins took a load off my shoulders. I don't know why, but I felt that it was true.

I'd been on the path of believing for quite a while, but mostly going to church had been a social experiment.

We finished our pizza and took the rest of it home.

When we arrived, we were surprised to find Uncle Aidan sitting outside our house in The Green Hornet.

Twenty-Eight

Two Hearts

"Hey, you two." His left arm lay on the open window and he looked young and handsome and as if nothing bad had ever touched him. Only those closest to him knew about the past alcohol abuse and broken marriages.

"Hey, Uncle A." The rhyme was silly and it felt good to be silly. "Why are you sitting out here at the curb?"

He smiled that wide smile that made him look like a teenager. "Just waiting on you girlsh to get home."

Girlsh? Did he slur his words on purpose, to be silly like me? I looked at Mom. A shadow of concern crossed her face.

She locked our car in the drive and approached her brother. "Why didn't you use your key, go on inside?"

He tilted his head to the side like a terrier contemplating the old *who's a good dog* question. "Janie's very upset."

Mom's gaze flicked toward the house. Janie's car was not in the driveway. "Did she call you?"

Uncle Aidan shook his head, opened his door. An empty beer can fell out at Mom's feet. "You've been drinking." Her voice sounded like a written accusation.

"Jus' a lil." Uncle Aidan got out. He staggered as he tried to shut the car door.

I'd never seen him like this.

Mom grabbed his arm. "Help me, Ben."

I took his other arm and he pulled me close in a clumsy hug. "My besht girlsh. I love you girlsh." His breath was warm and foggy. It smelled like yeast.

"Love you, too, Uncle A." I tugged him toward the house.

Mom groaned as he stumbled over the curb. "Remind me to make coffee."

We got him inside.

"I hope the neighbors weren't looking," she muttered. "Here lately we've given them enough to talk about to last a *lifetime*."

I'd never thought of that. I'd only been worried about school. Never about home, about neighbors. I peered out the window as we plopped Uncle Aidan on the couch. He immediately kicked off his shoes and stretched out. I got him a pillow and blanket from the hall closet. Probably the very ones he'd been using while he stayed with us those few nights. I recalled the plastic cup on the counter, the odor of rum. Wow. I wondered if he still went to AA.

Mom pulled his legs up onto the couch. "How'd you know Janie was upset?"

Uncle Aidan snorted and began to snore. I stuffed the pillow under his head and he smiled a goofy smile.

Mom just shook her head. "Lord, please. Help this man."

I listened with new understanding. All the times she'd said little prayers like this before, I'd brushed them off as facetious, sarcastic almost. Now, I realized she really meant them. I followed her to the kitchen. She laid her phone on the counter and touched Janie's picture icon in her favorites list. "Where is that girl?"

Her phone rang and rang until the voice mail message came on. "Speak now or forever hold your peace," Janie's voice said.

Mom hesitated, then blurted, "Call me, young lady. We aren't doing this again." Then she poked the END icon and grabbed the coffee pot and shoved it under the faucet to fill.

I wandered to Janie's room to see if she'd been there to get her things, then I realized I didn't even know if she'd unpacked from her near-elopement with Shawn earlier. Glancing in her closet, it looked the same as before, empty hangers and missing overnight bag. The bag was not on the bed, under the bed, or near the bed. I checked the bathroom. It wasn't there, either. I assumed her laptop was in the bag, too.

How did Uncle A know she was upset? She must've called him or been at the house at some point.

I hurried back to the kitchen. "Hey, Mom? Janie's laptop and overnight bag are gone. Should we look in Uncle Aidan's phone, to see if she called him?"

Mom slumped against the counter. "If we can, I guess it will be all right. Aidan would understand, right?"

"I'm sure he would. If he wasn't drunk." I let the word drunk fall off my tongue like a brick. "He's probably got it locked anyway."

In the living room, we were shocked to see his phone lying on the floor beside the couch. It must have slipped out of his pants pocket when Mom twisted his legs around on the cushions.

She grabbed it and pushed the home button.

ENTER PASSCODE

She looked at me. Desperation played at the corners of her eyes. "I have no idea. Probably shouldn't be doing this anyway. It's private."

I plucked the phone from her fingers, picked up Uncle Aidan's hand, and pressed his thumb to the home button.

The screen opened up.

Mom's eyes widened. She opened her mouth to say something—probably a protest about privacy or something—but I just mumbled, "He does work in mysterious ways," and then pulled up Uncle A's recent calls.

Nothing from Janie, but I did notice one from his ex-wife, Bree, that piqued my curiosity, but that definitely wasn't my business. I clicked over to messages.

Sure enough, there was one from Janie from an hour ago. "Uncle Aidan. I'm going to Gran's house in Oklahoma. I've already talked to her, she said she would call Mom."

I held up the phone so Mom could read it.

"She needs space," Mom said. "Is there more?"

I nodded. I'd already scanned the entire, short, conversation. "There's more." I handed her the phone, watched her as she read.

Her face crumpled. "She's pregnant, isn't she?"

"It sounds like it."

Mom pressed the icon to call Janie but once again, there was no answer. This time she didn't leave a message. "I'm going to call Gran; see if she's talked to her."

I sat beside Uncle Aidan a few more minutes, watching the rise and fall and of his chest. A drop of clear spittle appeared at the corner of his mouth. "Dear Lord," I said softly. "Please take care of my sweet—gross—uncle." Then I got up and went to my room to check my own messages. In the back of my mind I added, "And my stupid, stupid sister."

I had a message from Sam. "Hey. How's it going?"

As usual, I thought of a million responses. Finally settled on, "Pretty good. You?"

"I'm excited. Studying for my driver's test."

"Driver's test? Really?"

"Yeah. I can't wait to be independent. How about you?"

"Oh, sure. But I don't think I'll get my license any time soon. You know I'm only 14, right?"

"Wow. I'll be 16 soon," he wrote. "So you are really only 14?"

"I skipped a grade back in elementary."

He sent a smiley face with nerd glasses.

"Yep. That's me." I wondered if this would be the last time he bothered to call or text me. I didn't realize he was a junior already. For some reason I thought he was only one grade ahead.

Mom came in. "I just talked to Gran. Janie called her. Asked if she could stay with them for awhile."

"BRB," I sent to Sam. "Something's come up."

"Is she on the way there?" I imagined my sister driving through the gathering darkness toward the light of my Grandparents' house. I imagined her pulling over now and then for gas, and to puke with motion sickness. Mom once said her morning sickness with us had turned into all-day sickness—for the first few months at least. And forget about riding in a car, she'd said. Motion sickness was torture.

Of course now I knew what real puking torture felt like. But I wouldn't tell my mom that. Some things were better left unsaid.

"Yes." She wiped her hand across her brow. Her eyes were haunted, far away. "I imagine she doesn't answer the phone because she's in that long stretch of no man's land on Highway 84. The one where no cell tower exists."

"I'm sure you're right." I agreed, because what was the alternative train of thought? That she'd done a triple play, a hat trick, like me, like Dad? I'd once read that suicide was catching. That the idea could take hold in a small group and spread like wildfire.

Mom wandered back to her sanctuary with her phone. I knelt beside my bed. "Please Lord," I prayed, "don't make my mom have to go through this all over again." I started to rise, and then I added, "And please keep Janie safe. No matter what."

I rose and stood uncertainly. Shouldn't I be doing something to help? How had my poor little family come to this. Could I blame it all on Dad? It seemed we had imploded when he left, but no. That wasn't quite right. I'd been doing pretty much okay until Will and Kera did that to me at the party. But really, was that such a bad thing? It had hurt me; that was true. The two people I trusted most outside my immediate family had decided they wanted to exclude me and be together.

Should I have tried to accept it and remain friends with them? No. I'm entitled to my feelings. I shouldn't have to constantly put my feelings aside to make someone else happy. Should I?

I'll ask Dr. Blue. See what she thinks. Tomorrow would be my first group therapy session.

I strolled through the semi-quiet house remembering the storm of events that created this catastrophe. Paul. School. Kera and Will. The painting. My dad. Janie. My dad. Janie. Dad.

Suddenly, I itched to create something new. A picture that would let out onto the page all the pain and anger and confusion that gripped me with these evil talons.

My art supplies were all at school except for an old sketchpad and a box of Prismacolor pencils I'd gotten for Christmas. Where were they? Mom had scoured my room clean after my bout with the pills.

I peeked in on Uncle Aidan, snoring away on the couch,

and dashed back to my room. Pretty sure the pad and pencils were under my bed, but the narrow space was dark, empty, spotless. Where would Mom have put them? The sketchpad was large, it wouldn't fit in a drawer.

The utility room closet. Floor to ceiling shelves—it's where we stored everything that wouldn't fit anywhere else.

Feeling a sense of purpose, I passed back through the living room, dining room, and kitchen until I came to the utility. There they were, right where I'd thought, old friends who would never leave me.

I took them up and started back to my room wishing for an easel like the one in my art class at school. Another purpose. Get an easel. A good one.

I passed the door to the screened porch. Although it was dark, the door stood slightly open. I heard sobbing. Just like back in the days after Dad first left. If I opened the door wide enough for the kitchen light to illuminate the space, or if I turned on the string of soft lights draped around the ceiling, I would see Mom lying on the day bed, head in her arms.

My heart broke open as if made of glass.

Will and Kera seemed like pawns on a chessboard, but here was the queen, and she was in agony. Her children were falling apart; the love of her life had betrayed her not once, but twice—and now she'd never see him again—even her little brother, whom she'd always adored, had fallen into the quagmire that seemed to have trapped our entire family.

Setting my art supplies against the wall, I crept in and sat beside her in the dim light from the partially open kitchen door. We didn't say anything, we simply found each other's hands and sat there, touching, listening to the crickets in the hedges and a lone dog barking somewhere several houses away.

The moon hadn't reached its apex yet. It wouldn't shine on this side of the house for another few hours. The new darkness felt alien, alive, waiting.

"Can I get you anything—tea, coffee?"

She shook her head. I felt the movement more than saw it. "Chocolate milk?"

Mom smiled. I saw the glimmer of her teeth, briefly, against the shape of the pillow. Chocolate milk had always been our late night comfort food.

"I know we'll get through this," she said. "We don't have a choice." She hiccupped, a sob turned inward. "But I just keep asking myself what we did to deserve it? We're good people. We try to do good."

I squeezed her hand. "I thought I was the only one asking that question. I mean, it's like why did Kera think it was okay to start dating Will when I was supposed to be her best friend?" I wanted to add, or why did Paul think it would be okay to come over and "hang out" just because it got around that I wasn't dating Will anymore? Just because I looked at his hair a little too long? Was that one of those *mixed signals* I was always hearing about? Had it been my fault, all of it?

Something else to ask Dr. Blue, maybe. I couldn't ask Mom. It would just add to her pain.

"Yeah," Mom sighed. "I've asked myself a million times why wasn't I good enough for your dad. What did I—"

"You mean why weren't *we* good enough," I interrupted. "He left all of us. Tried to replace all of us."

Mom sat up. "He did, didn't he? No matter how we sliced it. How we tried to spread it on the bread, it always came back to that jar of 'we just weren't what he wanted anymore.'"

I broke down then. "That's it exactly."

"But it isn't true." Mom smoothed my hair, patted my back. "Now we see that it wasn't us, at all. There was something missing inside of him, like Grampa said. And his new family wasn't enough to fill it, either. I guess he was still looking when he got himself roped into something else. The gambling or whatever he needed that money for. It was something he couldn't divorce, couldn't get out of." She pulled me close. "I think I'm going to start going to therapy, too. I need to learn how to be happy again. I think I've forgotten how. But we *can* be happy again, the three of us. We've still got each other."

I understood what Mom was trying to say. But deep inside it didn't resonate. Janie wasn't here. She didn't want to be with me, anymore than Will or Kera—or my own dad. And if she wanted Mom, she had a very strange way of showing it. Of course, there were these extenuating circumstances I couldn't possibly understand.

Mom reached over and flicked the switch to turn on the string of patio lights. They gave off the sweetest childhood glow, like a string of summer fireflies. "I'm going to buy myself an easel," I said. "I think I'll set it up out here, if that's okay."

"Of course it is." Mom stood and stretched. "We're going to be okay. I'll make sure of it. Somehow." She patted me again. "Going to get ready for bed, how about you?"

"Yeah, in a minute." I followed her through the door and retrieved my sketchpad and pencils and took them to the porch. I propped the large pad against the head of the daybed and went to work with the pencils. The soft lighting lent the picture a cozy feel. Before I knew it, I'd sketched my entire backyard, the part visible through the wide screened windows, and there under the spreading elm that Dad had planted ten years ago for a future tree house, I sketched in the retreating figure of a man. The shape was slightly bent, ethereal, sad. In its center I left a blurry hole with light shining through. It made me cry even as it emerged onto the paper. But I couldn't stop.

When that one was done, with only shadows of color here and there to illustrate the darkness and the light, I tore that page off and started on another.

The second sketch came so quickly it felt as if the pencil had taken on a life of its own. This one showed a car driving down a long and lonely highway toward a distant point that may or may not have been a rising moon. Inside the dark interior of the car beat two hearts, one large and one small. The car's headlights lit up the nightscape like eyes peering into the unknown.

The only spots of color on that sketch were the two glowing hearts and the soft gold depicting the color of the car, and the bare hint of the moon.

When I finished that one, I almost crumpled it up. I knew Janie would understand it. I could never let her, or anyone, see it. So why had I bothered to make it?

It seemed I didn't have a choice.

Wearing a fine film of perspiration, I swiped my sticky bangs off my forehead and carefully tore the sketch off the pad and rolled it into a tube. My fingers were already itching to start another one. Something with twinkly lights and—

I yanked pencils out of the box and went to work on a new page. The other two sketches lay unfurled on the day bed.

This time, I dotted in twinkly lights, but they weren't the ones surrounding me on the screened porch, these were the lights that would be illuminating the live oak trees around the quad at school during prom.

Once I got those roughed in, I outlined a beautiful blonde girl in a sparkly off-the-shoulder dress and high heels. I put her dancing with a non-entity on a bare piece of ground under the lights. The shape of her partner was definitely male. It could have been Shawn, or it could have been The Beast from the old Beauty and the Beast fairytale.

The look on her face in the twinkly lights was the hardest thing to capture. I wanted a look that was both tender and defiant. Hopeful and resigned.

I didn't know if I captured it or not.

Once again, I used minimal color. A few of the twinkly lights I made clear yellow, a few were clear, see-through blue, and one, directly over her head, was my signature red. Like the little heart hidden in the folds of her prom dress.

Oh my God. When I finished it, I stepped away. Each picture was worse than the one before. What was I trying to do, ensure that my sister would never speak to me again? I thought of ripping them all to shreds, hiding the evidence. Wasn't it my art that had made me—us—into a pariah at school in the first place? Did I want to do that exact same thing in my own family—as if I hadn't already?

I reached for the sketchpad, determined to tear it off and tear it up. But Mom stepped through the door behind me. "I thought you were going to get ready for—"

Her words came to a stop.

She reached toward my hand, stopped it before I could tear off the picture.

"Oh, my." The amazement in her voice didn't tell me much. Was she amazed at the work, or amazed that I'd had the audacity to put it on paper?

"Mom?"

She looked past me to the two pictures lying on the bed. "Did you do these just now?"

Shrugging, I tried to pick them up before she could inspect them.

"Let me see." She brushed my hands away and took all three pictures into the dining room where she spread them side-by-side on the table.

I followed like a lamb, wearing my embarrassment like a coat of wool. "Mom," I said.

She shushed me and stared at the pictures. "I didn't know." She said. "I didn't know you were this good. I mean, I saw the one that created such a stir at school, but I thought it was maybe a fluke. But this…" She swept her arm through the air toward the pictures.

"Janie can't see them," I said. "She will freak. Just like she did about the one at school that embarrassed her so bad."

"Maybe it's a touch of jealousy."

I laughed harshly. "She said she hated me. That I was the reason dad did what he did. She said I should just disappear like him."

Mom turned to me, her mouth an O. "That awful girl. I can't believe she can be so cruel." She made her mouth into a hard line. "You know none of that is true, right? I mean we've already discussed your dad. It was nothing to do with us. He got himself in a bind out of greed and—that emptiness inside him." She pointed toward the hole I'd left in the middle of the dad character. "But Janie. Well, Janie has now got herself in a bind, too, hasn't she?"

She didn't seem to be actually talking to me anymore, just talking. "Yeah," I agreed. "She's in a mess, all right."

"Doesn't excuse her laying the blame on you, though. My

God. That girl. And still," she reached out and touched the two hearts inside the car. "You still depict her with such tenderness." She turned to me. "You are something special, Benji-girl. You know that?"

I allowed her to hug me. And I didn't try to destroy the pictures. I'd worry about that later. For once, I felt special. I felt strong.

In my room, I hesitated, then dug up some courage and messaged Sam to tell him good night. I told him there was too much drama at my house tonight and I would talk to him tomorrow.

He said he understood, not to worry. As I lay in my messy bed trying to go to sleep, it occurred to me to wonder if I intentionally kept putting off texting him because I was afraid if I didn't keep him at arm's length he would eventually hurt me—like Will. Or Paul. Or Keenan. Those scaly monsters.

No, I told myself. *No. I* am *strong. Tough. Like denim.*

Besides, once he really thinks about our age difference, he probably won't be calling or texting anyway.

Twenty-Nine

Group

The next morning Mom said Janie had made it to Gran's house without having an accident. Gran had called in the night and told Mom not to worry. They would sort it all out. That everything would be okay. Somehow.

At least it was peaceful at our house without her. Uncle Aidan sat up on the couch holding his head, looking sheepish. "I fell off the wagon," he muttered, reaching for his phone.

I didn't know what to say. We'd been depending on him and it seemed he was no stronger than any of us.

He glanced up and caught me staring. "It's okay, kiddo. Still just me, old Uncle A. Just a damn drunk." He punched some numbers on his phone. "Calling my sponsor right now. Get me to a meeting. I'll be fine. They said it might happen." He smiled at me and I felt like a grown up.

I went to the kitchen and made a fresh pot of coffee.

When I returned with a cup, he stood in front of the pictures still spread across the table. "You're good. You know that?"

I handed him the coffee and he made a big show of making sure it didn't drip on my work.

"It's just sketching," I said. "No biggie."

He slurped the hot coffee, grimaced, wiped his lip.

"No biggie, she says. Got the whole school in an uproar

with one fell swoop of her mighty pencil." He shook his head. "No biggie."

I gathered the pictures together, tired of the spectacle.

"Aren't you supposed to put something on them to keep them from smearing?"

My hands stopped. "How do you know that?"

Uncle Aidan shrugged. "I took art in high school. You ever think maybe the talent comes from your mom's side of the family?" He raised his eyebrows at me over the rim of his cup.

Well that was certainly something new. "You draw?"

He nodded. "C'mon. You've seen the detail work I put on cars. You think there's a pattern for that stuff?"

I laughed. "Yes, actually, I did."

"Nope." He grinned. "That's all me, baby. All me."

"My favorites are the flames and the skulls," I said. "Oh, and those tiny curly pinstripes you did on that girl's Charger. Those were so elegant."

"Why, thank you." He slurped more coffee. "Now, if you'll kindly direct me to the aspirin?"

I laughed. Even falling apart, Uncle Aidan always made me feel better. "Maybe I can get some Fix-it Spray this afternoon. You're right, they'll get all smeared if I don't."

"I'll pick it up on my way home," he said. "I need a few things myself."

"Thanks, Uncle A." I was touched. He really was the kind of guy I wanted in my life when I got older. Minus the alcohol, that is.

Mom seemed much better after her shower. Knowing Janie was safe at Gran's probably had a lot to do with that. Plus, she had a house to show so maybe that took her mind off things.

She took me to the hospital and dropped me off. "Call me

if you get out early," she instructed. "Otherwise, I will make it a point to be waiting right here in an hour and a half."

I agreed, of course, even though my insides felt like spun sugar—syrupy, brittle.

Group therapy with Dr. Blue.

Could I really tell a room full of strangers what I had done? And why I had done it? The doc said I didn't have to share if I didn't want to, but that I had to sit in on the group because it was important for me to know that I was not not alone.

Just then, I felt alone. I felt like a freak. Like everyone knew why I was there, what I had done. I didn't *have* to share. Everyone could tell just by looking at me.

Mom let me out in front of the hospital. The tall glass entrance doors were slightly tinted to cut the harsh West Texas sunlight later in the day. The rectangular fountain out front gurgled merrily, which I supposed was intended to cheer patients' families. There always seemed to be several milling around, talking on their phones.

The sidewalk from the circular drop-off drive to the front doors suddenly felt ten miles long. The morning sun rested on the top of my head like a warm cap. A drop of sweat tricked from my hairline down the back of my shirt.

Nails digging into my palms, I told myself I was strong— tough—and I forced myself to continue through the revolving doors, past the elevators, down the long sterile hall, right to Dr. Blue's office, a place that only yesterday had felt like some kind of sanctuary.

That's the problem, I thought, wiping my brow. *Just when I felt safe speaking freely in her blue-tinged refuge, she'd gone and thrown me to the wolves. Expecting me to start over, from scratch.*

As before, the office door stood open, and there sat Dr. Blue, waiting.

"Good morning." Like always, her voice was yogurt-smooth. "You look nervous." She smiled. "Don't worry. I wouldn't let you walk in alone. And you won't be alone, ever. I will introduce you. All that is required of you, today, is to sit and listen."

My whole body shivered. I took a deep breath, in through the nose, out through the mouth. It helped. A little.

Dr. Blue took my elbow and opened the door to the conference room beside the office. The place where a long table would normally sit was empty, encircled by a dozen folding chairs with blue padded seats. The blue seats made me smile. Then I realized the people already in the room—teens just about my age—probably thought I was an idiot to walk in smiling. Or simply mental.

But aren't we all mentally ill? Everyone here tried to commit suicide, after all. I grabbed the nearest chair and folded myself up as small as possible, knees together, hands clasped between knees, eyes on the floor, shoulders hunched inside my loose soul-protecting tee shirt. Only then did I allow myself to peek up through my lashes at the other half-dozen kids.

They looked the same as me, terrified and wishing they were any place else. Except for one or two who stared at the closed but sundrenched window blinds, all the others studied the floor or their shoes or something else of interest in that area of the room.

"We're expecting two more," Dr. Blue said. "We will give them another minute before we begin."

I glanced around. Why so many chairs if only one or two more are coming? Then it occurred to me that some of us would rather not sit side-by-side. Some of us—myself included—needed a bit more space on either side in order to avoid imploding. *Smart, Dr. Blue. Very smart.*

The door opened again and I sensed two people enter the room. One went toward the left and one came toward me on the right side of the doorway. The one coming toward me—I knew it was a he by the large Converse high tops I could see from the corner of my eye—did not keep going until he got to a safe chair unoccupied on either side. Instead, he sat down on the chair directly beside me.

"Hey."

I glanced up, somewhat alarmed (what kind of trick is this my fight-or-flight instinct demanded) and found myself staring right at the crooked-toothed smile of my new buddy, Sam.

"Hey," I responded, unable to hide my surprise. "I didn't realize it was a support group, too." I thought maybe Dr. Blue also counseled kids who'd had a family member commit suicide, like Sam's brother. Then it dawned on me that Sam and I had never discussed my attempt.

"Did you know I'd be here?" I asked.

He shrugged, just a little. "I thought you might." His eyes held my gaze. "I heard what happened. You know this group is only for those of us who have actually tried it." He turned his head to the side and allowed me to see the thin, ropy scar on his neck.

My brain wouldn't accept what my eyes were seeing. He'd told me his brother hung himself. He'd never said anything about—

"I'm sorry," he whispered. "I wanted to tell you so many times, but you were so raw. So much always happening. And it wasn't something I felt comfortable saying in a text. Besides, I didn't want to overload you." His smile had faded, but his eyes remained kind.

I couldn't decide how I felt about this new information. Was Sam defective like me? "I can't believe it." I looked at him when I said it, but it was like looking at the shore from a lifeboat bobbing on the ocean. "Have you been coming here for long? The scar looks old. How long ago—" All at once I felt such a kinship. Now I understood why he was so easy to confide in.

Dr. Blue raised her hands and welcomed us all to Group. "That's what call this," she said. "Just Group. In here, we are safe. We can say anything. We have no secrets. On the other hand, if you don't feel comfortable sharing just yet, don't worry. You will still be coming to me once a week on your own. All your fears are safe with me." She gazed at each face, and each set of eyes fastened on her as if she had just walked across the room on a layer of water.

"You'll be fine," Sam said under his breath. "I've been coming to group for several months. Even before we moved here. Dr. Blue is famous, you know."

"Did you really?" I pointed toward my neck, where his scar would be.

"Yeah," he said. "But I didn't. Just like everyone here, I tried, but I didn't." He smiled that smile and I felt as if he'd reached over and patted me reassuringly.

I unclasped my hands and took another deep breath. In my head the words, *yeah, but I didn't,* chased each other round and round, like a mantra come to life. *Yeah, but I didn't.* Not exactly a club, but maybe it should be.

"Now, who would like to begin today?" Dr. Blue let her gaze alight on the air near each person, nonthreatening, nonchallenging.

Sam stood. "I'll go." His voice came out deep, unafraid.

"My name is Sam Edgerton. I know most of you because we've been sharing this room once a week for a few months now so most of you already know I hung myself in my bedroom closet. Not very original. Not very smart—extremely stupid, actually—I could've wound up a brain-dead vegetable if my dad hadn't found me almost immediately and cut me down." Here, his voice finally faltered.

I saw his right knee spasm and jerk. Nerves. I pressed down on my own knees to keep them still. I couldn't believe he could say it out like that. Just like that. As if it was okay to own it.

"I tried to kill myself because my little brother, Tanner, killed himself in that very same way after being bullied at school. He never told me about it. And I was so self-centered I never noticed." He looked around the room. "I feel extra stupid now, looking back. How did I think killing myself would help? Well, I didn't. Not really."

He scrubbed his palms on the sides of his jeans. "It was guilt. Eating me alive. I was the one who was always supposed to look after Tanner. Ever since he was born, I was kind of in charge. Being four years older, everyone just expected me to take care of him. And I didn't. So, I wanted to join him. I wanted to punish myself. I couldn't stand the look on my dad's face every time my brother's name was mentioned, every time he walked by Tanner's bedroom door."

He straightened his spine and looked down at me.

"But it hurt Dad even more when he had to cut me down."

I noticed both his knees were shaking now.

"Grief is a killer. It comes with a packet of guilt attached. That's what I've found out from all my sessions here, and with Dr. Blue in private. Grief—and guilt—will kill us if we don't fight."

He sat down and my hand automatically went to him, squeezed his arm. Then I pulled it back and hung my head. No way I was going to make eye contact with anyone. No matter how brave Sam was, I couldn't possibly tell anyone what I had done. Uh-uh. Not now. Maybe not ever.

"Thank you, Sam. You are our rock. You know it was never your place to protect your little brother from something you didn't even know about. Even parents can't do anything if they don't know what's going on." She gazed around the group. "Now, having said that, I also know that a lot of us in this room—myself included—do not, or did not, have the ideal home life with two parents to take care of us, to teach us how to deal. That's bad. But it can be overcome. It can even make us stronger. As Sam said, we have to fight that grief, the grief of never having normal. Fight it with everything we've got. Then, our only job will be to take care of ourselves and no one else. Does that sound selfish?"

"Not selfish," the group muttered. "Necessary."

Dr. Blue smiled. "That's right. If I don't teach you anything other than that, I've done *my* job. We must take care of ourselves before we can take care of anyone else."

A girl in yellow raised her hand. "I'd like to say welcome to the new members."

"Thank you, Analise. Let's have each member stand and tell their name. You may choose to say more, or not. It's up to you."

"Analise Samarripa," the girl in yellow said. "I've been coming here for two months." She smiled and her face was so open, so kind, I could see how easy it would be for other kids—the cruel ones—to hurt her.

The next person was Carson. "I'm new," he said. Then he

sat back down. He seemed a little sullen, as if he'd been forced to come. To his right a boy stood, as jerky as a faulty marionette, and said, "Nathan." When he plopped back down, I felt certain I knew his problem. Drugs. His eyes were as shaky as Sam's knees had been.

The last person to introduce herself, besides me, was a slight girl of indeterminate age. "I'm T'nisha," she mumbled. As she was sitting back down she added. "I wanted to kill myself because I was so tired of my mother's boyfriends having sex with me." A sudden image of a scaly, horned shadow burst into my head. The young girl never raised her eyes from the level of our knees.

"One was my next door neighbor," she added like an afterthought.

"Mine was my uncle's best friend," Nathan said. "He took pictures and everything." He smiled and his entire face appeared to crack like an eggshell. I'd never seen a smile so horrific in my entire life. How had I never noticed these kids creeping through the corridors at school? Granted, a couple of them were still in middle school, but I recognized two of them from Lawson High—their faces at least—I'd just never bothered to really look at them before.

Suddenly, the near-rape in my own hallway didn't seem so bad. Not even the painful episode with Keenan when I was little. Some of these kids had been through Hell and back. Hell. Where the scaly horned monster ruled.

Everyone looked at me. Sam had already gone, so I was the only one left.

I stood in a half-crouch, ready to fall back in my chair as soon as I could. "My name is Benji." I raised my eyes to Dr. Blue, surprising even myself. "My molesters were both boys from school. One older, one the same age. But that's not why I tried to kill myself." I swallowed, hard. "At least, I don't think so. My dad took his own life. And my sister said it was my fault." I thumped back down in my chair, embarrassed, but somehow lighter. I could feel all those eyes on me. Why had I blurted everything out that way?

I became aware of murmurings. Everyone seemed to be saying something. "Welcome, Benji. Welcome to Group."

I felt Sam staring at me from the side.

"Welcome," he said. "It's going to be all right now."

Yeah, I thought. *It'll be all right. Welcome to group. The* Yeah, but I Didn't *group. Haha. So nice to be here. Right where I belong.*

All the air drained out of my lungs and I felt myself collapsing inward. But I didn't faint. My vision grayed, and then cleared.

T'nisha had the floor again. "Four in all," she whispered. "Each one thought he could come in my room whenever he wanted, as soon as my Momma was sleeping." She bit her lip. "I don't live there anymore. I stay with my Grams now. She thinks Momma got paid to let those men in my room." She hunkered down into herself.

Dr. Blue went to her, placed her hands on her shoulders. "We are fighting with you, T'nisha. You are not alone."

The rest of the session flew by as one after the other—except for Carson—stood and told horrid, torrid details of abuse and self-loathing. Between us we'd tried suicide through cutting, hanging, and pills. Even Dr. Blue had tried when she was a teenager and became clinically depressed.

I vowed to ask her in our next private session if she, too, had been abused in some way, but I didn't have the guts to do it in front of the group. Of us all, only Sam and Carson had not been sexually abused in some way. And compared to the others, my situation felt exceedingly minor. Except for the part about my father, of course.

When it was over, Sam waited until I stood. "Is your Mom picking you up?"

I nodded. It felt so strange to think he was the same boy at the funeral only two days earlier. How had I not seen that scar? "I can't believe you tried the same thing I did. Well, I mean, sort of."

"Yeah." We went through the revolving door together. "Most days, I can't believe it, either. Is that how you feel?"

"Exactly. It feels like some other girl did that. Not me. Like, I mean, I'm not a girl who would do something like that, you know?" I grabbed the silver pipe handrail to go down the steps beside the fountain. It was warm, but not scorching hot the way it would be in a few more weeks. "Summer's almost here." I knew it was an inane comment, but for some reason I wanted to keep him talking.

"Hey." He stopped by the fountain. "Do those boys still go to Lawson High?"

I knew which boys he meant. I sat on one of the benches facing the burbling water. "Does it matter?"

He sat beside me. "I want to know who they are, but I don't know if I should." He scraped his hair back with his fingers. "I wanna kick their asses, that's what I really want."

I liked that. It made me feel like a million bucks. "As much as I want to, I guess I won't tell you—don't want you to get in trouble." I wanted to say more, say something about how he was my knight in shining armor, but I somehow couldn't think with him sitting there in the sunlight so near. What came out instead was, "I'll never tell anyone their names."

I looked at him but he was in silhouette, the sun blocking out his face the way it had done Janie's at The Pizza Palace.

"I understand." He touched the back of my hand with his index finger. "I hate that you went through that." He didn't say anything else.

"Yeah," I said. "It was a shock, but I got away, both times. After hearing the stories in group, I realize it wasn't really that big of a deal—"

"No." Sam shook his head. The shape of his wild hair made dragon-like shadows on the cement walkway. "Don't ever say that."

I started to ask what he meant, but he continued.

"Don't ever say it doesn't matter, because it does. No one has the right to hurt you. Ever." He scraped an errant lock of hair back again. "There are mean people, stupid people. Like the ones who bullied Tanner."

"Yeah," I said. "It is a type of bullying, I guess. Not just about sex." And then my face flamed at the realization that I'd said something about sex like I knew what I was talking about.

Mom's car rounded the corner. "There's my Mom." I stood. "Thank you for helping me through that session."

"It's good for us." He grinned. "What doesn't kill us—"

"Gives us fodder for our art."

He laughed. "If you say so."

Mom didn't seem to notice Sam. She was tapping away on her phone as I climbed in the car beside her.

"Everything all right?"

She looked up, nodded. "Talking to Janie, a bit. It's easier through text, isn't it?"

I wouldn't know, I thought. "Probably. I hope she comes

back and goes to prom and stuff. At least graduation. She's so close."

Mom put the car in drive. "I'm trying to talk her into it. She already has enough credits to graduate, so she isn't in danger of failing or anything. They even said she could take her finals over the internet or something."

"Wow. The school is sure being accommodating."

Mom pursed her lips. "I guess they haven't had to work with a lot of parent suicides. They are bending over backwards for us."

I pressed my spine into the seat. "That's good. Isn't it?" To myself I thought, *Is it?* Letting Janie skip everything, all those high school rites of passage? I tried to imagine ten years down the road, or even five. Would she regret it?

Why do I even care? I leaned my head back. "How was your showing?"

Mom propped her phone in the drink holder. "They liked the house. We're putting in an offer this afternoon."

"That's great, Mom. I'm glad." And I really was glad. Getting back to normal. That's all I felt we could ask for at this point.

I twisted in my seat to see where Sam had gone, but he was no longer visible. We turned the corner and headed home.

Thirty

First Place

When we pulled up to the house, the whole street seemed extra quiet, waiting. "Well," Mom said. "Here we are."

I got out. *Yep. Here we are.* "I kind of hope that Homebound teacher comes soon, I don't really know what to do without school. I mean. This summer I was going to try and get a part time job. But I can't do that during the school year, right?"

"No, I don't think so." Mom looped her arm around my shoulders. "I'll call school right now. Get an update."

We walked in the house together just as Mom's phone rang. She glanced at the screen. "It's Janie." She hesitated, and then touched the speaker icon.

"Mom?" My sister's voice sounded way younger than it should have.

Mom placed her purse on the end table before she answered. "Hi, baby. How are you doing?"

A small sigh. "I feel awful. I'm just, I'm so nauseous all the time, and I finally did the test and it came back positive. But, I couldn't tell you in person. Not after everything—"

"I understand." Mom didn't look at me, but it was clear she had the conversation on speaker so I could take part if I wanted. "How far along?"

"Six weeks I think," Janie whispered. "Shawn said we'd talk about it. About what to do. Then he changed. Told me he couldn't. Couldn't do it."

"Couldn't deal with it, you mean?"

"I guess."

Mom drew in breath. "So what does he want to do? Just ignore it, hope it will go away?"

I winced. It wasn't like Mom to be sarcastic.

"We were going to either get married or get an abortion. I was hoping for marriage. In Vegas, remember?"

Mom's face paled. "Yes, of course. But we didn't know then. Why didn't you tell us?"

"I just said I didn't want to add more pain to the mix. You had all you could handle with Dad and then Benji."

I sat on the couch and tried not to make any noise. Mom might not know it, but I knew without a doubt that if Janie even suspected I was listening in, she would go ballistic. Especially since I would know what a hypocrite she was. I mean, she accused me of being pregnant, and all along, it was her.

"I always have time for you, sweetie. Please remember that." Mom cleared her throat. "Now. What do *you* want to do? Have the baby?"

"Shawn said we could still get an abortion." She let the statement hang in the balance and it reminded me of Sam's scar.

"What do *you* want?" Mom asked again. "After all, he isn't the one who would undergo the procedure. That would be you, no way around it. He isn't the one carrying the child, either, feeling life growing."

Way to go, Mom, I cheered. I was proud of her for letting her feelings about abortion be known without preaching. At least I thought that's what she had done.

"Right." Janie said softly. "I couldn't do that. I couldn't kill a baby. And Mom, I don't think I could have it and then give it away."

Crumpled silence filled the gap.

"I will support you, whatever you decide, Janie. We all will. Your family. Me, Benji, Uncle A, Gran and Gramps."

"I want to have this baby," she blurted. "But I want to go to college, too. Can I do that?"

Mom sighed. Then she appeared to regret it. "Of course you can. You will have to work, too. Babies aren't cheap. But it's doable. Women do it all the time."

"I don't know about Shawn, though. I told him I would call him after I figured out what I was going to do."

"Good. That's a good start. But first, what about finishing high school?"

It was Janie's turn to sigh. "I can do it online. Take my finals, I mean. The rest of it, prom and stuff, seems sort of superficial now."

"Can you bring yourself to walk across the stage?"

I thought it hurt Mom to ask that. I thought she was asking because maybe that's every parent's dream, to see their kid walk across that stage. I thought if I could hear that, maybe Janie could, too.

"Mom," Janie said, "Gran wants to talk to you."

Mom and Gran talked on speaker for a few minutes. Gran told her not to worry, Janie would be fine. She said we'll have a new little grandbaby and maybe that is God's way of making up for what my dad did. She sounded excited. I wondered how much of Janie's decision to have the baby came from Gran.

"Maybe you're right," Mom said. They spoke a few more

minutes, and then Janie got back on the phone and Mom told her to call the school tomorrow and figure out what she needed to do to take those finals.

"I will," Janie said. "And I may come home, if that's okay. I don't know if I want to stay here until it's born, or come home and face everyone." She hesitated. "I guess I definitely have to put off starting college until afterward. I can't imagine starting college five or six months pregnant."

I almost laughed at that image, but I managed to get control just in time.

"It's up to you, sweetheart. Just take it easy for a few days and pray about it."

Janie stayed silent.

"We'll be praying for you, here."

"O—Okay. Thanks, Mom."

Janie wasn't a church-goer. She wasn't a meat eater. She was something of an agnostic-tree-hugger-wannabe. At least when she wasn't mad at the world.

"Call me anytime," Mom said. "Do you want me to contact Shawn's mother? I mean, does she know everything about why y'all were going to elope?"

"He said he told his folks, but I don't believe him. I think he's lying, hoping I'll get an abortion and then they won't have to find out. You know he's got a scholarship to Tech, right?"

"Oh, I remember," Mom said. "It was in the paper when he signed the letter of intent."

Janie sighed again. "I'll call you tomorrow. I'm not going to worry about what he does or doesn't want. This is my body. My baby."

"Good girl." Mom hesitated. "But don't forget, it is half

his. He needs to take responsibility for half the cost at least. Research the costs of having children while you are online tonight. It may make you think twice about letting him be an ostrich."

"Okay." Janie didn't sound quite as confident as before. "I'll research. Beginning with how the heck I'm going to pay the hospital—"

"You're on my insurance until you're twenty-two as long as you're enrolled in college. So—you may have to start out with satellite or online classes even before the baby comes. To stay on my insurance I mean."

"Oh my God. So much to think about."

I felt my sister's pain, her confusion about the future. Once again, my problems seemed small. And I vowed not to ever let myself get pregnant until I was married and settled into the career of my choice. Geez. What a mess.

Mom told her to get some rest, and then they disconnected.

Not long after, Uncle Aidan called. "Tell Ben I'm bringing her a surprise after work."

Mom laughed. "You just told her, I had you on speaker."

"Good," he said. "I had a great meeting this morning. Been a good day at work, too. Sold a car just a few minutes ago, now I'm about to chow down at Whataburger. Hangover's almost gone. That's always a plus."

Mom shook her head and twirled her index finger around her ear. "He's kooky," she mouthed at me.

I nodded. He sure seemed recovered. I don't know why I found that suspicious. Maybe I just didn't have enough experience with drunks to know the drill.

"We'll expect you for supper," Mom said. "I've got to go start the paperwork for an offer on a house I showed this morning."

"Sounds like you had a good one, too." It was obvious his mouth was full. "Want me to bring anything?"

"Chips and salsa, please. I'm making fajitas."

"You got it, see ya around six."

Mom rolled her eyes and grinned. "I love that boy. He's always been like my child instead of my brother."

I smiled back at her. "I love him, too. I sure hope he's done drinking."

"Amen to that, honey. Amen to that." She picked up her bag and told me to take it easy and she'd see me soon.

Sometimes I wondered why she wasn't more worried about me. About leaving me alone, I mean. But then, why should she be? I'd learned my lesson. I was pretty certain I would never try to harm myself again.

I went to the kitchen and put a pan of water on the stove for Ramen noodles. I wasn't starving, but I knew I couldn't wait until six o'clock. Noodles would hold me. After checking all the doors to make certain they were closed and locked, I filled a glass with crushed ice and covered it with root beer. Then I began to wonder why it was called *beer,* so I spent the next half hour eating noodles and scrolling the internet to learn about the origin of root beer.

I felt a slight tug of curiosity about my old accounts on FB and Instagram. The others I didn't care that much about, but those two had tons of pictures that I hoped were still there. On the other hand, most of the pictures revolved around me and Kera, or me and Will, so maybe I didn't want them after all.

Lack of social media had begun to eat away at me. Like my sketched in dad-figure with the center missing, I felt incomplete. A stray thought struck me. Sam probably had to go right back to school after Group. How did he get there? I hadn't even asked. Boy, I had become extremely self-centered. Was my personality changing like my memory? If so, was that a good thing, or a bad thing? I didn't think I could be objective enough to tell.

Does anyone really know his or her own personality? I could tell you I have brown hair and blue eyes. I could say I like all kinds of music and I could name a million favorite books, but was that my personality?

I looked it up. There were a jillion definitions and they all varied. Some said personality means how nice or appealing you are. How caring, or callous. Another said personality means how you treat others and how you see yourself fitting into society, into the world. But I always thought it also included how you feel about yourself.

One study implied that a person's personality is almost completely developed by age five. If that's true, then I didn't know who the hell I was. At age five, I couldn't even look people in the eye.

I'm much stronger than that now.

Don't believe everything you read, right?

I pored over the internet a while longer. Should I make new profiles? Surely it wouldn't hurt to get on and just... check. I closed the computer and jumped up. I had to do something. Of course I knew I couldn't stay off everything forever, but maybe Mom was right. Maybe it was too soon.

For the first time, I thought of texting Sam. But he was in class. I didn't feel quite strong enough to go for another walk. What if I went too far, got lost again, forgot how to get back?

Finally I went to the bathroom, turned the shower on the hardest setting possible, stripped quickly, and stood under the warm spray until the water ran cold. Shivering, I lathered and rinsed my hair and wrapped a large towel around my body and another around my head like a turban.

Then I stood in front of the steamed-up medicine cabinet mirror and looked at my face. It looked familiar at first, same old me, but the longer I stared, the stranger it became. The stranger I became.

At last I closed my eyes and wiped away the blurry image. The thin girl there no longer appeared to have anything to do with Benji Marie Stevens. Nothing. I didn't know her at all.

In an attempt to turn off my escalating thoughts, I concentrated on combing out my hair and moisturizing my skin. Music, that's what I needed.

I pulled on baggy shorts and a tee shirt, and grabbed my phone. I started to press the music icon but the little number one beside the message icon caught my eye. A few weeks ago, that wouldn't have been a surprise, Kera, Will, and I had messaged back and forth constantly. Now, getting a message was quite a surprise.

I touched the icon and Jenny-from-Art's picture appeared. I couldn't think of her last name, but we'd always been friendly. Just not friends. She'd been at the funeral, but wasn't she also the one who had made me so uncomfortable at lunch the last day I'd attended school? The one who acted like I had the plague and then went and gossiped about me to the cheerleader's table? Or had that been Karma Jones?

Another thing I couldn't quite remember.

I looked at her message. Like so much stuff these days, it made absolutely no sense. "Hi," it read. "I wanted to be the first to say 'grats on the Art Show. Maybe I'll see you there."

Huh? I literally scratched my wet head. She was

congratulating me on some art show. WTH? She had been in my Art class. Maybe it was something we'd done and I'd blocked it out.

On the other hand, maybe it was a total prank.

I dashed for my computer as another message came in. Sam this time. He must be at lunch. I glanced at the clock. Lunch? Shoot. School was over for the day. I'd messed around ever since Mom left. Nearly five o'clock already.

I heard a key in the lock. Mom must've finished up early.

I looked back at Sam's text. "Way to go," it read. "You must be stoked!"

Double WTH! What did they know that I didn't? Typing a reply to Sam, I heard Uncle Aidan call out, "Hey! Where is everyone?"

I pressed send on my message to Sam—What are you talking about?—just as Uncle Aidan walked into the kitchen carrying a huge easel like the one I had at school. He also had a large cardboard folder thing under one arm that had a funky little black string tie to close the top. It also had pleated sides like an accordion—to allow it to expand I assumed.

"Is that a portfolio?" I took it from beneath his arm. A plastic bag fell to the floor and a can of Fix-It Art Spray rolled out. I grabbed him in a hug. "Is all this for me?"

He grinned. "Yep." He held up the brown accordion thing. "This is really called a Portfolio Binder. What you put inside will make up your portfolio." He pointed at it. "Looks like a giant file folder, doesn't it?"

"Yeah, and with those expandable sides, it will hold a ton of work." I peeked in the top. "I love it! It will even hold my big paintings like the one at school." I couldn't believe I'd said that. I never wanted to see that watercolor piece again.

"I went to your Art class and visited with Mr. Stanford. He told me what size to get. If you want one made of canvas or nylon we'll have to order it, but this is the one they had at Hobby Lobby."

"You're the best, Uncle A!" I ran to my room and brought back my sketches and unrolled them. "I'll have to lay them out with books to weigh them down, flatten them back out, before I put them in the binder."

My uncle stood near the table, watching me, scratching his head comically. "Don't forget to spray them, too."

"Oh, I won't," I said. "After they're smoothed out again. I don't want it to run into any creases or anything. I had that happen in school once—"

"Speaking of school—"

I grabbed books from the living room shelf and placed one on each corner of the Dad sketch. "What about school?" Something in his tone alarmed me.

"Mr. Stanford asked my permission to enter your heart painting in a Haute Young Artists show at Lawson Junior College."

"You didn't—" I said.

"I'm afraid I did," he interrupted. "He asked me at your dad's viewing. Remember? The two of us talked for a long time. He said he wanted something good to come of that work—that's what he called it, your work—because it was obviously very powerful."

My knees turned to Jell-O and I plopped onto one of the shaker dining chairs. "Oh, Uncle A. I don't know about that. I'm afraid people will just make fun of it all over again."

"Too late," he said. "I've already done it. Gave my permission right then and there. Lied. Said I'd ask you, then I sauntered right back over to him and told him you agreed."

He wasn't even apologetic. "But you don't know the things they said. Everyone made fun of it, made fun of me for making it. Oh, Uncle. You don't know what you've done." I felt hard tears prick my eyelids. They were tears of anger that he hadn't asked me. Just lied and said yes.

"Well, you can be mad if you want." He sat in a chair across from me at the table. "But it won't do any good. The thing is hanging in the Student Art Gallery at LJC right now. It has a giant blue ribbon on it. The instructors—three of them—were the judges." He waited for me to respond. When I didn't, he continued, "You won first place, baby girl. You beat 'em all. There were fifty-something entries and most were from the college classes."

My phone buzzed on the table beside my sketches. I reached across and poked the message. It was from Sam. "What am I talking about? Your first place of course! They announced it on the PA right before the bell rang."

"Oh my God," I said. And then I typed it, too. "OMG. My uncle let Mr. S enter it. I had no idea until JUST NOW!"

"Awesome," Sam wrote. "I told you it was special."

I sent him a big Smiley Face. "Thanks, Sam. I'm sort of in shock."

To my uncle, I gave a stern look. But I couldn't hold it. "They really thought it was good?"

He jumped up and came around the table to me. "Honey, they think it's great. And the best part is, there's a scholarship that goes along with it. The award ceremony is tomorrow. The media will be there and everything."

My phone buzzed again. This time it was a Congrats message from Steph, also from Art. I sent back a quick TY and a Smiley. "Now, tell me more about the scholarship.

Does that mean I can take Art classes at Lawson Junior College now?"

Uncle Aidan threw his head back. "I don't know about that. You'll have to find out tomorrow." He made a big show of wiping pretend-sweat off his brow. "I'm just so glad you're not mad at me. After I'd said yes, I began to doubt myself."

I hugged him again, and then socked him in the shoulder with my fist. "It worked out for the best, this time." I gave him a playful warning look. "But I still can't believe you lied like that!"

"I'm a scoundrel, what can I say?" He flinched as if he thought I might slug him again.

Mom walked in carrying a large plastic bag from Rosa's, our local Mexican restaurant chain. We both hurried to help her. "What on earth is going on? You two didn't even hear me come in." She put her purse on the counter beside the plastic bags of takeout. "The paperwork took longer than I thought it would so I decided to let Rosa's make the fajitas." She grinned. "I even got the chips and salsa in case my little brother forgot."

"Sure," I said. "Act like you don't know what's going on."

She looked seriously perplexed. "What do you mean?"

I glanced at my uncle.

"She really doesn't," he said.

"Well," I took paper plates someone had given us for all that funeral food and set them on the kitchen island since the dining table was in use. "Uncle Aidan told a big lie and allowed Mr. Stanford to enter my stupid painting in a college art show—"

"And it won!" he interrupted.

I shot him what I hoped was another scathing look, but I

couldn't keep the grin off my face. My phone buzzed again, but I didn't even bother to check it. The look on Mom's face was comical.

She hauled me to her in a swift hug. "I prayed for something good to happen," she murmured.

"It's even got a scholarship attached," I mumbled against her shoulder. "I don't know how much but, *ain't it cool?*"

She laughed at our old joke. "Very cool, baby. Very cool indeed." She immediately tore a corner off a paper towel and wrote First Place—Art along with today's date. Then she grabbed an old Mason jar out of the cabinet, unscrewed the top, and dropped the little note inside.

After replacing the lid, she took a Sharpie marker from the coffee cup holder on the counter and wrote ANSWERED PRAYERS on the glass. "Every time something good happens," she said, "we'll put a little note in here. By Christmas time, it will be filled." She looked at us, her eyes shiny with unshed tears. "And then when we celebrate Christmas this year, we can take them out and read them, one by one."

"I love that idea." I paused. "But there's just one thing—"

They both waited.

"I didn't pray to win a contest. I didn't even know—"

Mom nodded. "I've been praying for something good to happen. Something to ease this family's pain. I think this is it."

Uncle Aidan beamed.

"Oh." Could it really be that simple? "Well. I guess I'll take it, then." I picked up the Mason jar and hoisted it above my head like a trophy. "Now, how do I find out more about that scholarship?"

Uncle Aidan and Mom both laughed. "The award ceremony is tomorrow evening at seven," Uncle A said. "We will meet the art instructors at six-thirty and they will tell you everything." He grinned. "Mr. Stanford will be there, too."

"I still can't believe you did this." I shook my head. "I'm going to be so nervous."

"But we'll be there with you." Mom squeezed my arm. "I'm so proud of you. And I really do think God had a hand in it. Anyone who wants to join me at Mass tonight, feel free. I think I'll just go and say thanks."

Uncle Aidan shrugged. "Got nothin' better to do."

I had a momentary pang of doubt. "I've never been inside a Catholic church."

"It's up to you," Mom said. "Now, let's eat." She filled glasses with ice while I assembled the fajitas and chips on the island.

"Pass me that guacamole, Ben," Uncle Aidan said. "Can't have a celebration without guac, right?"

We laughed. It was the best celebration we'd had in forever.

Thirty-One

Bandages Across the Sky

The church was surreal. I'd never seen such opulence in my life. The stained glass windows were beautiful works of art. There were twelve of them; six down each side of the nave.

"The stations of the cross," Mom said when she saw me studying them.

That made sense.

The priest gave instructions to the sparse congregation—it was a weeknight, after all—and every mouth answered in unison. That kind of freaked me out. Then he read a gentle homily, a woman sang to her own guitar, the congregation sang another song along with her, and then it was time for communion. "I don't know—" I began.

"No, you don't have to." Mom patted my knee. "In fact, you haven't been to confession, so you shouldn't."

I nodded. I had no idea what she meant, but I was glad I didn't have to walk up there in front of everyone and take the bread and wine.

Mom did it, though. And I have to admit it was quite moving.

Uncle Aidan didn't take communion, either. He leaned over to me. "My AA meetings are held in the basement." He waved his hand around. "This is way fancier."

After services, Mom introduced us to the priest, Father Flanagan. I remembered his name from her *Daily Devotionals* book. He shook my hand and invited me to attend their youth classes on Tuesday nights.

I thanked him, but I couldn't imagine joining a room full of kids my age. What if someone from Group was there? Or worse, one of the uglies from school. One of those who had texted or messaged me?

In the car, we were all silent. Finally, Mom couldn't stand it any longer. "Well? What did y'all think?"

"Very peaceful," I said. "I loved those windows."

Mom laughed. "Of course, you did."

Uncle Aidan put the Green Hornet in drive and we roared away from the church. "I love it." His voice still had that jolly timbre. "Anything to keep me on the straight and narrow. At least until Miss Right comes along."

"Miss Right?" I giggled. "I heard you were already dating her at the car lot."

He treated me to a menacing look. "You did, huh?" His glance skated across me to Mom. "Now who would've told you something like that?"

I jerked my thumb toward Mom in jest. "We gotta look out for you, Unc. That's all there is to it." It felt so good to have something to joke about again.

"No worries, there." His voice lost some of its jolliness. "Neither of them are Miss Right. Both of 'em like to party a little too much. Don't young women want to settle down anymore?"

Mom reached over and patted his arm. "The right one will come along when you least expect it, little brother." She drew her hand back and looked out the window. I know she didn't intend for us to see the sad look on her face, but from the back seat I caught a glimpse in the side mirror.

Poor Mom. The love of her life deserted her, and then killed himself. Is that real love? Is there any such thing?

We drove home through the cool night. I had a momentary twinge of guilt for feeling happy. Should I feel that way when my sister is falling apart and my dad is—

Uncle Aidan made the turn onto our street before my brain could complete that thought. *You aren't responsible for taking care of everyone else.* Dr. Blue's words appeared in my mind like a little neon sign. *Just worry about taking care of yourself. Let yourself be happy.* Why is that so hard to do? Oh yeah, because I love them.

My thoughts surprised me. I loved them? Sure I loved my mom and my uncle—but Janie? I hated her. She hated me. It was that simple.

My thoughts were swirling around in my head so that I don't even remember walking in the house. Uncle Aidan came in with us, but he just kissed us both on the cheek and then said he was going to head on home for some shuteye. "I'll pick you girls up tomorrow for the awards ceremony," he called over his shoulder.

"I still can't believe he did that." I closed the door behind him. When I twisted the deadbolt, it reminded me of the day I'd run through the house after Paul left, locking all the doors. My fingers felt my forehead, where the lump had been, but of course it was gone.

"Honey?" Mom came up behind me. "You all right?"

I turned toward her, coming back to the present. "Oh sure. Just you know, shock."

Mom's eyes said she didn't quite believe that. "You sure?

For a minute there, I thought that headache had returned."

I shook my head, but it worried me, too. For a minute there, I thought the past had returned. "Nah," I said. "Sad things just sort of pop up in my head without my say so. Does that happen to you?"

Mom put her arm around my shoulder. "It sure does. That's called grief. It takes a long time to get over. If we ever do."

I told her what Dr. Blue said about fighting grief with all our might.

"I like that woman," Mom said. "I'm going to go, and I think the family therapy will be helpful, if we can get Janie on board with it."

I hesitated, and then spoke my mind. "You and I could go even if Janie won't. Maybe even Uncle A. He kinda has some things to deal with, too, doesn't he?"

Mom chuckled. "Well, I hadn't thought of that, but you know what? It probably couldn't hurt."

"I like having him close to us. Part of our family."

"I do, too," she said. "My little brother. I know he isn't perfect, but I will never stop loving him. I just hate that he couldn't be part of us while your dad was around."

I didn't know what to say to that so I didn't say anything at all.

"G'night, Mom." I touched my lips to her cheek the same way Uncle Aidan had done. It isn't what we ever did, but tonight seemed to call for a little more than just a hug.

Mom touched my hair. "Love you sweetie." She kissed me on the forehead. "Want me to come and tuck you in?"

I laughed and crossed to the hallway. "I guess not." I held up my phone. "I have a few messages to look through."

Her smile faltered. "Want me to do it first? Just to make sure they're all on the up and up?"

That stopped me in my tracks. "You know what?" I mulled it over. "That's not a bad idea."

She took my phone and opened messages, scrolled, handed it back. "Not a bad one in the bunch. How about that?"

My eyes widened and I glanced through the names. Ten messages had popped up. Most were people from my Art class, but a few were from Choir as well. There was even one from Karma Jones in World Lit. Gee. But they could all wait. First I wanted to text Sam and tell him everything was good.

"Hey, Mom?"

She stopped to listen.

"Maybe things are turning around."

"They are." She turned out the kitchen light. "I've been praying."

I didn't tell her I'd been praying from time to time as well. Why did it embarrass me? Was I afraid for people to know I believed in God? When had being a Christian become a bad thing?

Entering my room, I opened Sam's last text, but before I could type anything, another one *binged* through.

Janie's name appeared.

I immediately clicked it. "I'm sorry," it read. "I heard about your award. A couple of people from school said it came on the announcements. I thought it was a stupid painting, but I guess I was wrong."

"Thank you." My thumbs flew over the keypad. "How are you doing? Are you OK?"

"I guess Mom told you," she replied.

"Uh, yeah."

I could almost hear her sigh all the way from Oklahoma

before she wrote, "I'm all right. Gran is helping me figure things out."

"Good." I sent her a thumbs up icon. "Let me know if I can help." I hit send and immediately wished I hadn't. It seemed pompous of me to think I could help her, my big sister. But there it was. *Whoosh.* Sent. Oh, well.

Several seconds passed. I didn't even see the little pulsing ellipses that meant she was writing back. Maybe she thought it pompous, too. I went back to reading the texts from kids at school.

"Way to go!"

"Awesome award!"

"'grats Benji!"

And several more in that vein. Most had emojis accompanying them. A couple were *only* emojis, and somehow I liked those best. Words seemed scary now, after all the ugly ones I'd gotten before. But those hadn't been from these kids. Nope. This bunch had been mostly silent. Maybe they'd been there all along, just waiting for a cue from someone else on how to react. Like that old bullying commercial on TV: Teach Your Kid Not To Be a Bystander.

I knew I was grasping at straws. I'd prayed hard for understanding and this happened. Maybe this *was* my understanding, like Mom said about Uncle A. Not everyone is perfect. Many of these were the same kids who had come to Dad's funeral. And I'd automatically assumed they were there just to cut class.

My phone binged with another message from Janie. "Thanks," it read.

At least she didn't tell me to disappear this time. And if I hoped for anything more from her, like saying she regretted blaming me for dad's death, I could probably wait till icicles formed at the gates of Hell. That's what Gramps would say.

But at least she'd said sorry about my painting. That was something.

To make myself stop examining every single texter's motive—*allow yourself to be happy*—I opened Sam's message again. "Hey," I wrote. "You still up?"

He immediately replied. "Yep. Strumming my old gee-tar. Thinking about your award ceremony tomorrow."

Wow. Not what I expected him to say. "Cool. I didn't know you played."

He sent a pic of a beat up acoustic balanced on his knee. "Want to hear something?"

"Sure."

My Facetime rang. When I accepted, he was already playing "Operator," an ancient classic by Jim Croce. He had a nice voice, kinda rough.

"Why aren't you in Choir?" I asked when he finished.

He laughed and began to strum another. This one by Ed Sheeran. He didn't sing this time. I hoped I hadn't put him off with my Choir comment.

"You're good," I said. "That's one of my favorite songs."

"You mentioned you liked him one day." He strummed a few more bars. "Why do you think I learned it?"

Another surprise.

Then he said, "You sing, too, don't you?"

I turned the camera away so he couldn't see me blush. "I used to. When I still went to school."

"Tell me what to play so you can sing."

"No," I laughed. "I don't know you that well." I still had a deep fear of being humiliated again, like with my painting. I didn't think Sam would, but better to guard my heart.

Sam put his guitar aside. "If you change your mind, let me know. I love to play and sing. Don't know if I can ever make any money with it, but I'd sure like to do something with music, you know?"

"Yes, I do know. My little award comes with an Art scholarship and that's got me wondering if I could someday support myself with Art. It's kind of hard to imagine, being responsible for bills and stuff, you know?"

He laughed. "Yeah. You don't know what you just said. My dad is always on me about choosing a career. Figuring out what I want to be. How I'm going to make a living." He fell back on his bed as if in agony.

"Wow. So tell me, young man, what are your plans for zee future?" I laid a lock of my hair across my upper lip and peered into the camera, twirling the hair like a mustache.

Sam smiled and every time he did I marveled again at that one slightly crooked tooth. Is that what made me trust him; the fact that he wasn't perfect and he didn't try to hide it?

"Zee future? I'll show you zee future!" He jumped up, grabbed his guitar, twanged his fingers across the strings, threw his head forward like an 80s head-banger and said, "I'm gonna be a Rock Star!" And then he started wailing an old song about wanting to rock all night. I knew I'd heard it, but I couldn't remember the name of the song or the band—*but don't worry about not remembering*, my simple mind whispered, *it's probably nothing.*

He played and screeched so loudly I had to turn down the volume on my phone. When he finished, he said, "Thank ya, thank ya vera much. Elvis has now left the building."

I collapsed laughing. That was exactly what my Gramps always said; *Elvis has left the building*. For Sam to know that old line made me trust him even more.

"Okay." He fell back, out of breath, "Now about this awards ceremony—am I invited, or not?"

"Ummm. Do you *want* to come? I mean, I never thought."

He didn't hesitate. "I want to come. And soon I want to come over and get you and take you to a movie or something. I mean, when I get my license."

"Sounds good." I had no idea if my mom would let me go with him when he got his license. With Will it had just been hanging out together or with a bunch of friends. Our parents took us everywhere. This could be a real game changer.

Sam stared straight at the camera, unsmiling. "But until I get my license, maybe I could just come over and play games, or music?"

I pulled my knees up to my chest, looped my arm around them, and hugged myself. Tried to look at the camera like he was doing, but I couldn't make myself look directly into his face. "Okay. After tomorrow things might settle down a little. If you do come over, it will have to be when my mom is here, though. Not when she's at work."

"Of course," he said.

I unfolded myself and stood, stretching. My curtains were slightly open. I went to close them, but a breeze had sprung up and I couldn't resist pulling up the window sash a few inches. My old swings creaked a little under the rising moon.

What an eerie scene.

There were so many things back there that screamed *Dad* it felt as if I'd gone back in time. Back to when I was three and Dad had brought that swing set home. Now the chains were rusty and the slide had a loose screw that ripped your skin if you didn't know to avoid it. At least that's what I remember from the last time I tried it—two years ago.

In the corner of the yard stood the ancient tree house we should have taken down years ago. Even the mulberry tree itself had been planted by Dad. He and Mom had clashed over that, too. She'd told him to be certain he got a fruitless variety but he'd brought home this one instead. The patio had permanent purple stains from the berries.

For a while I just stood there, holding the frilled edge of the curtain, the creak of my old swing punctuating my thoughts. No matter how I tried, I couldn't wrap my head around the fact that my dad was gone. As if he'd never existed.

Of course, he'd left us earlier, left us like we didn't even matter. Somehow that made it both easier to accept his death, and somehow so much harder.

Sam cleared his throat. I'd forgotten all about him.

I looked down. "Thanks for coming to the funeral." I said. "That was so hard."

"You're welcome. I think it's important sometimes just to show up."

I thought about that. "Yeah, my mom said that very same thing recently. I guess sometimes that's all you can do. Show up. And stay."

"Yes," he agreed. "Sometimes that's the most important thing."

We were silent for a few seconds.

"What are you looking at, outside?"

I turned the phone around, pointed him toward the window. "Just my old swing. My dad bought it when I was really small."

"Ahhh. Good memories?"

"Maybe," I said.

"I know it's a stupid question, but... are you all right?"

Gauzy white clouds stretched across the dark sky like fresh bandages. Some of the tree limbs were stark, no bark at all. Probably need to be pruned or something. Who had been doing that? Funny I'd never noticed the dead branches until now.

"Benji?"

I kept him pointed toward the window. "I saw my Dad last night, Sam. He came and sat on my bed and looked at me until I woke up. But now he's gone. He's just no more. Do you think I'm crazy?"

"No. Not at all. I believe in spirits. Why is that any harder to believe than the fact that we are born from a tiny microscopic egg, and we live all our years breathing something we can't see, and our heart and lungs and brain work without us telling them to, and then one day everything stops working and we don't even always know why?"

"Thank you." My voice was low, but I kept talking, hoping he could hear me, also hoping he couldn't. "I just can't believe he did this on purpose. He broke the circle, again. This time, permanently. And he didn't even tell me anything last night. Didn't even say goodbye." I hesitated. "I'm super pissed at him."

"I'm not going to say I understand exactly." Sam's voice seemed even deeper than it had before. "But well, the circle isn't completely broken. I mean there's still you and your sister, part of him."

"That's the problem. He left us behind. Again. Like—like nothing. Like not even worth fighting for." My voice crumbled. "Whatever he was going through, he didn't even stick around to see me that night. He saw Mom. And he saw Janie outside in her car. He even told her he loved her, but not me, he didn't even bother—"

"No wonder you're so pissed."

"Yeah. I kept telling myself that's why he came by that last night, but now, I don't know. He's just gone like some animal run over beside the road. Like roadkill. Like no soul. No purpose. No nothing." I inhaled to keep from bawling. "Maybe we're all just animals, and religion and all that really is just a ruse. A—a panacea for the masses. Like it says in so many books."

"Religion is the opiate of the masses. That's the quote I read. Believe it or not, this I understand." He didn't wait for me to agree or disagree. "My mom died of cancer when I was only four. I barely have any memory of her. My grandparents took us in, my dad, me, and my little brother, Tanner. But after a few years, my grandparents retired to Florida and then it was just the three of us. Me, Tanner, and Dad."

He stopped talking.

"And then Tanner passed away."

"Yeah." His voice had a ragged edge. "I went to middle school, he stayed in elementary. I didn't even know what he was going through."

"Oh, God—"

"No. It's all right. It was last year. Dr. Blue has really helped. You know, I've been seeing her since we got here. She was recommended by my old doctor in Dallas. She really keeps me sane. Somewhat." He laughed a dark little laugh.

"I guess you do understand. I can't believe you listen to me go on and on about my crappy life when you've faced so much—"

"Nah. Everyone has crap, right? It's like that old Facebook meme. *Be kind to everyone you meet, you don't know what they're facing at home.*"

"Right." I suddenly wanted to change the subject. I didn't want to think about sadness and suicide anymore. "Like your friend, Bucky Tabor."

"Yeah, maybe. I know most of the kids pity him, look down on him. But Bucky's a pretty happy dude as long as people let him be himself."

"Really?"

"Yeah, he has tons of interests outside school. He plays guitar, that's how we first connected—he was playing air guitar at lunch—he does Karate, collects superhero comics, and he loves to cook."

"Wow. He sounds pretty cool."

"He is," Sam said. "As long as you don't expect him to act like everyone else."

I thought about that. How I never even thought about getting to know Bucky, or anyone like him.

"You know," Sam continued. "My little brother had some challenges. Dyslexia. ADHD. But to me, he was just Tanner, my little bro."

"Oh—"

"It seems like Bucky has become one of my best friends."

My breath caught up in my throat. I wanted to ask who his other best friends were, but of course I could never do that.

"I think you'd like Bucky once you got to know him. Especially since I consider you my other best friend."

There. He'd said it so I didn't have to wonder. That was the best thing about Sam. He didn't play games.

"Seriously? I'm your other best friend?" I liked the idea. But could I really be best friends with someone whose other best friend had autism? I'd have to think about that. Kera and I, and even Will, sometimes especially Will, always went out of our way to avoid Bucky and others like him. We weren't mean, or rude—not really—but we sure didn't sit with them or try to carry on a conversation or anything.

I'm a hypocrite just like Janie. I expect everyone to be okay with my idiosyncrasies—like my art—and yet, my first thought about Bucky is to avoid him because he's different. Jeez. Talk about needing to do some work in therapy. Or in church.

I finally took Sam and turned away from the sad window.

We talked for hours until I finally yawned so wide that he couldn't conceal his laughter. "I'm going to let you go to sleep," he said. "I will be there tomorrow. But you don't have to worry about me. I'll just be like, around. Okay?"

I thought that was about the nicest thing anyone had ever done for me, besides Mr. Stanford entering it in the first place. And Uncle Aidan letting him, that is. The fact that Sam wanted to come and see me get the award without even expecting anything in return, that floored me.

"For real?" I asked.

"Yeah," he whispered. "For reals. I'll see you tomorrow." He disconnected without another word.

Strange guy, I thought. *Maybe that's why I like him.*

Maybe there's hope for me yet.

Thirty-Two

If Not for That Pain

The award ceremony began at two o'clock in the fine arts gallery of Lawson Junior College. My painting had been framed and hung on the gallery wall along with the other student entries.

The talent hanging on those walls amazed me. The fact that my little piece of art won first place made absolutely no sense. I saw at least a dozen that were so much better. Especially in the technique department.

Seeing it up there in living color—all that red—filled me with an immense desire to take it down and start over. I knew it could be so much better if I'd only had a chance to work on it a little more.

A horrible thought crossed my mind as I sat there trying to listen to the president of the college as he gave his "wonderful opportunity for students" speech. *What if they only gave me this award because of my circumstances, because of what my dad had done, what I'd tried to do? What if this was nothing more than a pity ribbon?*

No, they wouldn't do that, would they? I wouldn't put it past Uncle Aidan to insert that idea into Mr. Stanford's head, but no, Uncle wouldn't have known anything about this, would he? Besides, bad things happened to good people all the time. I didn't have the corner on that market.

I looked at the rows of paintings and mixed media works. I wanted to ask Sam if *he* thought it might be a pity award. He'd tell me the truth. I think.

After the president of the college spoke, Mr. Stanford took the stage. It took a moment for me to focus on what he was saying.

"—very honored to present this award," he said. "The level of talent and passion in our college and high school art classes continues to amaze me."

I'd forgotten he also taught a couple of classes at the college. No wonder there were both high school and college students entered into this show. I'd be interested to know how many times his high school students had won.

"But this first place winner," he indicated my painting, "showed a level of maturity not often seen in one so young. In fact," he looked straight at me, "this year's recipient of the Young Artist Scholarship and Blue Ribbon is the youngest winner ever."

The applause startled me.

"Benji Stevens," he called above the din, "please come up and accept this award on behalf of myself, Lawson Junior College, and the Greater Lawson Community of the Arts."

Mom had to push me to get me out of my seat. My legs were encased in concrete; knees wouldn't bend at all. I glanced around for Sam and there he sat, smiling, just behind and to the left of Uncle Aidan. As I made my way to the podium, I saw the two of them stand almost simultaneously.

When they stood, so did the rest of their rows, and then the entire audience was on its feet, still clapping. I thought I might faint again.

Mr. Stanford stepped out to meet me. Maybe he saw the

panic on my face. He took me by the arm and guided me up the two steps to the tall wooden podium.

There, he handed me the over-sized blue ribbon and adjusted the microphone downward so that I could speak into it.

I thanked him and pulled out the index card with my mini-speech written in bold block letters. Mom had helped me come up with it this morning. I knew if I didn't write something down I would be mute when the time came to say thank you.

Standing in front of the microphone, I looked out over the sea of faces. I knew some of them, but most were families of the other students who had their work hanging in the gallery alongside mine. There were second and third place winners in the competition as well.

When I took my place in front of the mic, people began to sit down. I waited for the sounds of chair scrapings and program rustlings to abate before I spoke.

At last, I glanced down at my note card. "Thank you," I said. "This award is not only a tremendous honor; it is a tremendous surprise."

Chuckling from a few family members.

I looked out at the faces. "My family has been through a lot recently." I caught Mom's eye. "Art is one way I try to deal with things. Sometimes, it isn't enough, but with help, I think it is becoming one of my best tools." I swallowed, hard. "Please accept my sincere thanks for this honor, and for the scholarship."

More applause.

I started to walk back to my seat, and then I realized I hadn't thanked the two people most responsible. Twirling back to the microphone, I stuttered, "And, m-most of all, thank you to Mr. Stanford and my Uncle Aidan. None of this would have happened without them."

Everyone continued to clap as I made my way back to my seat, face burning with embarrassment. I felt several hands patting me on the back as I went, but I had developed tunnel vision. I couldn't see anything except my chair and the path to get back to it.

The ceremony continued. The second place winner was a college student who created paper collage art out of repurposed materials like old library books, menus, and other printed materials found in the trash. Her piece was a love letter to a dying earth. It was so profound it took my breath away. I could not understand how it didn't win first place.

The third place winner was simply one of the most gifted portrait artists I'd ever seen. His pen and ink portrait of an oil field worker, hardhat tilted back on his head as he stared up at the top of a drilling rig, was so lifelike I would have sworn it was a photograph. Once again, I felt his work outshone mine like starlight outshines a light bulb.

They were very smooth in their acceptance speeches, too. And afterward, they both came right off the stage and told me how incredible *my* work was. "It touched me," Su Lin, the second place winner said. "I could almost feel the heart beating in my own fist as I stared at the two figures."

I hugged her and told her exactly what I thought. That she should have won first place. And then I told Ronald Kovic the same thing about his oil field worker. "It's unbelievable," I said. "So lifelike."

"Photo-realism," he replied. And I nodded because of course that's what it was. It still didn't explain why my little watercolor sketch with a beating heart won first place over his. Not to my eye, at least.

"We are always harder on ourselves than anyone else. I've heard it's that way in most of the arts. We either think we've created a masterpiece each time we put down our brush, or we think everything we do should go straight to the trash."

I laughed at his description. He was a sophomore at Lawson JC, so he was getting ready to transfer to a bigger university. He had obviously been at this game a lot longer than me. "So, if you don't mind me asking," I began, "what are you going to do with your art? How will you make a living?"

When he laughed, it almost crushed me. "That is the big question, isn't it?"

I nodded, wishing I hadn't brought it up.

"I'm going to get a degree in Art History Education while I continue my other classes. That way I can always fall back on teaching if my portraiture doesn't support me."

Mr. Stanford had just come up behind him and I saw him wince as if the boy had struck him in the jaw.

"Thanks," I said. "I'm just trying to think ahead." I nodded toward Mr. Stanford so that the student would know he was there.

Ronald had the good grace to look sheepish as he bowed out of the conversation.

"If this is a dream, I hope I never wake up," I said.

My art teacher smiled. "You're a very talented young lady. Don't let Ron deflate you. He's one of those artists who are afraid to make the leap. I can easily imagine him painting portraits of first ladies if he could ever get past his own self-doubt."

"Whew. I can definitely relate to the self-doubt part. Is

that a prerequisite to being an artist?" I was being facetious, but Mr. S took me seriously.

"Creative people often do suffer from self-doubt or over-inflated egos just like Ron said." He stopped. "But there I go, making generalizations. Look at me. Happy as a clam in my fallback life."

I laughed. I knew that remark had cut him. "I think your life is remarkable."

He patted me, but a wistful look had crept in behind his eyes.

Uncle Aidan came up and grabbed me in a small hug. "Doesn't your painting look great hanging there?"

I glanced over my shoulder toward the wall where it held the place of honor. "I can't really stand to look at it if you want to know the truth."

"Why not?"

My uncle could be so dense. "It came from a place of pain." I whispered the words because even as they left my mouth I realized how arrogant they sounded. Like I really was some suffering artist and not just a 14-year-old high school kid with some watercolors and a brush.

"But look what it got you." Mom had walked up beside Uncle Aidan. "If not for that pain, you wouldn't be standing there holding a certificate that says your whole first year of college is paid for. And you're only in ninth grade."

I felt my face break into a giant smile. I couldn't help it. "Well, yeah. There's that."

Sam approached. He didn't interrupt, but he got close enough that I had to either ignore him or include him. I chose to include him. "Hey," I said, so he would know to join us.

"Mom, Uncle Aidan, this is my friend Sam. From school."

Mom looked him over. I knew she was trying to be surreptitious about it, but Sam must have realized it, too. He ran one hand over his hair self-consciously. It made me wonder if he'd been head banging before he came. His other hand was stuck in the front pocket of his jeans.

"Sam." She held out her hand. "So nice to meet you."

He stopped smoothing his hair and they shook. He smiled and I'd swear a tiny ray of sunlight glinted off those pearly whites just like a toothpaste commercial.

"How ya doin', Bud?" Uncle Aidan held his hand out, too.

Sam shook it much more firmly. "You drive that sweet green Roadrunner."

Uncle Aidan lit up like a Christmas light. "She's mine, all right. You the one with the Camaro?"

Sam nodded and they were off, just like with the texting in the car that day. By the time Mr. Stanford came back they had already made plans to meet at Sam's house to check out his engine.

"Sorry to butt in," Mr. Stanford said. "But the photographer for the newspaper is here, he would like to take a picture of our three winners."

I hardly even heard what he said. My eyes were fastened to the back of the room.

Janie lingered just inside the doorway. I couldn't tell if she was leaving or arriving. When she saw that I had spied her, she straightened her shoulders and came up the aisle. I met her halfway.

"I can't believe you came." My first instinct was to hug her; she looked beat. But her body language was stiff, unhuggable.

She smiled but it didn't relieve her tired expression much. "I had to leave at five o'clock this morning to get here. But I couldn't let this pass me by. Once more, you managed to get all the attention." She tried for a joking tone, but it missed the mark—just like her smile.

My initial response was a deep, red desire to lash out, either at Janie or myself, or both. I turned from her, toward my painting, toward the words First Place pinned above it. I could feel that cavernous well of hatred and self-doubt yawing open beneath me.

But then the quote from the little card Dr. Blue had given me stole across my mind like a veil. *You can't control how other people treat you. But you CAN control how you react. And that's how you take back your power.*

I dug my fingernails into my palms, turned back around, and faced my sister even though her words had stung like wasps. It was the hardest thing I'd ever done. My usual response would have been to throw something—even just a few ugly words, maybe a bottle of lotion—and flee before she could react. This time, I steeled my nerve and said, "Why are you always so unhappy, and why do you blame me for it?"

Janie's eyes widened. Her arms tightened, and her hands clenched into fists like mine.

I thought she would attack me right there in front of everyone. But I imitated her posture and threw up my chin. I refused to give her any more power over me.

She broke first. "Because everything is so *easy* for you." Her voice came at me like the hiss of a poisonous snake. I flinched, but stood my ground.

"Easy? Are you kidding, have you seen me lately?" My left hand flew toward my painting. "Do you think I painted that out of sheer happiness? I hurt. My heart was breaking. My so-called friends, and even my family, nearly tore me in two."

I meant Dad when I said this, but of course Janie assumed I meant her.

"I couldn't stand it," she said. "You were always the smart sister, the one who skipped a whole grade level. And when you made that—" she indicated my painting with a hard jerk of her chin, "and everyone kept talking about it." She looked away. "Even though some made fun, others kept saying how good it was. How much talent you had."

Her eyes came back to rest on mine. They were like flint. They cut right through me. "Most of them were acting stupid and making fun of the couple in the painting. It wasn't you they were making fun of—it was your subject." She stomped her foot. Not much, just enough to bring her a step closer to me. "Mostly they were in awe, Benji." She dropped her gaze. "Even after Mom came up and made the principal try to stop the teasing, they still kept talking about it. Only then, it was the other kids doing the talking. The ones who knew you and knew your talent."

I couldn't process her words. What did she mean they were in awe? "If that's true, why did it make you hate me so? Why didn't you tell me before? All you could say to me was how much I had embarrassed you."

She crumpled. Not all the way to the floor, but just inside her skin, as if her skeleton, the frame holding her up, had begun to melt. "Because I was jealous. It was one more thing you were good at. One more thing that came so easy to you." She glanced up at me and her eyes were still chips of flint. Or maybe obsidian. "I go to work, study my ass off to get a scholarship because there's no money, and I barely get by. Then you paint one picture and get a whole year paid for. Ever since Dad divorced us I've had to put off everything to look after you." She raised her voice in an ugly imitation of Mom: "Look after your sister while I'm at work. Take her to choir practice, take her to school, take her to Kera's house, to the movie, to the mall—take her, take her, take her." Her posture had hardened up again. "It's as if I don't matter at all."

Oh my God. When she said it like that, I felt like the world's biggest toddler, spoiled, self-centered. But at the same time, I thought of Sam saying he'd always been responsible for looking after his little brother, too. "And then," I whispered, "I did the most selfish thing of all and tried to kill myself." I wanted to hit her and hug her at the same time, but I didn't dare. She had turned back into hard Janie, about to break, like a rubber band stretched way too tight.

By now people had begun to notice our little standoff. They either stopped to watch and listen, or they flowed around us like slow moving water around jagged river rocks.

Once more, I took the upper hand. "I'm sorry, Sis. I really am." Then I turned away and left her standing there to deal with her feelings without me. There was nothing more I could do. That felt powerful. And I hadn't mentioned her *condition*. Not even once.

Sam wasn't directly behind me, but he stood off to one side, his face a mask of concern. I smiled to let him know everything would be all right, and he took my arm and ushered me out a side door into the art department's sculpture garden.

I swept through, my legs beginning to tremble. "Is she gone? Did she leave?"

"Yeah," Sam said. "She went out. Are you okay? What just happened?"

Shaking my head, I allowed my body to dissolve onto the nearest bench. "Now I know why my sister hates me so much."

Sam sat beside me. "I overheard part of it. I think every-one did."

"Oh, God. How awful."

"Not for you. For her. Everyone could hear the jealousy. It sprayed from her mouth like—"

"Poison?"

"I was going to say vomit. But poison fits, too."

I squeezed my eyes shut. "And I just stood there and took it."

"Yeah, it was the bravest thing I've ever seen." He clutched the edge of the bench with both hands. "I probably would have been screaming if it were me."

"I wanted to hit her. And then run."

"But you didn't. That took a lot of strength."

"There's more to the story than most people know." I took a deep, calming breath the way Dr. Blue had taught me, and then I exhaled slowly. The roses surrounding us were in full bloom. I reached toward one, careful of the huge thorns showing through the leaves. The blood-red petals were soft as velvet.

"Janie is a rose," I said. "A beautiful red rose with a mil-lion thorns encasing her soft center. I'll paint her that way. Someday, I'll paint her as a rose."

Mom came into the garden. "Never a dull moment is there?"

She sat on a bench opposite me.

"She hates me," I said. "And I'm beginning to understand why."

"It's my fault." Mom hung her head. "All this time I thought she enjoyed being an adult, a mini-me. As soon as she got her driver's license, I put her in charge of you and the house, the groceries—everything."

"Poor Janie. I had no idea."

"Me, either," Mom said. "I thought I had it all under control."

Uncle Aidan appeared. "Here you are. I've been looking everywhere. Mr. Stanford's photographer is ready."

My stomach fluttered with fear. "I don't know if I can—"

"Yes. You can." Mom took my elbow and pulled me up.

Sam took my other elbow and prevented me from sinking back down. He grinned that crooked-toothed grin that I liked so much. "We will be right there beside you."

When we walked back into the building, Ronald and Su Lin stood in front of our three pieces of art, which were grouped together on the wall behind the podium.

Mom and Sam ushered me to them and I took my place in the center. Mr. Stanford instructed me to hold my blue ribbon in front of my chest.

Janie was nowhere to be seen, but several of my Art and Choir classmates clustered off to one side like grapes. I was shocked to see Kera with them. I saw no sign of Will, and for that, I was grateful. But I couldn't keep my gaze from darting around the leftover crowd in search of Paul. There was no reason he should come, but seeing all the familiar faces from school made me think he might be there lurking, watching.

Would I have the nerve to confront him if he was? I might. I just might. Use up the remains of my Janie-adrenalin on him. Tell the world what he'd done. That would give the photographer something to photograph.

The idea for a new painting snapped into my head. I longed to rush home and take up a stick of charcoal, a pastel, even another red conté crayon, anything to capture the instant my eyes would have met his from the stage, across the podium.

My eyes would be huge from the photographer's flash; his would be shadowed, deep. And then the photographer would see something on my face and turn, spotlighting Paul, looking through him, or into him, show that scaly skeleton within his flesh, show him for what he really was. Use his camera like a moral x-ray.

Mom and Sam stepped back and beamed. Uncle Aidan grinned. Just before the photographer began snapping the pictures, a delivery boy hurried up the aisle with a basket of flowers. "These are for Benji Stevens," he called out. "Is Benji here?"

I raised my blue ribbon tentatively.

The boy smiled. "That makes sense." He handed me the basket and tipped his finger to his ball cap as he turned away.

"Who's it from?" Uncle Aidan asked.

I removed the tiny card. "You're strong," it read. "Sorry I couldn't be there today." It was signed, *Dr. Blue.* The stems of the blue and white flowers were nestled in sphagnum moss and tied up with a ribbon made of denim.

My eyes blurred. I hoped no one would remark on the odd ribbon. I touched the denim and then I touched the heart necklace that read, *Choose Life*. So many people cared about me. How could I ever doubt myself again?

The front door opened and Janie reappeared. She smiled through her tears. It looked like a real smile this time. I matched it, and even gave her a little wave with my denim basket. It didn't bother me that she didn't come up to the front of the room. Just the fact that she came back was enough.

At least it was a start.

*Y**ou can't control everything around you—or even how others treat you—but you can control how you react. And that's how you take back your power.*

A week after the awards ceremony, I invited Sam over for Sunday barbecue. Uncle Aidan made his famous baby-back ribs and Mom made mustard potato salad, Dad's favorite.

Janie stayed in town after the ceremony. She and Shawn were talking again, but she said she still intended to return to Oklahoma after she walked the graduation stage. Every now and then I noticed her smoothing her shirt down over her still-flat stomach, as if measuring how long it would be before she started to show, before she needed to hightail it to Gran and Gramps's house. It reminded me of that awful day when pregnancy rumors had swirled about me.

I didn't go back to school. No matter what Janie had said, I knew all the kids there hadn't been praising my art and laughing at my subjects.

The Homebound teacher came. She brought me all the work from my classes. I felt as if she'd given me back my life. Each textbook was a long lost friend. Even my bittersweet paperback copy of *Wuthering Heights* was there. I never had taken the final exam on it.

The barbecue was a success. Uncle Aidan and Sam were like two sides of the same coin. They talked cars and music the whole evening. After sunset, when the coals had died to embers and Janie had gone to lie down, Mom and Uncle Aidan went inside to see if we had the makings for root beer floats.

It was just the moment I'd been waiting for.

I pulled my letter to Dad out of my pocket. I'd been carrying it, folded into a neat square, all night. When I lifted the lid on the barbecue pit, I could see the still-glowing coals and feel their heat.

"What are you doing?" Sam brushed his hair back.

"I forgot to put this in before they lowered Dad's coffin into the ground, so I thought I'd send it to him another way." I took the barbecue tongs and tucked the little note down into the coals.

The paper caught instantly, the white corners folding inward like the wings of a dove preparing for flight.

Sam leaned back and together we watched as tiny sparks began to drift upward, toward Heaven.

"What did it say?" he asked.

I shrugged. "Oh, you know. Just how much I loved him, and missed him, and how I know I will see him again someday."

Sam wrapped one arm around my shoulders and pulled me to his side. Then he recited one line of the poem from Dad's funeral, "I am the soft starlight at night."

I added, "Do not stand at my grave and weep, I am not there. I do not sleep."

We both looked up as the tiny flickers of light disappeared against the magnitude of stars.

"Thanks for being here," I whispered.

Sam leaned over and kissed me in the soft starlight. "Thanks for letting me."

I melted into his side, within the shelter of his arm, reveling in the feeling of calm normality.

Later on I planned to put a new note in the Answered Prayers Jar. A thank you note to God for making me as tough as denim. A note acknowledging all the rungs on the ladder, those going up, as well as the ones going down. After all, without one, there wouldn't be the other.

Benji, 2018

Ann Swann has been a writer since junior high, but to pay the bills she has waited tables, delivered newspapers, cleaned other people's houses, taught school, and had a stint as a secretary at a rock-n-roll radio station. She also worked as a 911 operator and as a police dispatcher.

Her fiction began to win awards during her college days. Since then she's published several short stories, novels, and novellas.

She's always reading and always writing, but even if no one ever bought another book, Ann would not stop writing. For her it's a necessity, like breathing. Most of the time, it even keeps her sane.

Connect with Ann online at:

http://annswann.blogspot.com